FATHER OF THE MAN

FATHER
OF THE MAN

ROBERT MOONEY

PANTHEON BOOKS, NEW YORK

Pantheon Books and colophon are registered trademarks
of Random House, Inc.

Grateful acknowledgment is made to Ludlow Music, Inc.,
for permission to reprint an excerpt from the song lyric "This Land
is Your Land," words and music by Woody Guthrie. TRO–Copyright
© 1956 (Renewed) and 1958 (Renewed) 1970 (Renewed) by
Ludlow Music, Inc., New York, NY. Reprinted by permission of
Ludlow Music, Inc.

Library of Congress Cataloging-in-Publication Data

Mooney, Robert.
Father of the man / Robert Mooney.
p. cm.
ISBN 0-375-42204-8
1. Vietnamese Conflict, 1961–1975—Missing in action—Fiction.
2. Missing in action—Family relationships—Fiction.   3. World War,
1939–1945—Veterans—Fiction.   4. Fathers and sons—Fiction.
5. Hostages—Fiction.   I. Title.

PS3613.065 F37 2002   813'.6—dc21   2002022004

www.pantheonbooks.com

Book design by M. Kristen Bearse

Printed in the United States of America
First Edition
2   4   6   8   9   7   5   3   1

FOR MAUREEN

My heart leaps up when I behold
A rainbow in the sky:
So was it when my life began;
So is it now I am a man;
So be it when I shall grow old,
    Or let me die!
The Child is father of the Man:
I could wish my days to be
Bound each to each by natural piety.

—WILLIAM WORDSWORTH

"The child is father to the man."
How can he be? The words are wild.
Suck any sense from that who can:
"The child is father to the man."
No; what the poet did write ran,
"The man is father to the child."
"The child is father to the man!"
How *can* he be? The words are wild.

—GERARD MANLEY HOPKINS

FATHER OF THE MAN

PROLOGUE

George Conklin had been the kind of kid who ate baby toads whole for nickels on Catholic school playgrounds, and he didn't change much when he got to adulthood, where all antes are raised. He was the guy who put itching powder in your T-shirt, wintergreen in your jockstrap, garter snakes in your kip. A real pain in the ass. He loved to gamble and had a bad case of what he called Luck o' the Irish, *but we knew he cheated. He bet the farm nearly every time and died with enough happy cabbage in his pockets to feed the First Army. Who could mess with him? He threw out punches like he threw down beers, and even though he only came up to my shoulder standing at attention, what he had was enough. It was a body he treated like a jalopy he didn't care what happened to so long as it got him where he wanted to go. It'd been torn up from altercations in South Boston taverns—scars, welts, badly set bone-breaks, the whole nine yards. Most of his knuckles were jammed swollen for good. His nose had been flattened and his front tooth chipped in a way that made him look fifteen years older than he was.*

If he'd been stupid we might have liked him right away, but there was a mind in there that rankled us—and I don't mean the prickly smarts of the bookworm, though he'd memorized a lot of Irish poetry and had the vocabulary of an archbishop, if he needed it. It was the screwy moral code he lived by. Take our favorite subject. You could be really vile, like he was, with high-society British quiffs, but couldn't bad-mouth a prostitute. It was OK to say "cunt" in front of him, but not "vagina." He'd show a wallet photo of his wife like it was a holy card, but he went out on skirt patrol pretty regular while we were stationed at Stover. Just couldn't resist the light chassis. What made it tough socializing with him was that nobody told a better dirty joke, and he had a line of limericks from Dover to Bristol. But somebody joining in always ended up violating one of his personal Commandments and got the shit beat out of him if he wouldn't back down.

We figured it had something to do with religion, but who knew? He hated authority but loved God without question. He'd take communion after bothering the padre with confession, then go out after Mass and paint a penis with a face sniffing buttocks on the outside wall of the officers' club. Stuff like that. If you covered for him he'd get sore. There was just no reading the guy except finding out the hard way and trying to make heads and tails of it.

After a month of maneuvers in England we'd all had it up to here with him. Stewart owed him two weeks' pay on a poker game he said wasn't on the up-and-up. Goddamn Rokos, who'd won some middleweight title in Philly, had his face rearranged for no reason at all, and Rizzo's wrist hung in a sling for two weeks for asking Conklin how he did it with his wife. Klein was pissed at his own fear of him. Me? I thought the cocky little bastard needed to be taken down a few pegs.

It was through this scapular I really got to know him. He used to wear it around his neck with his dog tag and sometimes we'd catch him talking to it. Not crazy kind of talk—the man at least had pretty good control over himself that way. Just a whisper here and there, holding it up to his lips like you'd nibble on the collar of your T-shirt. You'd only catch him if you were real close, at a shoulder-to-shoulder crapshoot, say, or if you had the bottom bunk next to his, like I did. We knew enough to keep our mouths shut; it was just another Conklin thing. I'd always associated these scapulars with Catholic women. On my honeymoon just a few months before, I found one in the cup of my wife's bra, but I was too shy to ask questions. And I liked the mystery of this ribbony thing rubbing against her nipple all day long, like some sort of ecclesiastical lingerie.

Conklin would take his off only when he went to the showers. He'd place the squares of cloth together like a card shark lining up a pair of aces, loop the brown ribbon around them, and tuck it all under the folded dress uniform in his footlocker. When he returned, the first thing he did was dig the scapular out and put it back on.

One afternoon after maneuvers we were sitting around the barracks fucking the dog. We'd started practicing for the invasion with live ammunition and were a little on edge. Mail was in, and a group of us sat on our bunks reading letters out loud. I had one from Sarah tucked away in my front right pocket. Rizzo had a letter from his brother in the Pacific theater who planned to give Hirohito a taste from his hip flask, and Rizzo took up right away on how he was going to settle things on this end—you know, march right into the Führer's bunker and slice off Hitler's balls with the hunting knife the old man gave him for the job. Conklin laughed like a flock of geese and said Rizzo couldn't beat his own wop grandmother at arm wrestling.

"Fuck you," Rizzo told him.

"What are you going to do, Rizzo, cut my balls off?"

"If I could ever find them."

"Oh, well, see balls," Conklin explained, "sometimes re-ferred to as nuts, gonads, stones, rocks, cods, cullions, bollocks, family jewels, or—for the learned among us—testicles or testes, manufacture and store spermatozoa used during the reproduc-tive process—what you call 'fucking'—to fertilize the female ovum. They're located in a sac at the crotch of the normal male. Here, I'll show you."

Conklin had been standing beside his bunk undressing to take a shower, and he pushed his briefs down to his knees.

"Most everyone in this room has a pair," he said, jiggling his in his hand. "If you don't believe me, ask around."

Rizzo's face burned red. "Asshole," he said.

"No," said Conklin, "that's over this way."

He turned and mooned the group of us, finished undressing, took a towel, and headed for the shower. When they could hear the water running Rokos said, "Goddamn Conklin."

"Smartass," said Lopez.

"Thinks he's hot shit," said Stewart.

Weaver, the peacemaker of the group, said he was just bustin', and we knew that was true too, but Rizzo was sort of a man's man—a braggart, sure, but the fiction did no harm. He sat there fuming while the boys shouted down Weaver and I went over to Conklin's footlocker, opened it, felt around for a minute, and held up the scapular for the boys' inspection.

"He'll goddamn shit his pants, man," said Rokos.

"Then beat the shit out of the guy who took it," said Klein.

"What's he going to do?" I said, stuffing the thing in the pocket of my fatigues. "Beat up the whole platoon?"

One by one they nodded. Rizzo saw everyone else smiling, and he showed his yellow horse teeth and nodded with them. We waited, and when Conklin strutted back into the room singing his war song, his towel around him like a kilt, he joined the silence for a moment before saying, "Remember, Riz: the balls are located at the intersection of the thighs of the male."

He turned to dress, and the boys elbowed one another while he foraged through his footlocker. He patted his hand over his collarbone and stood with his arms at his sides.

"Something wrong, Mr. Balls?" Rizzo said.

Conklin looked back at us with his top lip moving like shivering Liz.

"Yeah," Stewart piped in. "Lose your rubbers or something?"

Rokos snorted like a stallion and Conklin turned and aimed himself at Weaver, a scrawny kid from Rhode Island, weakest guy in the platoon, last in everything, a bit lacy—if you know what I mean. We called him Wimpy, but we liked him so far.

"Hand it over," Conklin said, and Wimp said, "Me?" and started to say something else, but Conklin was already grinding his forehead into Wimp's and twisting the poor bastard's wrist behind his back. Stewart told him to back off and Rokos said yeah, back off, but no one moved. Conklin knew about pressure points; one touch in the right place and he could bring Goliath himself to his knees. He got Weaver just behind his neck and Weaver's legs gave out, but Conklin wouldn't let him fall. I dug into my pocket and held the scapular out like a ticket to the fair. He let go of Weaver and snapped his fingers and I laid the thing over his open hand with Wimp gasping like a radiator on the floor between us. He put it on without taking his eyes off me, returned to his footlocker, and got dressed. He took his time. When he finished lacing up his groundhogs, he turned and said, "Potter, outside." I looked at the boys looking at me and followed Conklin out of the barracks.

My fatigues hadn't dried from maneuvers so the rain didn't much matter to me, but by the time we reached the end of the long row of Quonsets and were heading along the road into town, Conklin was drenched again. His shoulders were hunched and he looked like he was about to dive on a loose football. All the way into town and he didn't so much as look over his shoulder at me.

Paignton was a seaside village of the type you see in paintings except the preparation for war intruded everywhere you looked. Half the people were in uniform. Planes tore up the sky. There were billboards that said things like "Be like Dad, keep Mum," and just like a poem gathering in my head a boy stepped out of a doorway and said, "Got any gum, chum?" We walked right past him, but then Conklin stopped so suddenly that we nearly collided. He dug into his trousers pocket, pulled out a pack of Juicy Fruit, and tossed the whole thing. The kid bent down to pick it up and yelled "Bloody 'ell, chum!" but putting on the humanitarian thing wasn't going to take the white out of my knuckles.

Down on the beach waves grabbed at the land as if water itself could drown. The wet sand was loose under my feet and we kept going until Conklin hefted himself onto a boulder and sat staring out across the Channel with his arms wrapped around his knees. I just stood there with my boots taking in water. If I went back to the barracks without anything to tell it might look like I just ran away. Conklin had this look of tranquility about him and it would have been stupid to provoke him. A four-engine Lancaster flew low and when the racket passed Conklin pulled the scapular out of his shirt.

"You know anything about these?"

I shrugged. "My wife has one," I said, and I felt for the letter in my pocket, still there. "It's like a religious medal, I guess."

"It's what's technically called a badge of religious confraternity," he said.

"So what."

"So to you it's just a rudily-doo piece of cloth. Why should it be anything else? But it means something to me. I think you should respect that."

"Oh, get off it, Conklin. You're the jokester in the outfit. Can't you take a little of it?"

He turned the scapular around and around in his fingers and said, "If you die wearing one of these, you go straight to heaven, no questions asked. That's what my mother told me, anyway, when I was a kid. I walked in on her once when she was dressing and saw it. I figured it was a woman's thing. Like part of the business of undergarments or something."

I moved my boots over the mud and he went on.

"She would never part with it. Believed in its powers and wanted me to believe, too. She used to tell the story of how Mary appeared to Saint Simon Stock at Mount Carmel and gave him one of these, saying if he died piously wearing it he would not suffer eternal flames." He squinted out at the water for a long time. The tide moved in a little with every third or fourth wave. "Of course, she would have gone to heaven anyway. As good a human being as human beings come. Raised six boys singlehanded for the last eight years of her life on a policeman's pension. It was even harder, though, when the old man was alive. He was a good man, don't get me wrong. But there was whiskey. Other women. And yet she never said one bad thing about him."

He tucked the scapular into his shirt pocket, slid off the rock, and started walking down the beach away from town. I let him go—what else could I do?—and watched him shrink in the distance. The wind sent a shiver through me and I thought about home. I took the letter from Sarah out of my pocket and smelled the envelope before opening it and removing the single sheet of pink stationery. The first sentence nearly knocked me off the rock. I looked over the rest of the letter without taking a breath, then went back and mouthed each word of the first line again and then again and then the wind took the envelope from my hands and I leapt off the rock and ran. Conklin turned when he heard me shouting and saw me waving my arms and weaving over the beach so that later he said I looked like the Flying Dutchman sailing the seas.

I ran at him with the wet letter clenched in my fist and he backed off, fists up, head cocked as I shouted over the roar of the tide. He couldn't hear me and so I threw my arms around him and pressed him to my chest. He fell back and we rolled on the beach and when he fought loose he started swinging, landing wild punches on my shoulders and face. I tried hitting back but I was laughing too hard and we ended up fighting until we were both bloodied and out of breath. "I'm going to . . . I'm going to be . . . !" The letter had been blown by the wind down the beach and I spotted it snagged against some sea heather, then let into the air by another gust that bore it over the water. I pushed myself to my feet yelling, "Father! Father!" and tried after it against monstrous waves storming the shore like an army.

History is bunk.

—HENRY FORD

Ford is history.

—JONATHAN POTTER

—*Dialogue scrawled above the urinal in the men's room of the Belmar Lounge, Main Street, Binghamton, New York, circa 1968*

ONE

BINGHAMTON, NEW YORK, 1982

I n the bed Dutch Potter fought darkening thoughts with the word "No." They came to him in voices other than his own, in voices of the dead, some of them famous statesmen and generals but most just men he had known, like Rokos, Conklin, Klein, and a score of other foot soldiers laid to rest in a zigzag path eastward across Europe from the Channel to the Elbe. Words that might be useful in the shaping of stories he'd tell that afternoon. But voices of other dead came less welcome: his father, the mother of his dead grandson, an old man who stepped in front of his bus on Robinson Street. They cajoled, accused, asked questions he could answer only by breathing the breeze the room hailed through an open window. Somewhere out there a car backfired, Leroy Street or maybe Grand Boulevard, its engine berserking into the distance and leaving a purer silence into which his wife, Sarah, ceded exclamatory phrases of air.

She lay on her back, jaw thrust upward, hands resting on the pillow just above her head as if she were being robbed. Together their bodies formed a terrain of linen that brought him back to the droning engines, the boom of mortar shells, the beat of rifle fire, the shrieking of broken men. Germans fired from the cliffs. Geysers roared out of the tide. Flicks of sand rasped kaleidoscopically among mayhem. His buddy Conklin, a South Boston madman responsible for Dutch's nickname, yelled that name, and it was his last word. His body, or the torso of that body minus one of the arms, flew through the air in slow and perfect geometry, the face bursting with interrogatory wonder— as if caught cheating at craps—yelling *"Dutch!"* even as it arched over him raining blood and smashing onto the sand some twenty yards back toward the shore. The mouth was still gulping air when Dutch lifted the head from the tide to see not Conklin's eyes but those of his son Jom, flickering out of consciousness.

Dutch had been born in February, but the sixth of June was the anniversary of his life as he understood it, a way of ordering memory in time. It began with Wimp Weaver, who would call just that one day, collect and drunk, and the two of them spoke in a code no one else would have understood. With a simple phrase Wimp threw open worlds. "Klein in the hedgerows" or "raining eighty-eights" or "Riz's cullions" or "them cliffs," and Dutch could be certain it *had* happened as he remembered it, and that those who were lost meant something. And Wimp never failed to ask if there was news of Jom—he was the only one left in Dutch's life who would inquire or even say his son's name aloud—and when Dutch answered no, not a word, Wimp's commiseration was real and unguarded. The simple honesty with which he said, "Jeez, Dutch, just jeez," or "What a thing," meant all the difference, and with hope and dread revivified Dutch would begin a new year.

But last year Wimp didn't call on the sixth and instead Dutch had been contacted a few days later by a cop in Providence who'd found his phone number on the corpse of a homeless man. There was the service in the empty funeral parlor, which Dutch paid for, then the drinking in tavern after tavern where Wimp might have been known, until he plunged into a gap in his memory of three days—two of them in the hospital he woke up in. It was as if he had followed Wimp into oblivion and climbed back.

But the life to which he returned had changed. The people and his circumstances were the same, but there was an eerie feel to things, something ethereal, intermitted, as if he had become a ghost in his own life as he was living it. He eventually returned to work, got suspended from work, went back to work. Winter and spring came again. No news of Jom, again. More days happened, and they kept happening as if without him, and he remembered it now as a year composed almost wholly of nights, when, tired of sitting on the edge of the bed looking at his heavy face thrown back at him from the dark window, he would dress quietly and free himself of the house's cluttered rhombic divisions, bursting out as if from shackles, to walk the streets of the city. There, cadencing, he'd count sidewalk cracks, telephone poles, streetlamps, stop signs, anything—counting things to count. Sometimes he would pause at a house and spy through lighted windows a couple at late supper or a mother tucking in a child or college students swilling beer in a kitchen. He'd wonder if a pedestrian had ever paused in front of 43 West End Avenue to observe his sister-in-law Ruth, a sharp-tongued hypochondriac who had moved in for good, smoking on the sofa, her back stiff, her poodle at her feet standing guard. Or Sarah, crocheting beside her on the rocker as if sitting for Whistler. Or his divorced daughter and her five-year-old son in front of the television like Buddhists at a shrine. What would such a passerby make of Dutch pacing and wringing his hands, his footfalls rattling china in the hutch two rooms away? How did he fit into this scene? At some point Ruth would suggest that he take his heavy feet out to the sidewalk, and he'd have words for her that would fade into senseless mumbling out on these lanes and boulevards and drives and avenues that crisscrossed the valley, graded hillsides, bridged rivers, curbed, tree lined, potholed, oil stained, glass spackled. Streets with history snapping like synapses through neighborhoods sleeping heavily after a gritty day's toil at making shoes, computer parts, Cold War munitions, any of a number of small manufacturing afterthoughts that towns in upstate New York have been assigned by history, gray and quiet, unplanned in the way that families used to be— just happening, going where they were most needed.

The moon served as referent, if there was one, and he'd wonder if Jom's face, perhaps unrecognizable, was condemned against the same impassive light in a bamboo hut a world away. He would be thirty-eight, missing for twelve years, and the thought of such a life plundered from promise could be mollified only by Homeric fantasies: Jom outwitting the slant-eyed demons, Jom's makeshift raft windward over the South China Sea. Block after block he'd fill in every conceivable detail, imagining himself a one-man army going in to free his son, fantasies so vivid his heart would thrash in his chest and the echolalian gasps of his son's name would abate only after re-entry into the world he had come to loathe—the one Wimp, once the unlikely hero, finally couldn't take—the real one, where the logic Dutch demanded from other men in turn demanded he admit the rat-tat-tat of bullets was only the monotonous percussion of a student up late at a typewriter, the blood-chilling screams merely a couple in a distant bedroom.

Or he would follow people, sometimes unaware he was doing so, taking one turn and another at a distance of ten or fifteen paces, and on more than one occasion women, as it turned out, pivoted back and warned him away in voices ionized by terror. He would often find himself sitting under the viaduct on the East Side where he found Jom, who had run away for the first time at the age of four, waiting for a train that would take him, he'd said, to the end of the world. Or at the triangular table at the Belmar where he told Dutch he had enlisted to make him the responsible human being he had yet to become. Or staring at the carousel horses in Recreation Park, or the tree in the backyard they had planted together, now tall enough for an adult to climb. Dutch would attend these places as one might say the Stations of the Cross in church, often finding himself at one or another with no forethought, as if his body took him there of its own accord. But they gave less and less back to him, these Stations, slowly reverting to rock and dirt and wood and steel, sucked dry of meaning except what they simply were.

Talking helped, and if he saw a light on in the rectory of the Lutheran Church of the Redeemer on Main Street he might pay a visit to Pastor Philips; likewise with his friend Zulik, the city councilman, at his home in the First Ward, or Sammy Corcoran over on Murray Street. But a man's singular sorrow can never sustain pitiless interest in another for very long, no matter how close they may be or have been, and at some point during the past year, he couldn't remember when, Dutch began avoiding their wary scrutiny of the ache inside him, the one Wimp's death somehow set free to course through his every thought, or so it seemed, like a dislodged clot.

"If he was gone," Dutch would say to Pastor Philips, "if I knew Jom was dead, I maybe could rest. Sounds cruel, doesn't it?"

The pastor would give no indication what he thought. Classical music was forever entering his study through speakers set on cleared sections of the bookshelves: the twinkling of piano keys or rich heraldic brass, sweeping strings, arias. They would sit in two chairs facing one another at an angle across a Persian rug in the high-ceilinged room starkly lit and overcast with pipe smoke where the pastor had, over the long years of their acquaintance, digested into lay terminology concepts and stories from many of the books he had read, dropping names of characters from antiquity as if they were acquaintances living down in Wilkes-Barre or Montrose.

"I try to put him out of my mind," Dutch would tell him, "but I have this feeling inside that he's alive. Stronger now than ever. It's something I can't explain. You know how close we were. We had our differences, sure, but at heart we always had this *connection*. And always some hope resurrects him—an article in the newspaper on MIAs, or a letter from some bureaucrat answering one of my questions, you know. I'm just about to give up, put the whole blasted thing behind me, and bang!" Here he would slap his hands together, or slam his heel onto the floor, and Pastor Philips would arch his white eyebrows to warn Dutch that Mrs. Philips was asleep upstairs.

He had been doing so well and here he was back to the desperate hope that should have been corrected by the odds long ago. That's what the pastor was thinking, because his appetite for puzzle and conundrum did not include problems of a personal nature. Instead he preferred his challenges abstract—nameless, or buried under centuries like the pea under twenty downy mattresses. He'd fold his lanky frame back into the armchair, run his fingers through hair that stood stiff as the comb of a bird, then cross his legs at the thigh where the robe opened to the plaid production of his pajamas. Once settled, he'd reignite his pipe and, with smoke rising around him, say something about God's will and faith.

"Oh, I have faith, Dieter. Like a cancer. I pray. I attend church services at two denominations, for cripe sakes. Like any good Christian I look to the Bible for answers."

"And what does Scripture tell you?"

"It laughs at me. It tells me God is the kind of guy to torment a good man on a wager with the devil. It tells me God is the kind of guy who commands Abraham to sacrifice his only son to prove his *faith*."

"Don't forget the God of the *New* Testament. Besides, God loved Job, and rewarded him. He wounds, yes; but His hands make whole. Job 5:18. And He did not, after all, force Abraham to kill his son."

"Don't I know it? Abraham and Isaac, saved by the bell—or I should say saved by the ram in the thicket. Very nice."

"So you look for your ram in the thicket."

An image of Jom bucked out of the shadows in the pastor's study, or from Dutch's memory of being there one night last winter—a memory from a memory from a personal history far more meaningful to him than the pastor's teeming millennia: Jom's naked body stretched out on the queen-sized bed, arms and legs leashed to the four posts with clothesline, a brown woman straddling his pelvis, growling like a beast, her black hair shrouding her face and Jom's. Dutch, on a split instead of his usual straight run at work, had thought Jom might be up-stairs roughhousing with his best friend, Meehan, or maybe left his bedroom window open and another pigeon had flown into the house, and he was not sure how long he had stood at the door of his own bedroom holding a badminton racket, witness-ing their furious motion, before the woman turned her head.

She was in her twenties, though favoring her teens or thirties he could not tell; her face—narrow, hungry—delivered itself in a defiant leer.

"Off," he'd said to her.

She kissed Jom on the forehead before dismounting. A welt-colored tattoo on her left buttock grew in size when she bent over the hillock of clothes in front of the dresser: a cracked heart over blue letters spelling the word "love."

"You think this is funny, young lady?"

She zipped up her white shorts and buttoned the top button before turning around. "Well, it ain't the end of the world, is it?"

Her top was a turquoise sleeveless thing and she slid it over her torso. She pulled her hair free, flipping it back over her shoulders, and checked herself in the mirror.

"You little tramp. Out of my house!" Dutch pointed to the door with the racket.

"Are you going to let him talk to me that way, Jommy? 'Tramp'?"

"Out!"

She shrugged and said, "Nice old man you got. Call me."

"He'll do no such thing."

She sauntered past him out of the room, and on her way down the stairs her coarse giggling rattled the hallway like a murmuration of starlings.

"Neanderthals were the first human species to entomb their dead," the pastor was saying. "They discovered death, you might say, and so, in all likelihood, discovered religion."

He had nestled back in his chair with the hubris of a baby in its mother's lap, oblivious to all but the labyrinthine path of his reasoning.

"What's your point?"

"Do as the first men had the good sense to do, Jon. Face the hard facts and ease the pain they inflict by steering back toward the faith from which you're drifting. Find your peace in the Creator of all things."

The silence that followed was so complete it seemed to shout Dutch's response: a hush, like gas leaking into the room. The pastor, eyes screwed, head cocked, poked the stem of his pipe into the air and said, "You know, he falls asleep on the job at least twice a week."

Dutch squinted up through the strata of smoke and said, "God?"

"No! Oh-ho, *heavens,* Jon! No!" A smile burst onto his face and he shook his head. "Oh-ho!" he said again, bellowing now, pounding his fist down on his thigh as if to work out a cramp. He jabbed the stem of his pipe upward again, toward the speaker on the shelf closest to Dutch. "I mean Hawker. The night fellow on WSKG. Sometimes I call the station and wake him. God falling asleep on the job! Oh-ho, Jon!"

Dutch formed a smile to match his friend's and the pastor said, chuckling and wagging his finger, that, yes, sometimes it did seem that way—"Didn't Christ himself wonder for a moment?"—and, suffused with mirth now that the tension in the room had been punctured, reloaded his pipe and launched into a story of how, late one night a few weeks back, he had to awaken this man Hawker with a call so he could hear the second half of Mendelssohn's *Reformation* Symphony. But as he droned forth about his conversation with this fellow on why the composer's reputation had come round full circle by the mid–twentieth century, Dutch did not follow his detailed narrative, preferring to stay behind, as it were, with the image of the cruciform, momentarily forsaken son.

They were streets through which by day he drove a bus, taking on and letting off the people of Binghamton and the adjoining villages of Johnson City and Endicott, the "Triple Cities"—neighborhoods of Square Deal clapboards in the shadows of once clamorous factories now strewn like toppled monuments along the Susquehanna River near the Pennsylvania border. His bus served as a conduit to their errant lives of gathering goods, commuting to work to earn money for those goods, to school for certificates entitling them to better jobs: a modern chain of being to Dutch as aimless as the 35 Endicott route he skippered them through, running from BC Junction in downtown Binghamton through Johnson City and all the way out to Grippen Park in Endicott six miles west, turning around to face the same route back (like turning a slide around in a projector, he thought), dodging potholes through car-clogged streets, starting, stopping, validating coins, tokens, passes, dog-eared transfers, roaring forward, climbing the gears through Endwell and Johnson City, stopping and starting in spurts and fits back to Binghamton, only to turn around again.

Poised in the driver's seat, broad shoulders squared—one hand on the steering wheel, the fingers of the other pushing back through iron-gray hair—he would squint at the choreography of traffic thinking, sometimes, how frighteningly easy death could come. How turning the wheel a mere ten minutes left, directing the coach to an oncoming truck or concrete abutment, could end a story six decades in the making, like *that,* launching him from his seat into shattering glass and the other world. A jerk of the arm!

But these thoughts were only what they were, what so many years had been to Dutch. If ever, on a given day, he found them difficult to shake, he might get off at a stop, walk around a little, light a cigarette, breathe a breath of air. Let the people in the bus wonder. Let them check their watches, wrestle their own anxieties. Or he might eavesdrop on a conversation, if one was in earshot, for often the people just sat alone at the center of their thoughts, staring out of empty eyes, their heads bobbing to the motion of the bus. When they did speak to one another their conversations were like stones skipping across the shiny surface of things: sports, politics, clearance sales, the weather.

One afternoon the previous October while sitting behind the wheel of the bus waiting for the light to change on the corner of Oak and Riverside, Dutch injected his opinion into a conversation taking place just over his right shoulder. "Time was," he said, "the weather meant more than a spoilt wedding day."

The eyes of the middle-aged women met his in the long mirror over the windshield.

"Yeah, you two," Dutch said. "Folks today, they look at things as how they threaten pleasure. There's other ways of seeing, though. Take your rain. For you, it's nothing but a ruined day at the park. For the farmer—Old McDonald turning over rocks down there in northern Pennsylvania—it's a gift from heaven. Hey?"

The women looked at one another and then at those around them, aware, suddenly, they had been yanked into an arena of attention as long and as wide as the bus, Dutch's raspy baritone working on a frequency that easily cut through murmuring dialogue, window rattle, and traffic—a nasal upstatese with *a*'s italicized as though pronounced through the probe of a tongue depressor, sharp alarming vowels commanding silence, or at least whatever silence possible in an idling old bus. The woman with the blood-red kerchief wrapped around her head, tightening the collar of her jacket, felt compelled to say, "Whatever are you talking about?"

"Let's look at it this way," Dutch said. "Take Noah—you know, the guy with the ark? For him, the rain was something else altogether, hey? It wasn't just a nuisance but the beginning of a whole new world through the destruction of the old. Creation's second chance, so to speak. But the people around Noah were empty-headed jerks. 'Every intent of the thoughts of their hearts was only evil continually,' right?"

"I'm sorry," said the woman in the kerchief. "I don't get what you mean."

"Hey!" someone shouted from the back. "The light's been green forever!"

As the bus lurched into the right-hand turn Dutch could see

in the mirror a wonderland of faces, alert, averted, looking out the windows or at the floor, all of them familiar to him by dint of his habit of studying each as they entered the bus, searching their expressions as if looking through disguises, memorizing them so that, late at night, they showed up in these floating thoughts, as clear and as detailed as the black-and-white snapshots taken at a Woolworth's photo booth—ragged factory workers, weary mothers, sleepy students, mall rats, disgruntled clerks: the spectrum of worn-out humanity—or at least the segment of it that, for whatever reason at that point in time, had no car.

"'And the Lord was sorry He had made man on earth,'" Dutch hollered down Riverside Drive. "'And He was grieved in His heart!'"

Those sitting in certain seats could see Dutch on the other side of that mirror, if they chose to observe him navigating a turn or waiting at another light, the gray eyebrows thatched over eyes intent enough to want to believe in what they saw, blue as souls. His large face, ruddy but not of the broken-vesseled hue characterizing drinking men of his age, was heated by earnest corpuscles to all possible emotions, as if Joy, Sorrow, Anger, Pity were characters in a drama ready to storm the scene if cued by the right phrase or gesture. The hooked nose, broken twice—"faking left, going right" he'd say—tempered each unguarded expression to something curiously interrogatory, almost friendly, so that on other runs people who had never ridden his bus before, sitting in the sidelong seat opposite, might chance a conversation, opening themselves up to the same overwhelming philosophical agenda.

TWO

His suspension from BC Transit on D-13,642 (a method of recording time he would calculate to mark momentous occasions, good or bad) was unwarranted, unfair, just plain mean-spirited, and for months afterward he could not look at H. Richard Petoski, Director of Operations, without feeling a blast of wrath. So he'd failed to make a few stops. So he'd expressed an opinion or two. What harm?

With nothing to do for a week he was no better than the old-timer at the Tally Ho Diner on Main Street, the dishwasher with St. Vitus' dance who once leaned over the counter at Dutch and stuttered in a fusillade of halitosis: "time is nerves"—and if it weren't for the luck of happening into what he would later refer to simply as "the movie," there is no telling what he would have done. He had been walking down Main Street, fists in the pockets of his coat, slush splattering at his boots, when he was halted by a line six or seven deep in front of the Crest. He lingered only to rest his legs but stayed to purchase a ticket when he saw the color glossies of grease-faced soldiers on a mission in the jungle. The poster in the glass case promised ACTION! ADVENTURE!

YEARS HAVE PASSED SINCE THE FALL OF SAIGON. AFTER
LEARNING OF AN INTELLIGENCE REPORT CONFIRMING
THE EXISTENCE OF A POW CAMP IN LAOS, A RETIRED
AMERICAN COLONEL, WHO BELIEVES HIS MISSING SON
TO BE AMONG THOSE ENSLAVED THERE, RECRUITS
SEVEN OF THE BEST MEN WHO HAD SERVED UNDER HIM
AND TRAINS THEM FOR ONE LAST MISSION . . .

On the screen: A rice paddy. Gunfire. American soldiers
sprinting toward choppers, Vietnamese in pursuit. Some GIs
are shot, others captured. Then silence and blue light. A man,
middle-aged, awake in bed, wife beside him asleep. A sound,
and he squints. Nothing. The bedroom, suburban in its com-
forts. He leans against the headboard, massages the bridge of
his nose, opens his eyes again and sees a boy in pajamas beside
the bed. "Daddy," the boy says, but vanishes when the father
reaches to touch his face, and the boy's cries echo across what
all present come to learn are the years.

Dutch returned the next night for both showings. And the
night after that. On the weekend, he added the matinees. By
the time he returned to work he knew the dialogue by heart,
and the movie played in his head as he navigated his bus
through the hilly lanes of Vestal. The dashboard was a cockpit;
danger lurked route-side in dark clusters of pine; passengers
were depleted troops. He encouraged chatter, to calm them. He
called them by the nicknames of the movie's characters—
Werner, Sailor, Rookie. Potholes were artillery taken.

For weeks he told no one about the movie and it developed
inside his head like a roll of pictures in a darkroom. Sarah was
out of the question; his daughters Catherine and Georgia would
fret about his health; and his sister-in-law Ruth would be sure to
find something untoward in his recommendation. Sammy, and

maybe some of the boys at work, would be OK with it, but without any sex scenes Zulik would give it the thumbs-down. Pastor Philips would call it a simple adventure film exploiting the latest special effects, and, as he would do whenever he caught Dutch quoting from *Battleground,* say, or *The Longest Day* or *The Dirty Dozen,* admonish his friend's appetite for this particular "cinematic confection"—as if staying up to watch old war movies could cause an indigestion of the soul. And his son-in-law, Bummy Bumgartner? Forget it.

But this was no Rambo fantasy, no comic-book plot; it was believable to the very end when the helicopter punches through the jungle air carrying what's left of the makeshift platoon and surviving POWs, and the cheers in the theater would fill Dutch with a sanguinity he had thought expunged forever from his life. All along he had not been alone, and love of humanity flooded his heart.

He'd attended the movie three or four times before the girl behind the ticket window took notice. She was terribly thin, perhaps anorexic, with mouse-brown hair dropping to her shoulders. Her hunger sometimes looked like curiosity, but when Dutch greeted her with the familiarity of acquaintance she'd simply push his ticket through the window slot as though she were feeding an animal at the zoo. He tried drawing her out, not succeeding until halfway through the second week when he mentioned that she looked a little like his daughter Margaret.

"You have a daughter?"

Her voice was deeper than he'd expected, slightly hoarse.

"Three, actually."

The next night she asked him what his daughter did, the one that looked like her. "Does she go to Johnson City High School? Maybe I know her."

"Oh no, no," he said. "She's thousands of miles away. In

Oregon. Hitchhiked out there with nothing but the pack on her back. Got a job at a bookstore. Has no telephone, no car. We're waiting for her to come to her senses."

Dutch had never talked about his daughter's fall from grace to anyone but Pastor Philips, and the ease with which these lines slipped out surprised him. Excited him, even. He wanted to tell her more, as though he were falling in love and needed to tell his whole life.

"Do you think I look older than sixteen?"

She turned and squared her shoulders.

"Only sixteen, is it? My goodness, I thought you were, jeez, older than that."

She showed Dutch a row of teeth that could only have been achieved through hundreds of dollars paid to an orthodontist, but it was not clear if she was teasing or just ignorant of her charms. He was treated to that same smile every night she worked for the duration of the movie's run as she posed questions so formally and ill-timed that Dutch knew she had composed them in her head before his arrival. These exchanges never lasted more than a minute, but piecing them together she would have been able to form a composite of his character. She learned that his name was simply "Dutch," that he had been married thirty-nine years and had four children. Though he could quote the Bible and went to church every Sunday—in fact, because he had converted to his wife's religion, had actually practiced two faiths—he was quick to say he wasn't a "Holy Roller" but only a man who knew enough of things so he didn't have to make converts to prove it. Yes, he loved his daughter very much, the one who went out west for no good reason but to be there, but she had to grow up and realize she was wasting her life. Chocolate was his favorite ice cream, and he thought politics since the 1950s a complex game of deception.

The girl also learned things about Dutch that were not true, or were at least exaggerations of the truth. He was a war hero, decorated by General Eisenhower himself. He knew a great deal about national defense, and officials from the Pentagon occasionally contacted him on matters of some importance. Of his job he only said it involved moving people around "from one position to another." She asked if this meant he was some sort of director, and he said that was close enough.

Talking this way to an inquisitive high-school junior did no one any harm, and it excited him to embellish his life to receptive ears. So much so, it always surprised him to discover how much he missed these fleeting exchanges when, on Sunday and Monday nights, a dour middle-aged woman worked the ticket window, and he found his concentration interrupted by thoughts of the young girl, whose name was Suzy, while viewing the movie. She did not remind him of Sarah when she was young—this girl wasn't beautiful or sassy enough—but the teasing brought him back to their courtship, the feeling that suffused him in those early years when he could think of nothing but the swirl of dark hair at Sarah's shoulders, the way she held her books against her chest, fingers splayed, as if in light embrace; the easy loll of her gait and how it furled and unfurled the pleated skirt of her school uniform; the smell of soap and peppermint and the soft voice that sounded like singing even when upbraiding him for bad manners.

They officially met, it was later decided, during the end of sophomore year in high school, but he went to North and she to Catholic Central, one of the fundamental differences that both challenged and solidified their determination to spend their lives together, and so they did not begin to date until months afterward. He was from stern Lutheran parentage of German stock with a modest but well-kept home on Liberty Street; her family, larger than his by four children, rented a three-bedroom apartment in a duplex on Howard Avenue off Robinson on the East

Side, "the Patch," where, Dutch's father said, the shanty Irish coagulated like muck in a sewer.

It was a late spring evening on a Thursday, when downtown stores remained open until ten and everyone in the city, or so it seemed, strolled the environs of Court Street looking at the displays in the windows of Fowler's or the Fair Store or Drazen's or Bern's, purchasing an ice-cream cone at the Tastee Freeze or a burger at the Pig Stand, talking to one another about the start of the Triple Cities Triplets' season, or the prospects for the Yankees or the Giants or the Dodgers down in the City, or some recent development in the Europeans' latest war—what with Herr Hess falling out of the sky over Scotland and the *Bismarck* at the bottom of the Atlantic. That's what was in the air in 1941 when he was walking past the Riviera Theater with Dave McCarthy and Marty Lawson and a sun-spangled quarter came rolling down the sidewalk so quickly he did not have time to think before scooping it up with one hand like a shortstop.

"Money from heaven, fellas!" he said, but when he stood he was face-to-face with a young woman saying, "Thank you, kind sir." Her eyes were dark as loam, fixed on his, no-nonsense, but something mischievous in the way they didn't move. Two older girls stationed like acolytes were her sisters, all of them on their way to see *Citizen Kane,* which was opening that evening. She wore a light blue cardigan fastened with one button at her chest, and the sight of her standing there with her hand out to him, he confessed much later, in the safety of marriage, could have caused his legs to give out.

Suzy leaned into the circle cut out of the glass and, wrinkling her nose in playful conspiracy, asked why he kept seeing the same movie over and over. She had seen it, and thought it was OK and everything, but, you know . . .

"Well, I shouldn't tell you this," he said, looking over one shoulder, then the other, "but I know somebody in the film."

"Really?"

He nodded.

"A friend?"

He leaned forward and his words fogged the glass. "My boy. My son."

"Really?" Her mouth stayed open for a moment and then she asked which one.

Dutch felt a presence behind him and he winked at Suzy, turned, and entered the theater. On subsequent nights she pressed him, and each time Dutch simply placed a finger on his lips. She would make a guess, he would smile. Some nights she would go through name after name, making half of them up, and when he heard his own he looked up to see that he was not in front of the glass booth at the Crest but standing barefoot in pajamas before Jom's bedroom door in the upstairs hallway of his house. Sarah was standing in the doorway of their bedroom rubbing sleep from her face with the heel of her hand, asking if he was all right.

"Yeah. Really. Go back to bed," and, he added softly, "OK?"

The door to his right opened and there was his sister-in-law Ruth pushing her face at him. Her poodle growled from inside the room and then began yelping and Dutch told her to quiet that thing. But it was too late: from the bedroom down the hall Catherine's child cried out, and then Catherine appeared at the door wearing one of her ex-husband's T-shirts.

"It's a little late to be going out, isn't it?" Ruth's lukewarm breath on his neck.

"Can't a man stretch his legs in his own house?"

"As long as he doesn't keep going out into the streets to his hooker friend's."

Sarah ordered everyone to bed in a tone they were not accustomed to hearing from her, and Dutch watched the slits of dark swallow each of them, Sarah last. Blue street light from the hall window tracked the woodgrain of the door to Jom's room. He dabbed his fingertips over the scar between the lock and jamb he'd repaired many years ago, fifteen, after kicking in the door only to find the room as empty as it was now, in fact arranged exactly as it had been then—same green bedspread, the Baby Ben alarm clock on the nightstand, *Sgt. Pepper* on the open hi-fi, Jimi Hendrix eating his guitar on the closet door, Janis Joplin sweating on the far wall. A shrine to hope, or a museum to what hope had once been. He couldn't say.

Jom. He possessed the blood of Aryan warriors and Hibernian bards, Thor and Ith, Saxon and de Danaan, an oxymoronic composition he bore with a relaxed dynamism—though the wedding of which he was the immediate result might have portended a different character altogether. There had been resistance to the marriage from both sides of the family, the excuse being youth—the couple was only just out of high school. But the real reason was religion. Though everyone behaved themselves at Saint Paul's Church, the reception at the Elks was a disaster, one insult after another and the couple leaving in the middle of a brawl for a three-day honeymoon in a Catskills cabin owned by one of Dutch's more beneficent uncles.

The thick dust on the bookshelves and desk and album meant that Sarah didn't come in here anymore, or at least hadn't for quite some time. She could not bear to hear his name mentioned and would leave the room without a word. The not knowing stunned them to silence so sure it was as if he'd never lived.

The colonel in the movie received word, at least. He had that advantage over Dutch. His band of soldiers find the camp they are looking for, but after the battle that liberates the POWs—during which some of the brave mercenaries are slaughtered—and all the survivors are aboard the helicopter, the colonel's son cannot be counted among them. He had gotten sick, one of the rescued prisoners tells the colonel, weeping; and the colonel, also weeping, holds the emaciated man in his arms as the chopper slices through the jungle air. Without the Dolby blasts of guns and grenades, the orange explosions, the enemy bodies bursting, Dutch reflected on the colonel's loneliness and recognized it as his own, except the colonel had the gift of knowing; his son's life was a memory that could finally take shape with a beginning, middle, and end.

Dutch had discovered that a new movie was coming to the Crest while flipping through the *Sun-Bulletin* on a Thursday morning in late February. There was an ad for some stupid love story, a picture of buxom women smirking as if they knew what you were thinking. Zulik's kind of film.

"Well, Dutch, this is it," Suzy had announced when he went up to the ticket window that night.

He counted out four ones and slid them into the stainless steel tray under the window.

"Dutch?"

"Just gimme my ticket!" He struck the counter hard enough to jangle coins in the cash drawer. Her fingers trembled when she tore a ticket off the roll and slid it under the glass. He did not wait for his change.

A path of street dirt bisected the carpeting of the aisle sloping to the screen. Seat covers hung like the skin of dead animals, row after row. Two wall lamps had burned out; the paint on the ceiling was flaking. He remembered when, for a piece of change in a mother's purse, going to the moving pictures meant entering a palace. Ushers like royal guards, patrons in fine clothes, and the camaraderie of anticipation.

As the houselights dimmed and the Cinema National anthem blared, he calculated he had spent nearly $150 on the movie and pondered a list of the more sensible things he could have done with the money. Where did most of his earnings go anyway but running a house of females who saw him as a necessary disturbance? It was his cross to bear, or one of them, so why couldn't he lighten the load for himself every so often?

Sitting through the parade of coming attractions was as tedious as waiting at a railroad crossing. The boys who had finally settled in behind him commented loudly on a clip showing a man and woman kissing in bed, and Dutch let out a loud *shhhhhh* that only fanned their revelry. He turned to stare them down. Three teenagers in Binghamton Central varsity jackets stared right back at him. The one on the end, the blond, elbowed the boy next to him and both snorted like hogs.

He turned back to the screen, where American soldiers were making a desperate run across an open field toward helicopters. Gunfire and grenades, quiet at first, grew in amplification until they exploded from the speakers.

"*Chic*-ken!" one of the boys behind Dutch yelled. The words of his friends were drowned out by the whirring of chopper blades and the burst of mortar fire, and it was not until the next scene, a quiet dawn in the colonel's bedroom, that Dutch turned to face them.

"You think this is a *joke?*"

They stared back at him for a moment and then the boy in the middle said, "OK, OK. Sorry."

"You punks," Dutch spat. "Life's a party, isn't it. All fun and games."

"Hey, old-timer," the blond boy said. "Frankie said sorry. We're sorry. Chill out, huh?"

"Do you have any idea—" Dutch started, pointing back at

the screen, but a bright light shone in his eyes: the usher, wanting to know what was going on.

"This guy's going bonkers," one of the teenagers said. "He's losing it."

"I'll show you losing it," Dutch said, reaching back over the row and grabbing a loose piece of clothing—the collar of one of their jackets. He pulled the boy in close enough to strike his face with his fist. Someone jumped on his back and dragged him over the back of his seat onto the row of chairs behind. A woman screamed, then another, and the usher called for help. In the narrow row Dutch's body became entangled with the arms and legs of the boys, his face buried in a seat cushion. They were locked in that knot and it took the ushers and a few patrons a minute to pull them apart. A smear of blood stained Dutch's coat, and in the blue lambency of the screen he could see the blond teenager holding his head back and pinching the bridge of his nose.

A party of men escorted Dutch roughly through the emergency exit beside the screen, and once outside one of the ushers pushed him against the brick wall. The crisp air cleared his head and he thought of Sarah.

"I saw the whole thing," a patron said. "The boys were making noise, and this jerk overreacted. Went apeshit. Just turned around and—"

The manager, a burly bald man with severe eyes, cut off the good citizen and said, "All right, mister. What's your game?"

Dutch stood silent, breathing hard. And someone standing behind the manager said, "He's OK. Let him go."

When the manager turned and ordered Suzy to get back to work, Dutch broke out of the huddle and ran through the back lot like he hadn't moved in years, down a snowy embankment across an open field toward the railroad tracks that ran between Main Street and the EJ warehouses. The bow of a quarter moon splashed through clouds. Cold air hammered his lungs. In the growing distance, footsteps pattered on the shoveled pavement behind the theater until he heard a man shout, "Let the asshole go."

But Dutch continued running, his open coat flapping behind him, the dry snow so thick and his legs so heavy pushing through it he felt as though he were running in the slow-motion desperation of a dream that knew his name, one from which he opened his eyes to find himself in the attic of his house, out of breath, as if time were space and he'd run the full distance of three and a half months to get there.

THREE

Stooping to accommodate the slant of ceiling at the top of the narrow stairway, palms on knees, eyes narrowed, waiting for the dark to make enough sense for safe negotiation to the arm-chair in the corner. Then he felt his way along the oak dresser, the open Bible on the lectern, the chimney. He gripped the polished edge of the credenza, on top of which sat the Philco he and Jommy once repaired, then the coffee table. When he reached for and found the arms of the chair he turned and fell back.

The attic was his refuge in the house and it contained in careful arrangement those things that were privately his own. Boxes of every piece of correspondence he had ever received were stacked and ordered by correspondent and date beside a four-drawer file cabinet containing papers as essential as the deed to the house and family birth certificates and as sentimental as his children's report cards and school projects. The footlocker beside them contained war souvenirs and memorabilia; the oak dresser opposite was stuffed with bills and receipts and canceled checks from every financial transaction he had been party to for four decades. The room was a physical manifestation of the furnishings of his memory, but the arrangement of furniture around an imitation Oriental rug was that of a poor man's version of the pastor's study.

He lit a cigarette. Three-thirty-three on the digital clock, a number the pastor could lecture on—the unity of form and content, say. A number as perfect as God, lasting only a moment before dissolving into the very thing it recorded, gone into a dimension a man could not physically attend. Like that archipelago of hours exactly thirty-eight years ago when he, Dutch Potter, belly down on the deck of a ship yawing across the Channel, tried not to think of landfall and what awaited him there. But he had failed, just as, for so many years afterwards, despite desperate supplications to Saint Withold, he'd failed to expunge the recurring nightmare of running in slow motion across that mortar-rocked beach, naked and unarmed and cold under the sky, cupping his balls in his hands.

There was a cassette player on the side table to his right and in it was a tape recording of the NBC radio broadcast of the invasion of Normandy. He'd ordered it out of a magazine in the 1960s and listened to it on the anniversary every year since. The news didn't render the day as he remembered it unfolding but rather in the frigid factuality of history's proclamations. But it put the enormity of what they had done in a context, and there was also a prayer the announcer said for the troops that Dutch thought would be appropriate for grace before the lunch they were having at the house that day. He pushed the Play button and John MacVane's voice rose through the static.

"Operation Overlord," it had been called—the attack on Hitler's "Fortress Europe" from nine Allied army divisions, three airborne and six infantry, 130,000 men, Dutch among them. There had been more than five thousand ships and a thousand aircraft used to carry it out. Sarah heard this broadcast hours after Dutch and the First and 29th Infantry Division hit Omaha Beach, the hot one, the one taking the greatest toll on the Allies, and she wrote to him that day in a fantod of desperation. He did not receive the letter for three weeks, they were nearly in Paris, and it arrived with four others from her. These and the envelopes of every other letter she sent during his three years in Europe, bound in brick-sized parcels with twine, were as crisp as money. Inside, her professions of love looped in Catholic-school cursive through the smallest details of life at home with her parents—details he had lived for, and loved her more for sending, if such a thing could have been possible then.

They had married between boot camp and his shipping out to southern England in August of 1943, and after the three-day honeymoon she returned to her parents' house as if the whole thing were a date that had gotten out of hand—except things once mortally sinful were now their duty to her church. It was a duty she carried out with shocking fervor, and after he'd gone she focused all that energy on doing her part in the war effort, working in the stitching room at EJ's Avenue C building until the seventh month of her pregnancy. Most women were getting jobs, she'd written, so he shouldn't be sore about it, and the doctor said it wouldn't hurt the baby. The factory manufactured boots for GIs; she had started in the boxing room and quickly worked her way up. The labor exhausted her, but she thought of her monotonous toil giving some comfort to her Jack and brave men like him. Like her brother Liam, God keep him, who'd died the year before at Guadalcanal. Rationing was not easy. She went to the movies on Saturday nights with her sisters Eileen and Ruth and some friends from work. Abbott and Costello were her favorite; they made her laugh the laugh he said was his favorite in the world. Did he get any of the new songs over there? Her favorites were "You'll Never Know" and "Mairzy Doats"—excepting, of course, their song, which was "I Don't Want to Walk Without You" and which made her cry whenever she heard it. She would often write out the lyrics to a new song, or the plot of a movie, underlining her favorite parts. But all that was ballast for exclamations of love she could not keep herself from expressing, she just couldn't, and he, in a foxhole or bivouac, could not resist reading again and again.

He'd ordered the letters by date, starting from the second week in England and through the campaigns into the months of limbo after V-J Day: exercises in southern England, Ike's hard and humble voice, the invasion, bivouacking through Brittany, Paris, Belgium, Holland, Germany (Jonny's colic, Jonny's first word, Jonny walking!) as his father marched and crawled and fought his way across a wrecked continent, and succeeding, achieving victory, only to begin preparing to train for the invasion of Japan. Every day had been an entire life back then, and hope had been rewarded. "As bright as the sun, they say," Sarah had written about the explosion across the world that did in a place called Hiroshima. Then another, and he was coming home. Home, Jack! *Home!* It was the word then, on everyone's lips as if it were newly minted slang.

He'd returned a different man—more introspective, inwardly less sure of things but outwardly more abrupt, or less apparently concerned about how others perceived him. He was closer to friends who had also served, but his marriage was less passionate than the honeymoon had portended. It did not help that during those first months he could not make love. His body wouldn't respond and he didn't know why and he mostly didn't care why. Lying with Sarah was all he thought about for two and a half years, when he could think, and then this. There was much to work out, and the way to do it was in his cups at the VFW on Robinson Street, which was frequented by men who had discovered that life at home was in some ways more difficult to handle than the day-to-day of the campaigns, where, though death reigned, at least the ambience was masculine and the code of conduct among soldiers as sure as the purpose they shared. When he and Sarah finally did resume the physical love they'd initiated before his departure—more the result of osmosis, it seemed, than choice—the process was cautious, muted, self-conscious, fumbling.

She witnessed fits of temper she did not realize he was capable of, often over the smallest things—a dish in the sink, stale bread in the box, a few dollars spent foolishly. It would have been hard going financially in those first few years anyway, but it was made worse by Dutch's erratic employment, moving from one job to another before finally settling in with Triple Cities Traction.

These difficulties took focus in the rearing of the child. At four years old Dutch knew that they were in for a rough ride. That was the year Jom ran away from home for the first time. He'd made a hobo stick, as he had seen done in the movies, and took off down the driveway of the East Side apartment house they were living in, surprised that his parents were actually letting him go. Dutch waved to him from the porch, holding Sarah back with his free arm. When Jom—called "Jonny" then, before his youngest sister's mispronunciation rechristened him—got to the end of the driveway, Dutch told him to write them a postcard once in while, and directed Sarah back into the living room.

"You didn't have to say that," Sarah had said. "You didn't have to enjoy it."

After fifteen minutes Sarah suggested they go look for him. Dutch, sitting on the sofa reading the newspaper, didn't answer. Ten more minutes passed and Sarah, pacing the room, said they should do something.

"He'll be back," Dutch said, turning a page.

Sarah waited as long as she could and then stood before him and said, "Jack, if you won't go out there and bring him back, I will!"

"Says here," Dutch said, "the Russians are working on getting the bomb."

"It'll be dark soon," she said.

"The Russkies get the bomb and it's goodnight, Irene. That Stalin—"

Sarah tried grabbing the paper from him, but he pulled it back. "Get out there and find him!"

"You baby that kid," Dutch finally said. "You give him everything he wants."

"He's just a child, Jack!"

He squeezed the newspaper as if it were the collar of a man who had insulted him, holding it to his face and listening to her footfalls across the carpet to the foyer, the whining of the screen door.

Sarah's eyes would burn at him sometimes in those days, as if she'd saved what little capacity for anger she possessed just for Dutch, eyes as dark as a man's worst fear that seemed to say that they were doing just fine together, mother and child, before he returned from Europe and why didn't he go back there and leave them alone? Sarah would never even have thought such a thing, he knew that even then, but the look on her face was so direct, so full of spite against gentle features unprepared to support it without becoming grotesque, that he could not belabor the point and pretended to go off on some urgent chore. But she would follow him, she wouldn't give up, and no matter how heated the next phase of argument, no matter what he said to her to hurt her to the marrow of her bones, she never failed to end her part of it by saying that however angry he made her, she loved him and she would never stop loving him. Did he hear her? Ever!

What defenses could Dutch—or, he believed, any man—muster against that? But the more he fell back into love with her (if, in fact, he had ever fallen out of love), the less he felt worthy of the love she returned, and he remained disoriented, at best, and sometimes angrier than he had been before the argument began. Sarah knew her Jack, or believed she did, and she knew it was the war, whatever he had seen or done, or some interrelation of both, and she never brought it up but one time, telling him one night after making love that she respected his silence but if he ever wanted to talk she would listen, no matter what he had to say. But he never spoke of it except to explain briefly his insistence on such an odd name for their first daughter.

So why break the silence on that day as he planned to do all these years later? He wondered this sitting on the floor in a nest of letters, tangled in the coils of Sarah's script, looped among its loops, as if he were something written upon the attic among his things. He never needed to talk about the war, never wanted to talk about the war except to Jom, man to man, when the time seemed appropriate, when it might do him some good. But not saying something aloud on the sixth this year, in his state of mind, would make it simply another day, a Sunday in a June in a year in a decade, and that shouldn't be, couldn't be, if he could help it.

Souvenirs from the war were neatly packed in the footlocker to his left. A deck of Conklin's marked playing cards bound by the scapular he wore at his death; a small Bible, metal-plated, with a crease where it deflected a bullet from the aorta of Lopez, who had it in the pocket of his fatigues; a strip of cloth with Klein's blood; a laminated copy of Ike's letter to the troops before the invasion; his 1939–45 Star, his France and Germany Star, and his War Medal; a Nazi flag folded in a square; a music box that played "We Gather Together to Ask the Lord's Blessing," taken from a house in Essen, where he later discovered his ancestors, then the Pfannenschmidts, to have lived; his disassembled haversack and under it his field jacket, wool ODs, HBT fatigues, rubberized raincoat, web gear with X harnesses, olive drab helmet, boots. And at the very bottom, the serious hardware: a Luger taken off a soldier near the Elbe; two bullets for it; Rizzo's hunting knife, which he, and then Dutch, were going to use to cut off Hitler's balls; a hand grenade, what they used to call a pineapple.

He could hear Sarah cough in the bedroom below him, then the familiar complaint of the bed and another cough from another room. Catherine. It was Ruth, then, running the faucet in the bathroom, and he noticed by the light at both attic windows now that dawn had come and passed without his knowing, the day waking over the letters and artifacts strewn like trash across the floor. The light had been gray at 0600 on D-1; Dutch had stared at the sky from where he stood in the crowded LST and watched the low drab sky before the door fell open to bedlam.

There would be ten of them at the table with him, and he knew where each would sit. He would stand at the head with Sarah to his left and Sammy Corcoran to his right and clasp his hands together just as they were clasped now and when he bowed his head it would cue everyone to do the same. But even in his imagining Bummy Potter-Bumgartner would refuse to put his hands together for any God, and sit, arms folded, at the other end of the table waiting for them to finish. They had been at odds since Jom dragged him home from high school as a friend—a designation his son made with pathetic ease but one Bum saw fit to take personally. At times he seemed affable enough, even silly, playing nutty pranks to entertain his children or his friends, as if he were trying to be Jommy in his absence. But a sinister calculation worked overtime behind that baby face, and Dutch was not fooled by the earnestness with which he expressed his opinions. He'd look down the length of the table that served the same purpose as the hyphen between their surnames and shoot him a look he deserved, then soften his face for Georgia, their three children, then Ruth, Sammy, Sarah, Catherine beside little Joseph, nodding at each like a sergeant at inspection, and begin.

"Whoever it was of the test tube and the print, who joined molecules and dust and shook them till their name was Adam; who taught worms and stars that they could live together, we beseech your blessing on this food and upon those of us about to share it. And when we do, let us remember those who gave their lives so that we might live free. If from every place of worship, from home and factory, from men and women of all ages and many races and occupations, our supplications rise, then may those souls which have gone out before ours to make such a gathering as this possible never be forgotten."

It would be so moving that it would shock Bum into saying "Amen" and meaning it, and then Dutch would sit and as they ate tell stories he'd never chosen words for. It would feel odd, purgative, set him free, return him, somehow, to the daily world and its concerns. He'd sing songs of unsung heroes—Conklin, Klein, Rokos, even Wimp, who died just last year but really ceased living during the war—and by singing them, bring them back. It was important he emphasize that it wasn't about heroism. They had no choice; there was only one way to go. It was beautiful in its simplicity. Something in the world needed fixing that only risking everything could achieve. And it certainly wasn't about him. Finer men than Dutch Potter—better sons and brothers and soldiers, men who'd had it in them to be better husbands and fathers and grandfathers and uncles, who had much more than Dutch's two cents of talent to spend in the world—were decomposing in the soil they fought for on the coast of France. Wimp would have understood this was not false modesty or self-pity; it was true for him as well. Wimp, who was only a lowlife bum to anyone who saw him on the streets of Providence. But who knew that he had saved five lives in three countries by risking his own? How many knew Rizzo dived on a grenade in Belgium, that Moulton took out a sniper in Saint-Lô and Lopez hopped on a Panzer tank in the Ardennes like a cowboy at a rodeo? Saying their names in the context of these moments was a way to bring a little of them back— that was all. Return a bit of the life stolen from them—the flesh made word, so to speak—so that memory itself might not decompose in the minds of those served by their deaths.

But even as he arranged each article of his dress uniform on the armchair—the trousers, the shirt, the tie, the jacket, the hat, his three medals—so that it looked like the ghost of Dutch the soldier facing Dutch the old man, even as he did this he might have felt himself heading into a day that held disaster befitting the anniversary it marked. How, for example, could Bummy Potter-Bumgartner, a former radical and conscientious objector cum stockbroker who still played hippie on the weekends, sit and listen to Dutch's stories without comment—for the sake of the children around them, he'd claim, so that war not be glorified and more made possible in that glorification? Hadn't two new wars just started that weekend? But how could Dutch not defend the telling for the sake of the dead and their sacrifice? How could Sammy, a veteran of the Pacific theater, not side with Dutch? How, in the din of rising tempers, could Vietnam not be mentioned, and then how not Jom's name and all hell breaking loose? Wasn't it such stories that gave Jom the idea that enlisting was a viable option for him? Didn't Bummy dodge the war not because he actually believed in anything other than himself but because he was a coward? It was an old argument but one they'd never had. Sarah would fall apart and Ruth would come to her aid by going after Dutch with what she thought she knew about his night in the city lockup and the shame it brought upon the family. Catherine had already been stunned to irrelevancy by a disastrous marriage but Georgia, defending her husband, would say she hated this house and all of them hated this house and the only honest one among them was Margaret who did something about it by moving as far away as she could. How could all of this not burst in Dutch, not freeing him to be a part of life again but to finally say the things he'd pent up over the years, clearing his mind by clearing the room one by two by four, even Sammy, every adult but Ruth in tears, the children agape, leaving Dutch alone amid the smoldering ruins of lunch?

But at that moment the possibility never occurred to him. With his pajamas discarded, he dressed himself in the clothes he had lain across the chair. He had to suck in his paunch to accommodate the shirt, and the trousers were tight at his thighs and backside. Before buttoning the fly he took his penis into his hand. Creator and snake, like Job's God, he thought. Before he left that cabin in the Catskills to return to Fort Dix, Sarah had fished it out of this very uniform while they were standing in the kitchen—just unbuttoned his fly with alarming dexterity when they were kissing goodbye and she saying, her tongue moving at his mouth, "One more thing, buster," and stroked him gently, slowly at first, her other hand working over his scalp, kissing him with her warm open mouth that had become as his own in those few days because it seemed they'd shared more breaths than they took apart, tasting his lips, breathing his breath again. When he was full in her hand she lifted her skirt and rubbed him along the inside of her thigh, looking down at what she was doing and then up at him with those eyes and when he could no longer stand it he lifted her by the buttocks and she wrapped her legs around him and he was inside her again, standing in the middle of the kitchen of his uncle's cabin as if doing it in midair before they landed against the cupboard by the sink, her kisses so full and her embrace so tight he thought he might enter her so completely they'd be gone. She breathed words on his lips and neck and ears; she was saying that he better not dare not come home, that she wouldn't accept that at all, not at all, Private Potter, and that was an order from Mrs. Potter, who loved him and would always love him and would be waiting for him every minute of every day and that he'd better come home, and he said he was, right then, and laughing out the words as he breathed them, but she was crying, her tears were wet against his forehead and cheek, he could taste them as she said over and over he'd better come home, he'd just better come home to her.

In the attic his penis was a warm mass in his fist. He tucked it back inside his trousers, buttoned his fly, and joined the clasp across his girth. He saluted the opposite wall and whispered, "Good luck!" in impersonation of Ike. "Let us all beseech the blessing of Almighty God upon this great and noble undertaking!" He brought his right arm down straight at his side, frozen at attention, staring ahead at nothing.

Does sound go on forever as a sound?

No sound lasts forever as a *sound*. The waves that
carry the sound become weaker and weaker,
and finally our human ears can hear them no longer.
Nor is there any scientific instrument, no matter how
delicate, that can record sounds after a certain length
of time has passed. The waves that have carried the
sounds to our ears have ceased being audible.
The energy of sound-waves, however, is never lost. If
we had more delicate instruments for the measuring
of sound, we might find traces of sound-waves in
the movement of air particles long after the sound
had ceased. Although the sound has ceased as
a sound, the energy of its waves must go on
in some way forever.

—FROM *QUESTIONS AND ANSWERS FROM
THE BOOK OF KNOWLEDGE*

FOUR

Heaving forward, the bus roared past Main Street facades and, through the racket of window rattle and engine strain, as if on another frequency, Hulda Lambert could hear the driver grumbling in a tone more calculating than the climbing and declining gears. She wondered if the man was still thinking about the truck idling at the stop where she had boarded back near the Triumph Supermarket in Johnson City, and if so, why he'd carry the grudge for more than a block. She'd left her umbrella there, befuddled by the ruckus he'd made, and wasn't happy about that, but she'd gotten over it, or would eventually.

The driver's army uniform fit poorly. He could have been the veteran at the Normandy cemetery featured on the cover of *Parade* magazine in the *Sunday Press* the day before—the very photograph that had inspired her to take this trip to her husband's grave in Hillcrest—and she thought of the signs of apocalypse a Jehovah's Witness recently advised her to watch for. The headlines in the newspaper dispenser at the bus stop announced that war had erupted in the Middle East—a sure sign, she remembered this Mr. Walsh saying—and then she boarded the bus to see the driver dressed like this.

It was a few minutes past six, the first bus of the morning, and there were only three other people back of her from where she sat opposite the rear exit—a gentleman in a suit, a young waitress in a dirndl, and a man in a white T-shirt writing furiously in a notebook about the size of the paperback on Hulda's lap. The one person sitting up front, an albino, probably couldn't see clearly enough to have paid much attention to the driver, and in any case he was eased back in his seat with the sports section of the *Sun-Bulletin* held full span to his face.

The bus farted to a halt just past the granite arch marking the border between Johnson City and Binghamton and three people boarded after the young man with the notepad got off. First was a handsome woman who jammed her coins into the fare box, followed by a large black nurse who had taken the three steps with some effort and complained about being cut in front of.

"'Sides that you're *late*," she said to the driver, passing the fare box without paying and heaving her weight into the first seat, just behind the driver—the one facing sideways across the aisle. She touched at the lavender cloth wrapped tightly around her head and smoothed her uniform over her thighs as she told the white man who had come up behind her to pay for them both.

His name was Andy, and when the door slapped shut and the bus lurched forward a few coins spilled from his open hand. He steadied his black-rimmed glasses against his forehead and scanned the floor, but the woman told him to forget it.

"It's lost," she said. "And get me a transfer, too."

Andy counted aloud as he poured coins into the fare box, and when he got the transfer he passed it over to the woman before sitting beside the albino in the seat opposite. The albino put his paper down and squinted at him.

"I'm gunna be late again and I'm gunna get canned," the woman said.

"You'll be OK, Grace," Andy said.

"Whatta *you* know, Mr. Unemployed? All you got to do is call Meals on Wheels when you need something on the table."

She folded her arms under a dauntless bust and asked the driver what the hell time they could expect to arrive at the place she could get the 28 Robinson. Andy looked from the driver to Grace, back to the driver, and when nothing happened turned to the albino and said, "When we get there, I guess. Huh?"

"Hey, GI Joe!" Grace yelled. "I'm acksin' you a question." But the driver said nothing and Grace ratcheted her arms under her breasts and said, "That's it. Ignore the nigger."

She demanded the time from Andy, who opened his mouth to say something, but stopped, tapping on the watch with the stem of a corncob pipe he had taken out of his pocket.

"I got five after, but it must've stopped. Nuts."

He put the watch up to his ear, and Grace rolled her eyes. "That's not *all* that's stopped," she said to the albino, rotating her finger at her temple.

Andy leaned toward the albino and said, "I'm fine," and then, in a grave tone, "Grace thinks *all* her neighbors are crazy. She just plain hates Carhart Avenue." He winked and leaned back against the window, dug into the pocket of his trousers, and came up with a foil pouch of Half & Half. "She thinks I'm a little, you know, because they had to put me on medication for a while," he said, loading his pipe. "But it wasn't serious. I caught my wife with another man right in our own bed. What a thing *that* was. It takes the wind out of your sails, I tell you. But anyways, that was two years ago, and I just got depressed for a while."

He planted the pipe stem in his mouth, struck a match, and fed the flame to the bowl. "This new morality gets me confused," he said, puffing. "I know it's how things work now, but I liked it better the old way."

The bus stopped so suddenly that the albino hit his head against Andy's shoulder and rebounded against the backrest of his own seat. In the mirror above the windshield the driver's eyes were burning like gas jets and he was saying something about smoking on vehicles of public transportation in New York State in a hoarse voice that made you want to cough for it.

"Don't look at me," Grace said to Andy. "I woulda never lighted the goddamn thing in the first place."

Andy grimaced when he jammed his thumb into the bowl of the pipe, then lifted the digit as if to wish all the passengers luck. "Sorry," he said. "Sorry."

The driver's eyes vanished from the mirror and the bus roared forward. Andy packed away the pipe and pouch and mumbled something that, from back where she was sitting, Hulda couldn't hear. She opened the paperback on her lap and the spine cracked like a set of knuckles. It was called *Questions and Answers from the Book of Knowledge*. She'd chosen it from the others in her apartment because it said things about the world that made good sense. It was the only one in Peter's collection that did, and she wondered how it ended up on his shelves with all those others. Reading it sounded to Hulda like conversations she and Peter should have had but couldn't. The questions were good ones and the answers were clear. It was science told like a good story, because the authority in the author's tone didn't make you feel stupid for asking, and some of the explanations left a little room for mystery, even magic. Her favorite was the one about the inventor Guglielmo Marconi's attempt to make a special kind of radio that could broadcast sound waves that have been traveling through air particles for centuries— Lincoln's Gettysburg Address, for example, or Christ's Sermon on the Mount. If he had succeeded in inventing such a gadget she would have used it to listen endlessly to her father tell the fairy tales he reconfigured to landscape her world, or simply study the excited tone of Peter's voice as he talked his gobbledygook about the workings of the universe.

The pages of the book were yellow, almost brown; many of them had come unglued from the spine and were collected loosely among the others. Her fingers whispered through the margins, page after page, as she looked for something that might be especially interesting to know. "How does a dog sweat?" "What makes the poison in a snake's fang?" "Why is the sky blue?" "Are there other worlds like ours?"

Many astronomers believe that there are probably other families of planets like our own solar system. It seems very likely that if our sun, which is just an ordinary star, has planets moving around it, other stars may have planet families too. Astronomers have not been able to prove this, however, since even the biggest telescopes are not large enough to show other planets which might be revolving around stars.

In the three and a half years since Peter's death her memories of their life together filled her with as much anger as longing. He was a man of great passion that had little to do with her. She met him in the middle of his religious phase, between Unitarianism and Buddhism after an unpleasant foray into Calvinism, and stuck with him through various stages of mythology before he finally discovered cosmology and its glorious "theories of everything." It was he who chided her for not finishing anything, but in the wake of his foaming interests it was she who was still around with no chance to resolve what had been left between them. He once analyzed her character as a symptom of the paralyzing dread of death, which he claimed not to fear himself.

"*What?*"

"Look at you. What do you ever finish? You toss out magazines before you're halfway into the first article. There are romance pulps all around the place with bookmarks stuck in the pages. Look at the size of those cigarette butts in the ashtray! You never finish the dishes—you always leave at least two or three cups or utensils rotting with crud in the sink."

"I don't finish the dishes because I'm afraid to die. That's precious."

"Think of it. If something is completed it's over. Done. And you can't deal with it. Endings, small to grand, scare the hell out of you."

"Here's an ending," she'd said, picking up her drink from the coffee table and draining it.

"*That's* an exception. And for a hypochondriac, a pretty strange one."

"It's only gin."

"Hardly a nutritious beverage."

"Grain and juniper berries. Protein, I'll bet. Look it up on that chart you got hanging in the alcove over there. The gas-and-liquids thing."

"You won't find spirits on my periodic table."

"I don't dine at your periodic table."

Science! What he called his "quest for truth," his "religion of curiosity and wonder." He was an elementary-school teacher who thought he was Einstein, thought that with a shelf of incomprehensible books and enough drive you could find out how and maybe why the universe was made. But you can't fool a wife. His quest, whatever it was, had more to do with escape than search; you could tell by the way he treated her, or didn't treat her, camouflaging his fear of being intimate with highfalutin theories. "What about the part of the universe that's me?" she'd ask, but it just pushed him further into his theories.

They stopped at the corner of Crandall and a young woman boarded wearing a scarf so yellow it was as though the sun had risen in the bus. Her black blouse and slacks highlighted other colors—the green sash, the orange fingernail polish and lipstick, the rouge across her cheeks. Crescent rainbow earrings swung at her neck as she lugged a handbag larger even than Hulda's, also streaked with rainbows, down the aisle.

Are there other worlds indeed, Hulda thought. She tried to resume reading, but this new passenger began humming a tune so beautifully she couldn't concentrate. Grace craned her neck to see what was happening, and when their eyes met, Hulda tapped her temple exactly as Grace had touched her own to define Andy to the bus—then pointed at this rainbow girl. Grace nodded and Hulda did the same.

She placed her reading glasses in their case and packed them, along with the book, between the wrapped sandwiches and pint of Gilbey's gin in her purse. She took out her compact, opened it, and dabbed powder on her nose and cheeks, wondering how she might look to a stranger. Her face had character for a woman her age, if she did say so herself. Her nose was as Roman as Julius Caesar, sloping to the square Scandinavian jaw her mother bequeathed. Her eyes, her father's, the blue jewels of her countenance, still held the luster Peter had fallen for so long ago. It was all that was left of her youth, the essence of her, before wonder became confusion, trapped inside her now, looking out, plaintively, whispering the past in a voice harder and harder to hear. She shut her compact and buried it in her purse.

The bus stopped at Cedar Street for a woman toting a screaming infant and again four blocks further to let them off, and then didn't stop again until they got to the corner of Front Street, where the driver turned on the hazard lights and sat with his face in his hands. No one boarded and none of the passengers had pulled the cord to request a stop, and just when Hulda was certain Grace, at least, would say something, the door of the bus slapped open and the driver pounded down the steps to the sidewalk, where he paced in front of the Binghamton Optical Center for a few moments and then disappeared around the corner. The rainbow girl hummed in harmony with the idling engine and the heads of the other passengers bobbed as if keeping time until Grace demanded the time from Andy, who had to remind her his watch had stopped. The albino brought his wristwatch to his eyes but Hulda couldn't hear what he said because a boy shouldering a boom box boarded the bus and paraded the amplified racket down the aisle. He wore vein-colored jeans and a tattered T-shirt and when he passed Hulda she could see the blond bristles over his lip. He fell into the last seat and stared at the passengers with his jaw raised over the contraption on his lap.

When the rock song short-circuited into a commercial about acne, the man in the suit across the aisle from Hulda looked back over his shoulder and said something to the boy. He was holding a set of papers in such a way that Hulda could see the letterhead for a law firm with many names.

The driver came around the corner dazed, it seemed, his arms at his sides in those short jacket sleeves. A new song roared through the bus just as he boarded and he stopped at the top of the steps looking down the aisle at the boy, who volleyed glare for glare until Andy tapped the driver's arm and pointed at the fare box.

The driver threw himself behind the wheel, flicked off the hazard lights, and sent the bus into a hard right turn onto Front Street instead of continuing down Main. The passengers looked out the windows and then at each other and then out the windows again, but even after they veered left onto Riverside and swung left again onto the loop near the Arena and the Collier

Street Bridge, no one said anything until they were across the Susquehanna River barreling up Pennsylvania Avenue, perhaps thinking, as Hulda had, that the driver was taking a shortcut to BC Junction to make up for lost time.

But as they rocketed into the countryside, no one could be heard anyway. The driver, his shoulders cramped over the steering wheel, moved only to navigate or, if someone stood up, as Andy did twice and the albino did once, threw the bus into swerves that sent them back into their seats. At one point the lawyer lifted a hand as if he had the answer to all this and his briefcase crashed into the aisle. Papers spilled and as he reached to catch some of them Hulda lip-read his furious curses. The plastic cord moved wildly overhead, Grace flailed her arms like the ululating Arab woman on the news the night before, Andy watched her with an expression that looked something like elated terror. Hulda turned to the lawyer and yelled for him to do something, jabbing her finger in the air, calling him names that she couldn't hear herself saying.

Sweat on his forehead looked like condensation on glass when he finally did rise to take hold of the ceiling rails on either side of the aisle and pull himself forward against the motion of the bus. But when he got to where he could shout into the driver's ear, nothing happened. They kept hurtling south toward the Endless Mountains like an airplane falling out of the sky. Hulda grasped the safety rail in front of her and kept her feet planted wide apart but still smashed her shoulder against the window when they turned off the road, and then, some time later, when they turned again—this time onto a dirt road where dark woods digested the bus whole. Branches slapped at the sides and roof, rocks and ruts stuttered their speed. When the lawyer reached for the ignition on the dash, the driver struck his face with the back of his fist and he fell back, landing flat on his back near the long seats facing the aisle. It took him a few moments to pull himself up into a sitting position, but when he tried to stand he fell back down again.

They dove into a clearing at the pinnacle of a hill overlooking a shaded valley, and Hulda would remember how pretty it all looked—remember proudly how even then, in the throes of terror, she'd appreciated beauty—and what would Peter think of *that*? Sun breaking through clouds splayed streams of light she once believed to be heaven's grace pouring over creation, gilding the flanks of the plush hillsides of what her father used to call the end of the world, and if you were there to catch that grace, feel it, and you believed, you were blessed.

But when they began their descent into the valley, gathering speed that could not be controlled because it was not the engine's but gravity's, and then near the bottom when they swerved off the dirt path and shot straight into the deep and pathless woods, she knew they couldn't keep missing trees at this velocity and she braced herself, remembering the only other accident she'd ever been in—her father driving her to see the fireworks in Endwell on the Fourth of July, 1926, a white truck running a red light, the screaming of brakes, crumpling of metal, shattering of glass into blackness.

FIVE

"Is everyone all right?" It was the young waitress, named Heather, whose soft voice lilted through the early-bird specials at the Red Oak but here shattered the silence around them. Her fingers trembled at the backrest of the seat above the lawyer, Matthew, who lay on his back in the aisle with his leg twisted under him. He did not know if he had blacked out and, if so, for how long. When he struggled to his feet the pain in his left ankle nearly brought him back down again and he figured it to be broken. The large nurse and the woman with the rainbow earrings were also up, and they looked back at him and then at one another through sun-spangled dust, touching their bodies with the flats of their hands. The old woman that had been sitting across from Matthew crawled back into her seat and sat folding and unfolding her hands on her lap.

The front windshield had been demolished by the branch of an oak now splaying leaves through the front third of the bus. When the albino rose through them he was squinting so hard a pink blush glowed on his cheeks. He ran his hand over the branch and then stroked his goatee, tilting his head to one side as if straining to hear something in the distance. He wore a blue T-shirt upon which the words KEEP YOUR SOX ON were written in white across the chest and, across the paunch, TV 38. It was a size too small for him and the fly of his dungarees was at half-mast, but his expression suggested a measured intelligence.

"There's blood all over," Andy announced. "Head wound. Pretty bad."

He was wedged between the branch and the fare box, leaning over the driver, and through the rearview mirror now dangling over the broken windshield Matthew could see him place three fingers on the driver's neck and hold them there. Then he lifted the driver's arm, and when he let go the hand bounced off the dash and swung freely at his side.

"He's gone," Andy said, shimmying free and moving back down the aisle toward Grace. "Dead. Gone."

"Try the door," Grace said, and when he did not move she pushed him into the branch until he ducked under it and crawled to the stairwell. He was out of sight for a moment, then resurfaced, dipping his shoulder into the door and grunting.

"It won't budge! Something's blocking it. From the outside."

He gave it three more tries and then crawled back under the branch to Grace.

"Help me look for my batteries!" It was the boy, on his knees in the back of the bus. "I hope it ain't broke . . . the batteries came out . . ."

"I think my wrist's broke," Grace said.

Heather covered her face with her hands and began weeping and Hulda, staring at her, then at the empty seat beside her, said the word "purse" over and over until Matthew rummaged through the debris on the floor and came up with two of them. She took the larger one and fell silent. The handsome woman, smartly dressed, her dark hair falling into her face as she bent forward to take the other, put a hand on Hulda's shoulder and said her name was Erica and that Hulda should take a deep breath.

"What about the back door?" Grace said. "Let's try that."

"Just wait," Matthew said. "Sit for a minute. Let's get our bearings, make sure everyone is okay."

"I got a broke hand," Grace said.

"What about you?" he said to Heather.

She rubbed her cheek with the knuckle of her index finger and shook her head.

"That branch up there just missed putting my lights out for good," Andy said. "And I got racked in the you-know-whats."

"You?" Matthew said to the girl with the rainbow earrings.

"Rose," she said, the wings of her nostrils at full span. "And I'm aghast, if that's an injury. I mean, what in the world?"

The albino, who told them to call him Whitey, suggested they put the kibosh on the medical clinic and get the hell out.

"I got one!" the boy shouted, holding up a battery. "Three more to go!"

"Get over here and sit down," Matthew said.

"Make me, asshole."

Matthew looked for a place to be sick, if it came to that, and tried to steady himself, until he realized that it wasn't him but the bus, tilted at an angle, port over starboard.

"This is incredible, right, Grace?" Andy said. "I mean, one minute we're just going downtown—"

"Save it for the papers, Andy."

"We'll have to get help," Matthew said, "but it's not wise for all of us to go. We may be a ways from any house, certainly from a road with any sort of traffic—especially at this hour. The terrain is pretty rugged. Maybe some could go and the rest just sit tight."

Grace looked out the window and shook her head. "There's snakes out there. Rattlers."

"Yeah?" Andy said.

"Bear, too. Worse thing, though, for me, is rednecks. They see a nigger stomping through these woods, they go for the gun."

"Well, *I'll* go," Rose said, and the albino said he'd join her.

"I'll stay here with you, Grace," Andy said.

"I'm afraid I wouldn't get very far with these," Erica said, indicating her high heels.

Matthew nodded and then called to the boy in the back, who didn't answer him.

"All right, then," Rose said on her feet.

A small boulder lodged against the bottom of the rear exit jammed that door, too, so Andy and Matthew pushed out the emergency-exit window near the back. Rose crawled out first, and Whitey tossed down his knapsack and followed. Everyone watched them hike across the clearing, Rose taking brisk strides through the tall grass and the albino slogging as though through water. He said something and Rose replied without looking back and then they disappeared into the woods.

"I'm gunna get the creeps just sitting here," Grace said.

"I guess this is OK now," Andy said, taking out his pipe and matches.

"Got another one!" the boy shouted. "I'll have the box in action in no time."

"So what do we do?" Erica said.

The crystal of Matthew's Rolex was smashed and he could not make out the time. "It might be a good idea to gather our things together," he said. "It'll give us something to do while we're waiting, and we'll make sure none of us lose anything. Does that sound all right?"

They surveyed the mess on the seats and floor—papers and manila envelopes, loose pages from Hulda's *Book of Knowledge* and pages of the morning newspaper, Styrofoam cups, ballpoint pens, tissues, a tampon, nail files, rolls of Life Savers, a legal

pad, loose Tic Tacs, tubes of lipstick—everyone's inside para-
phernalia there for everyone else to see. When Matthew spied
his pocket Dictaphone under one of the seats, he picked it up
and brought it to his mouth as though he were going to record a
message before placing it into the briefcase he had set on one of
the seats. The leaves of the oak branch rustled when he made his
way to the front of the bus. He paused at the partition behind
the driver's seat, took a deep breath before working his way
around it. There, just in front of him, the dead man, one arm
dangling, the other set at an angle on the steering wheel beside
his head. Blood had splattered across the dashboard and among
the shards of glass, and when he moved closer he could see
where it had runneled across the driver's cheek and neck. He
thought he heard the corpse swear and jerked back, hitting his
elbow against the branch, but it was only the boy, who was
standing near the stairwell studying the body through the other
side of the plumage of leaves. "Y'know?" he said, and Matthew
nodded.

When Matthew moved in, glass cracked under his shoes like
small bones. He found the microphone hooked on the side of
the radio console and brought it up to his mouth. When he
squeezed the lever nothing happened, so he leaned closer, keeping his balance on the good leg, and flicked each switch across
the console. Perhaps it only worked when the bus engine was
running, and he reached for the same key he had tried to disen-
gage before the crash. But when he turned it nothing happened,
so he worked his way to his feet, careful not to touch the body,
and placed the mike back into its holster above the dash. It
fell out and knocked against dashboard and steering wheel
before resting against the driver's shoulder. Matthew reached
into the back pocket of the driver's trousers and removed the
wallet, weighing it in his hand for a moment before opening it.
A twenty, two tens, and a five. A yellowed newspaper clipping

that fell apart when he tried to open it, something about the CIA. A poker hand of credit cards. A BC Transit ID and New York State driver's license: Jonathan R. Potter, 43 West End Avenue. Photos in plastic pockets: a wife, daughters, a son—a Marine. Grandchildren. Matthew had seen this driver every morning for three weeks, and at various times before when he'd had the 35 Endicott route, and he knew absolutely nothing about him. He looked down at what was left of him, a broken body in a war uniform. He took a breath and turned to make his way back down the aisle.

"What *is* this shit here?" Grace was saying. She held up a loose page from a paperback book. "They're all over the place. Question-and-answer stuff—like, look here, 'Does a hen know that a chicken will come out of her eggs.'"

"These papers aren't trash," Matthew said to Heather. "Here, let me take those."

"Well, lookee here," Grace said, holding up an airport bottle of Gilbey's gin. "It's happy hour!"

The boy, working his way down the aisle to the back of the bus, reminded everyone to keep an eye out for his batteries. Two were still on the loose, he said.

Grace held the little bottle by the neck and moved it back and forth in front of her face. "Anyone mind?"

"Just take it," Hulda said.

"*You?*" Grace said.

"Somebody gave it to me for a joke and I forgot to take it out of my purse."

"Well, thank the Lord," Grace said, twisting the cap. "I really do think my hand's broke, you know. This'll help that." She drained the shot and ran her tongue around her lips, eyes closed, then stopped, shifting her head to one side. "What was that?"

"What?" said Heather.

A squirrel rattled a statement from a nearby tree. A breeze played on leaves and then died.

"Bear," Grace said. "I bet."

Andy leaned to look out his window. "I don't see nothing."

The boy let out a raspberry and called them all chicken shit. Erica rose from her seat and walked to the back of the bus and asked him if he wanted company. She sat next to him before he could answer. Pipe smoke sweetened the air, and Matthew took a deep breath of it. Hulda had slipped something from her purse, and in a moment Matthew could see that she had another bottle—this one a full pint, or nearly full. He watched her turn the cap as though breaking the neck of a chicken. Erica was speaking to the boy again, asking if he was OK.

"What's it to you, lady?"

"I'm just wondering. A lot's happened here and I'm wondering if you're OK."

"What're you, my goddamn mother?"

"Can't I be friendly?"

"Yeah, right."

While they waited the bus accrued the stifling ambience of a waiting room. Every so often Grace would sigh, and when the silence got to be too much she read the answer to the question on the page of the paperback she'd found. Andy's smoke floated around them as they listened to Grace say that hens had no idea that fluffy little chickens would come out of the shells, though they were pleased when they did; they only knew that things like eggs were pleasant to sit on. It was instinct, she read, chuckling, one of the most important points about which was that an animal goes through the action without knowing what its purpose is, or what will come of it. As she read on about reasoning and intelligent beings and knowledge of the use and purpose of any given action, Matthew thought it might be nice to have a shot of

Hulda's gin, to dull the pain in his leg. But he did not move from his seat until a scream shot through the bus.

Heather was on her feet, her back to them, and through the dangling rearview mirror beyond they could see the matted head of the driver. He was buttressing himself against the branch, which shook against his weight. His mouth opened and blood trickled onto his chin. Hulda gasped and the driver's eyes flashed in her direction. The right side of his face was a mask of blood, and when he shook his head exclamations of it flew against the windows and seats.

"Bad-*ass*!" the boy said.

Grace turned and said, "You'd make a great fuckin' doctor, Andy."

The driver looked around the bus, dazed, as if he'd landed on his feet from a great height.

"Are . . . you OK?" Heather asked him.

When he did not respond, she took a step toward him, but backed away as though she had been pushed, and when she did they could see the gun shaking in the driver's hand, the barrel pointed at Heather, then at Hulda, back to Heather in a stammering sweep of the arm. Phlegm boiling in his throat released a word that sounded like "bitch," or "beach," as he jabbed the thumb of his other hand to indicate something behind him.

"Tell him OK," Matthew rasped, and Heather sputtered two "OK"s and an "all right," but they were hardly audible. When he barked his order again, the gun still trembling, Matthew said, "OK, Mr. Potter. OK."

The driver looked at him, head tilted, as if the voice he'd heard might have come from his own thoughts. "John long mustache!" he said.

"Yes," Matthew said, working his way up toward Heather. Dry blood cracked around the left side of his mouth; his yellow eyes moved beneath stiff, untended hair. "Dabrich ba dar . . ." he said. Not a question but a simple statement of fact. He said something else, louder, equally incomprehensible, then nodded, arched his back, and cast a suspicious but fatherly gaze at the passengers before issuing a complete oratory of nonsense ordered in some kind of syntactical pattern of sound.

Every so often an actual word popped out—"day," "boy," "sun" or "son," and then "God"—like streetlights flicking on at dusk. Perhaps coincidences of sound, except it kept on happening—"imp," and "us" or maybe "bus," and "beach" again; and then a gang of polysyllabic words rushed out of him—something about evening and morning and afternoon. He indicated the ceiling of the bus as if to prove a point. He must have felt the gun against his ribs then because he looked down at it and backed away as if someone else were pointing it at him. He held it up against the light, squinted fiercely, aimed it at the window to his right, and fired. The bus itself seemed to shriek, and in the quiet that followed someone whimpered. Matthew was crouching behind a plastic seat and just in front of his right foot a page from the dismembered paperback shouted at him in boldface: "What is Greenwich time?"

As the earth spins around, the sun seems to rise sooner, the farther east we are. So the apparent time, judged by the sun's rising . . .

He peeked over the edge of the seat and saw the driver ringed in sulfurous smoke, confused and fascinated, as if he'd just been born into the harsh light around him. Words from the page cadenced themselves foolishly in his thoughts, and then he heard himself speak.

"Mr. Potter? Please put the gun down."

"Hnh?"

"We're on your side, Mr. Potter."

"Mister?"

Matthew did not know military stripes and in desperation was about to guess sergeant when the driver said, "Dutch."

"Dutch?" he said, standing to face him.

"Dutch."

"OK, Dutch. We're on your side."

"Mission," he said.

"Of course," said Matthew.

"Course," Dutch said, lowering the gun to his side. "Where are you?"

It was his first real sentence, and the diction frightened the passengers more than the babbling. He was leaning forward, squinting fiercely, and it became clear that his right eye had been impaired, maybe blinded. Behind him, the plastic windowpane, fissured in gossamery chaos, refracted light like stained glass. He made his way down the aisle so stiffly, dragging his right foot, Matthew thought perhaps he *had* risen from the grave. When he stopped to shake the fog out of his head a drop of blood hit the top of one of the backrests like a correction on a term paper. He stopped and placed a bloody hand on Hulda's shoulder and said, "OK?"

"Scared," she whispered.

"Ha!" Dutch said, patting her cheek and straightening up. "Biggest club in the war!" When he turned to Heather his boot dammed a rivulet of urine snaking across the aisle. "You?"

She nodded without taking her eyes off his.

"Ah! Beckworth!" he said, flicking Matthew's tie. "S'down."

He proceeded down the aisle, leading with the left side of his face, the gun held casually in front of him. Matthew watched him pass within a few inches of his elbow and thought of rushing him, but didn't.

"Johnson!" Dutch bellowed at Grace.

She glared back at him but Dutch continued dragging himself

down the aisle. "Get dressed, sold-er," he mumbled, indicating Erica's stockinged legs with the barrel of the gun, and then spotted the boy standing in the back. "Kevin!" he shouted, raising his hand. The boy lifted his own hand, then quickly holstered it in his pocket.

Dutch turned and lumbered back up the aisle, mumbling, and then turned around to face them.

"Thank you. For coming," he said. "Got what it takes. Bond between you. I feel it. Like my son and me."

The passengers waited, but he said nothing else. He just stood there with his eyes closed and Matthew reached over and picked up the wallet on the seat beside him. He set it on his lap and flipped through the photographs again. The boy in military uniform stared out at him. The same blue eyes as the driver, same jaw, chin.

"Know why?" Dutch said, picking up a conversation in his head. "You lost!" He opened his eyes. "This world, it's bankruptcy. Boof!" He pointed at the shattered window with the gun and Hulda plugged her ears. "Forget. 'Bout you. *You.*" He pointed the gun at Heather. "Cost too much. *You,*" he barked, aiming at Erica, "no profit." He shrugged, lowering the gun. "Nuts," he said. "My only regret is . . . is I haven't had time to get to know you. Personally. Despite circumstances deprived you of your original commander, I feel you've given me your confidence. Co-op . . . eration, I mean."

His rheumy eyes smiled at them through the raccoon mask of blood. He took a step back and the leaves on the branch hissed at him. "Who . . ." he said, looking right at Hulda.

"Please don't," she said.

"Are you?"

"Hulda Lambert. I live at 47 Endicott Avenue in Johnson City. Please . . ."

But his attention had shifted to Heather, then Matthew—

focusing on one person for no more than a few seconds. He squinted to see beyond them. Sweat glazed the blood at his temple. He looked at one set of windows, then turned to look at the windows on the other side.

"Dutch?"

His head swung around but he could not see who had said his name.

"You're OK," Matthew said. "Everything's OK. Let's just stay calm."

"Beckworth?"

"My name is Matthew. We're on the bus, remember? The 35 Endicott. We've had an accident."

Dutch looked down at his boots, then at the gun in his hand.

"You were driving the bus. We had an accident. You hit your head."

"Accident?"

Heather nodded and her curls danced across her shoulders. "Two people have gone for help," she said. "Help should come soon. OK?"

"Help?"

"Soon."

"You've been hurt," Matthew said again. "Your head. We're only passengers. On the bus."

Dutch touched his forehead with the tips of his fingers and pulled them away to look.

"We want to help you," Matthew said. "Can we?"

Dutch shook his head, perhaps trying to clear it.

"I want to help you," Matthew said again, rising slowly from his seat. "OK?"

Dutch studied his hand, then put two fingers into his mouth. He pulled them out and licked his lips. The taste seemed to revive him. "Back!" he shouted.

"OK. OK. I'm going back. See?"

Dutch watched Matthew slide slowly into his seat and then studied the faces of the others. He licked his lips again under fiercely dilated nostrils. Without taking the gun off them he backed up toward the front of the bus, sidling backwards between the branch and the seat facing the aisle on the driver's side, mumbling to himself all the while as if in conversation with the rustling branch, moving his head at one angle or another to assess the shattered windshield, the blood on the steering wheel, the crisp glass on the floor. He leaned over and put his index finger into the bullet hole as if it were one of Christ's wounds, pulled it out and looked at it for a moment, and then shouted "Let's go!" so clearly it chilled the air. But he lowered himself onto the seat, the gun in his hand and that hand on his lap, staring straight ahead so vacantly it was as if he had himself gone but left his body behind to guard them.

SIX

When the pastor knocked at the front door, the poodle, already in high gear, fired off another round of vowels and one of the two men standing in the foyer turned and squinted. Pastor Philips heard his name in the turbulence and when he opened the door he thought of Dutch's greeting the day before. "Bless me, Father, for I have sinned," he'd said through the screen, and then broke into laughter louder than the quip deserved.

Inside, Sarah introduced the Reverend Philips as a friend of the family, hesitated, then apologized for forgetting the men's names already. The tall one with the shock of brown hair stepped forward and introduced himself as Detective Curley. He shook the pastor's hand without making eye contact, but Detective Lynch, old enough to be his partner's father, nodded when he said his own name.

Sarah clasped and unclasped her hands at her chest, saying, "Oh! Come in. Here. Please," and the poodle herded them into the living room with a fresh fusillade of barking.

Sammy Corcoran was sitting in one of the armchairs, and Ruth, from her rocking chair, said her name over the noise. "Perhaps you boys have heard of my Gerald? On the force forty-one years, six months. Retired maybe before your time. Gerald Flynn."

Neither detective gave any indication that they'd heard of him; they sat at either end of the sofa while the pastor offered the remaining chair to Sarah and stationed himself near the fireplace with his hands clasped behind his back.

"The detectives say they want to ask some questions about Jack," Sarah said.

"Right," Detective Lynch said. "You apparently know everything we know. The bus Mr. Potter was driving this morning is missing. We don't know where it is. We don't know what's happened."

"Mr. Lynch asked me has Jack called the house," Sarah said to Pastor Philips.

"We're covering all bases," Lynch said.

"Dollars to donuts the lummox has gone nutsy again," Ruth said.

"Excuse me?" Lynch said.

"Well, after yesterday I'd believe anything of the beast. He's not right, you know."

"Ruth, stop it."

"What happened yesterday?"

"He went bonkers. Right over there in the dining room. We were having a D-Day party. Can you imagine? It was Sarah's idea, I think. If it was to calm his nerves, it didn't work."

The detectives looked at one another, then back at Ruth. Georgia was talking on the phone in the kitchen; her tone was anxious, irritated, and then she hung up.

"He just got a little upset," Sarah said. "A disagreement with our son-in-law."

"And daughter and you and me and the deep blue sea," Ruth said.

Lynch removed a pen and notepad from the inside pocket of

his sport coat and asked what it was about, if they didn't mind him asking.

"Oh, goodness," Ruth said. "Where do I start? The world, I guess. But who really knows what's bugging the old ox. He wanted to talk about the war and apparently we didn't respond like he wanted us to, so he threw us out like trash to the curb. But not before making the most godawful accusations."

It hadn't been Sarah's idea but Dutch's, very casually mentioned only a few days before, as though it were no big deal, but she sensed it was important and tried to make it special. Bummy didn't want to come over, of course, but Georgia put him on his best behavior. They seemed to be getting along—they even took sides with the children playing soccer in the backyard, while the women prepared dinner. Sarah had an eight-pound spiced pork roast in the oven, assorted sweet rolls from Wagner's. She had baked German stollen herself that morning before Mass. She had peapods with almonds, golden-crumb broccoli, orange-glazed carrots. For dessert she had the three pies she'd made the day before: gooseberry, strawberry glaze, and Dutch's favorite, apple crumb. It was to show her husband that she knew it was important to him even if she didn't understand why. It came out so well, Ruth said, interrupting her sister, that she sat tortured at the table because she could not eat until Father Toibin came to give her communion on his rounds for the parish infirmed.

But when Dutch talked about what had happened that morning thirty-eight years before, the children kept interrupting him—wasn't Omaha in Nebraska? is a hedgerow a line where hedgehogs wait for their hedges?—and his story got as bogged down as the invasion itself until Sarah could tell he was straining to keep his temper. It was when Dutch told the story about his friend George Conklin's violent death and the children began asking real questions out of real curiosity that Bummy took issue, and it was only a matter of time before they let out everything they had been keeping in over the years about war and sacrifice and glory and shame and then, finally, Jom.

"He's had a rough time of it lately," Sarah said. "But he wouldn't do anything bad. Not Jack."

"That's a crock of the well-known article," Ruth said. "I told you he was heading for trouble again, Sarah. There comes a time when you must take a bull by the tail and face the situation squarely."

"You said 'trouble again,' Mrs. Flynn?"

"Yes. You fellas had him in the lockup not one month ago."

The detectives looked at one another again and the pastor's white eyebrows arched over his glasses.

"No charges were filed," Sarah said. "It was nothing."

"Pah!" Ruth said. "Whores and the like is nothing? Tell that to the monsignor and see what *he* says."

"Ladies of the evening?" Sammy said, shaking his head. "That doesn't sound like Dutch."

"You check it out," Ruth said to Lynch. "Some China girl. Broke into her apartment and wouldn't leave, is what I heard."

When Catherine and Georgia came in from the kitchen and stood under the archway separating the foyer from the living room, the poodle scrambled to her feet, looked at the girls, and slid back down onto her stomach beside the rocker.

"About this lunch yesterday and Mr. Potter's displeasure— could you be more specific?"

Lynch was a working-class man who had forged a smoother persona later in life—that's how the pastor read him. The shape of his nose was not the original, and set deep in his face above them his gunmetal eyes were all business.

"Just a little angry," Sarah was saying, "that's all. It just . . . Stan Zulik called to say he couldn't come, something had come up, and the reverend here had to leave before we ate—but that was my fault, because . . . I . . . ."

"What was this about an army uniform?"

"He's a veteran," Sarah said. Lynch shifted his head a little, waiting.

"Jonathan's been under a great deal of stress lately," Pastor Philips said. "A good friend of his died last summer and it seems to have had a strong effect on him. He became ill at the funeral, in New England. Had to be hospitalized—am I right, Sarah?"

"But he left before they could do the tests they wanted to do," Ruth said.

"Among other things," the pastor went on, "I think the experience caused him to re-evaluate his life, and he's been mired in a depression he's had difficulty negotiating. His son has been listed missing in action from the Vietnam War for a dozen years or so, and this understandably has aggravated his mind-set."

"How, exactly?"

"His job performance hasn't been too good," Sammy said. "I know that. He's been a little spacey, you know. I think he was suspended for a while, over the winter, right, Pastor?"

The pastor shrugged. "Under it all, Jonathan is a good man with a good head on his shoulders. I can't believe he'd do anything rash, Detective."

"Is he a member of any political organizations?"

"He thinks he's in cahoots with the President of the United States," Ruth said. "He writes to the White House and gets letters back. But I doubt he's on real friendly terms with the executive branch."

"Do you know the nature of the correspondence?"

"It no doubt has to do with the son," the pastor said, cutting Ruth off. "He's been more or less active in the POW-MIA issue for years."

"Active?"

"Well, letter writing, mostly. Just as I think any parent would be. He's been down to Washington a few times over the years, I

believe, Sarah? And he's visited veterans who knew his son during the war and kept in some correspondence with them as well.
All, I would imagine, common for people in his situation."

The telephone rang again and Catherine went out to the
kitchen to answer it. The interruption broke the rhythm of the
conversation and Georgia took advantage to introduce herself
to the detectives and say that her father was a very good and
responsible man who would never hurt anyone.

"What frame of mind was Mr. Potter in this morning before
he left the house, Mrs. Potter?" When she did not answer, Lynch
went on. "I mean, did he say anything that might lead you to
believe something was amiss? Had he calmed down?"

"I didn't speak with him this morning," Sarah said. "He gets
up before dawn. First shift . . ."

"*I* don't believe he even came back last night, did he, Sarah?"
Ruth said.

"Back from where?" Lynch asked.

As soon as Catherine returned from the kitchen the phone
rang again and, rolling her eyes, she went to answer it.

"He wasn't here for the rest of the afternoon nor evening,"
Ruth said.

"He walks," Sarah said. "It isn't unusual for him to go out.
For long walks."

"Did he come back last night, Mrs. Potter?"

She looked down at the carpet and said that she supposed he
didn't.

"Do you have any idea where he might have gone?"

She shook her head.

The doorbell rang and Georgia went into the foyer to answer
it, the yelping poodle right behind her. Over the noise Lynch
asked Sarah if her husband kept a diary or journal, and she
shrugged and mumbled an apology for not knowing.

"Try the attic," Ruth said. "If he keeps one, it's up there."

The detectives looked at one another and then Lynch asked Sarah if they might take a look.

"Jack's things?"

"This is only a preliminary investigation, Mrs. Potter. We're looking into all options. This is just one, and we'd really appreciate your cooperation."

Sarah nodded, looking down at the carpet. Georgia was talking out in the foyer. The screen door creaked open, breathed shut.

"Can't get up there," Ruth said. "He locks the door and no one knows where the key is."

"I'll show you," Sarah said, and stood, squared her shoulders, and led the way up the stairs.

The man Georgia had let into the house had a mop of graying chestnut hair and an untrimmed mustache and he followed them upstairs to the second-floor hallway without a word, just filed into line, and while they waited for Sarah to find the key to the attic—hidden somewhere behind the molding near the door—the pastor tried to recall his name. An old friend of Jom's, he remembered. Something Irish. Moran or McMahon.

Only the men went up, detectives first. The few times he visited, the pastor had never been up in this part of the house. When Dutch had made references to his "study," or sometimes his "office," the pastor envisioned paneled walls, thick carpeting, bookshelves, a hardwood desk. But the only furniture in the oddly configured room was a rumpled green armchair, a battered chest of drawers, a card table at which was set a single folding chair, a walnut lectern showcasing an oversized Bible, a coffee table, a pinewood credenza. And scattered throughout were sheets of paper and magazines and clothing and all manner of bric-a-brac, as though the room had been ransacked by thieves who didn't get what they were looking for.

"That his son?" Lynch asked, jerking his head toward a framed photograph on the wall near the armchair.

"Yes," Pastor Philips said. "Jonathan Junior. Enlisted in the late sixties. Declared missing in action in the early seventies during his second tour of duty. Some of these things are his effects, returned by the Marines."

Detective Lynch went over for a closer look. He tugged up at one of the legs of his trousers before crouching again, and began picking up one or another of the items scattered there, looking at each of them closely before putting them back down. Sammy joined him, like a child imitating an adult.

There were old copies of *Time* and *Life* magazines folded open to pictures of soldiers in action, decades of homemade Father's Day cards and birthday cards, yellowed paper clippings on battles in World War II and Vietnam, a wrinkled T-shirt neatly folded, British shillings and pound notes, a piece of cardboard with the word "South" written across it in black Magic Marker, K-rations cardboard—all strewn as though they had erupted out of the open footlockers and cardboard boxes banked against the armchair under the south slant of roof. The pastor had never figured Dutch to be a pack rat. He was too organized, too no-nonsense, too unsentimental. A clothbound book lay facedown on the coffee table as if shot from behind, and on closer inspection the pastor saw that it was a copy of the *Odyssey* in the original. Beside it was an Ancient Greek–English dictionary, and with its help Dutch had scribbled a rough translation amid the text of the epic's first three books, circling a word—"ευχαρίστησα," or "άνθρωπos o," or "πατήρ o"— and writing its English counterpart above or below or beside it.

Lynch fished the T-shirt out of the bewilderment of memorabilia, letting it fall open to reveal a bloodstain on the front in the shape, the pastor thought, of a human face—as though it were some badly botched forgery of the Shroud of Turin. Detective

Lynch looked at it quizzically for a moment; the shirt was too small to have belonged to Dutch, at least in this half of his adulthood, and the blood was discolored, more brown than red. He refolded it with ceremonious care before putting it back.

"Look," Detective Curley said from the corner. He held up a cartridge for a Luger. "This belong to anything around here?"

Lynch took it from him and held it up in the dust-moted light, then handed it back to Curley.

"Bill, I want to take some of this stuff back to the station. Make sure Mrs. Potter doesn't have any objections."

Detective Curley moved around Jom's friend—Meehan was his name, Pastor Philips now remembered—and stepped gingerly through the mess to make his way back down the stairs. Lynch resumed sifting through the papers on the floor around the chair. Sammy rummaged in the corner by the window, every so often saying "Jeez!" or "Sheesh!" Dutch had written in the large Bible and the pastor moved closer to take a look at the degree to which the raw intelligence he admired in his friend had gone awry. In Genesis 21, in red ink, he had underlined "God has made me laugh, so that all who hear will laugh with me," and in the margin had scrawled, "He makes me laugh too." In Genesis 25 he had underlined "And Abraham gave all that he had to Isaac," and above that, the phrases "I will go" and "bowing himself to the earth." He had circled 25:21 and bracketed 43:26–28. There were question marks and exclamation points in all the margins through the rest of Genesis. When the pastor saw the words "You see how this world goes" scrawled in red ink across the first page of Job, which had been bookmarked, he realized Dutch wasn't Hamlet, as he'd thought, but Lear.

Meehan was at his side reading over his shoulder and the pastor asked him if he was here on business. "I mean," the pastor said in a louder voice, "you aren't going to write this up in the newspaper?"

"What's that?" Lynch said.

"This fellow is a reporter for the *Sun-Bulletin,* I believe? Or is it the the *Evening Press?*"

"I'm not here as a reporter," Meehan said.

"A reporter?" Detective Lynch said.

"The education beat, Detective," Meehan said. "I'm here because I've been a friend of the family for many years. Jom was my best friend."

"Who?"

Meehan pointed to the photograph on the wall. "We went to school together."

An amplified voice crackled in the room, accented and excited. It took a moment for anything more than the odd word to come clear.

"... *We who remain in this land can most effectively enter into ... subjugated Europe ... and fortify the determination of our sailors, soldiers, and airmen, who go forth to set the captives free ...*"

"What is that?" Lynch said.

Sammy held up a portable cassette player for him to see. He put it back down on the side table, shut it off, ejected the tape, and lifted that up too.

"It says, 'Radio Reruns, for private use only.' Um. Oh, here. '*The Normandy Invasion.* Various NBC newscasts, 6/6/44."

"Tell me more about this guy," Lynch said.

The pastor opened his mouth, but Meehan spoke first.

"He's fifty-eight years old. Was in the army from '43 to the end of the war. Came home a father, had a number of jobs—cab driver, EJ's, security guard—before he started with Triple Cities Traction in '50. Stayed on when it became BC Transit in '68.

Has four kids. Kind of a gruff guy, very opinionated. But responsible and conscientious. Always was."

"The other three kids," Lynch said. "They all live in town?"

"His two daughters downstairs do. One of them is divorced and moved back into the house with her child a few years ago. He's got another one that lives out west. The youngest. Margaret."

"He a religious guy, Reverend?"

"He was raised Lutheran but converted to Catholicism in the 1950s. He thought it would be best if the family shared the same religion, but he remained an active member of the Lutheran Brotherhood and he attended my services on and off until recently. He reads Scripture." The pastor indicated the large book on the stand beside him.

"What do you mean 'until recently'? His attendance drop off?"

"The past three, maybe four months."

"You know why?"

"We haven't had much occasion to talk lately."

The detective stared at the photograph of Jom he had removed from the wall, and in a moment said, "What do you know about him being brought into the station last month?"

"That was news to me," the pastor said.

"You?" he said to Meehan, who shrugged and shook his head.

"News to me, too," Sammy said. "But it just don't sound right."

"I see that Mr. Potter has kept carbon copies of his correspondence with various government agencies regarding his son. It seems he's quite angry with what he calls—" Detective Lynch squatted and ran his right hand over the mess of papers at his feet, taking one of them up—"'pansy-ass, diddly-do efforts to save our boys,'" he read. "And here he says, 'You know some of them are alive and we know some of them are alive and you shit-ass bureaucrats who could actually do something are just letting these heroes rot in an Asian jungle while you have your power lunches over more personally profitable issues . . .'" Detective Lynch looked up from the sheet of stationery. "That's dated May 15. Just a few weeks ago."

"Jommy's birthday," Meehan said. "He'd have been thirty-eight."

"This argument at the get-together yesterday," the detective said, rising. "Was the MIA issue a part of that?"

"I guess," Sammy said. "I mean, the subject of Jommy came up. Yeah."

He told them what had happened, beginning with Dutch's anger at Pastor Philips for leaving after only a brief visit, then, when they were all sitting at the table, who said what and how the argument got out of hand. "I ain't never seen Dutch so mad as he was when his son-in-law said Jommy enlisted and then reupped because of such stories he was telling his children at the table, and to please his father, which he always felt he failed to do."

"Bummy said that?" Meehan asked.

"He got pretty mad, too."

"And Mr. Potter kicked everybody out?" said Lynch.

"He had a crack at everyone," Sammy said. "Even me."

Detective Curley came back up the stairs and said that it was OK with Mrs. Potter if they took some of Mr. Potter's effects, and after Detective Lynch called him over to help load some of the things into the empty footlocker, he mentioned there was no sign of a gun.

The pastor watched them for a few minutes, noting that Lynch was selecting only certain letters and items. Sammy came up beside him and said, "I hope I didn't say nothing to get Dutch in trouble."

Meehan had drifted over toward the wall near the armchair and was examining the bloodstained T-shirt.

"Look what I found," Sammy said to the pastor. He held up an "I Like Ike" campaign button with the L scraped off. "It was over there."

The pastor turned away and began flipping through the pages of the Bible. He hadn't gotten much sleep and was on edge. The incident the day before had affected his golf game and preoccupied him during the drinks and dinner afterward. He'd just stopped over for a cup of coffee before the best-ball tournament. He'd misunderstood Sarah's invitation or would have mentioned the tournament. He'd thought of stopping at the Potters' on the way home to see if Dutch had calmed down, and he wished now that he had. Instead he waited until eight o'clock that morning to call Sarah to see if everything was OK.

When Detective Curley saw the writing on the pages he told Lynch and they put the Bible in the footlocker, too, and then secured the fasteners. He lifted his end of the footlocker and his suitcoat opened at such an angle that Pastor Philips could see his shoulder holster. Detective Curley lifted the other end and together they moved toward the stairs.

Down in the foyer, over the noise of the poodle's excitement, Lynch thanked Sarah for her cooperation. He said he would be in touch and promised to send a uniform over to keep the press at bay. Some reporters and a cameraman had already gathered on the front lawn, and Detective Curley told them to back off as he descended the front steps with his end of the footlocker. "Leave these folks alone," he said. "C'mon. Off the property."

Pastor Philips followed the detectives down the driveway to the unmarked Ford parked in the street. Detective Curley opened the door and, with Detective Lynch pushing from his end, guided the footlocker into the backseat. Once it was secured, he shut the door, went around to the driver's side, and got in.

"Please keep in mind . . ." the pastor said to Lynch, but trailed off as though he'd misplaced his thought, and the detective took the opportunity to thank him again.

Meehan watched them shake hands from the window of Jom's bedroom on the second floor of the house; then Lynch slid into the passenger seat, shut the door, and left the pastor standing on the curb looking around him as though the car had vaporized into the morning.

SEVEN

How much time had passed before Dutch roused from his stupor to ask them their number Matthew couldn't say; no one except the boy had so much as coughed for what seemed a long while. A congress of birds had convened in the clearing, where light patterns shifted with the movement of clouds, and burst into flight when Dutch barked his question a second time.

"There's seven of us," Matthew said. "If that's what you mean, Dutch."

"Women? Men?"

"Four women, two men, one boy, and you."

"Boy?" Dutch said. He rose to his feet, steadying himself on the branch, and the leaves whispered in the bus when he turned to scrutinize them with his clear left eye. "Get him up here."

Erica was sitting in the last seat with him but no one moved until Dutch ordered everybody to slide back against the windows; when they did, he started down the aisle, pointing the gun one way, then the other, as if shining a flashlight in the dark. He stopped a few feet in front of the boy and ordered him to his feet.

"Name's Bad," the boy said, folding his arms. "I wouldn't mess with me."

"I gave orders."

"Bad don't take orders."

Dutch nodded and walked back down the aisle. He stopped beside Andy's seat and pulled a white glove out of the pocket of his jacket. He looked at it for a moment, shook it, went back over to the boy, and slapped it across his upturned face.

"That's a quote from George Patton."

The boy's jaw hung open and he touched his cheek, then looked at his fingers as if he expected to see blood. He was not very tall, and when he stood Dutch had to lean back to study his face, which he did by touching the very cheek he had struck. Then he turned and strode back up the aisle, barking over his shoulder that he wanted the men outside.

"You want us out of the bus?" Andy said.

"Up," Dutch said, turning around at his station beside the branch. "At 'em." He pointed the gun at the side rear exit.

"That door's stuck," Andy said. "We already tried it."

"You mean when he was *dead,* Andy?" Grace rasped.

"The front door is, too," Andy said. "Stuck, I mean."

Dutch looked over at the emergency window exit hanging loose on its hinges and asked what that was all about.

"Two people went for help, Dutch," Matthew said. "A man and a woman. A while ago."

Dutch nodded and took a few steps toward the side exit, where he bent to look out through the windows on the door. "OK, Werner," he said. "I got a mission for you."

"Me?" Andy said. "Is he talking to me?"

"Yeah. You'll be the ferret. Out the window. Unblock the door. C'mon. Just a log." He waved the gun at Andy, then pointed it at the window. "You run, I'll get mad."

Andy did not move without first announcing every movement. "I'm going over to the window now. OK? Here I go . . ." He described how he planned to kneel on the empty seat, which he did, and back out feet first. He hung on to the sill and looked back into the bus and then let go. "I'm out," he shouted up. "And I'm not running. I'm right here, OK?"

A rotting log was the culprit, and Andy tried moving it, all the while offering his play-by-play, but part of it was submerged in the earth and it wouldn't move.

"I'll have to dig a little bit around it," he said. "Then maybe I can get it out of the way. OK?"

"Do it," Dutch said.

They could hear him grunting under the strain of what labor was involved. Dutch watched him through the window on the door and after a while went back to the front of the bus, where he disappeared into the branch's dense foliage. The passengers sat still as wax likenesses of themselves. The shoelaces of Matthew's left wingtip hung loose as cursive. The yellow page in the aisle a few feet in front of him, blotted with Dutch's hocked phlegm, now asked, "What is . . . time?" and he remembered a sermon given during a high-school retreat that took a crack at trying to answer that question. It was his last year and the Catholic retreat was mandatory and the sermon was really a pep talk to excite them about making a difference in the world. "Life is brief," Father Logan had said. And then, leaning forward in the pulpit for emphasis, started again, saying, "Brief is life," as if the cumulative law Matthew had learned from him in algebra were applicable to the balanced syntax insisted upon in English class. "Less than a millisecond in all of time. Much less. The universe is billions upon billions of years old, and our lives are, at best, a mere threescore and ten. If cosmic history were reduced to a single calendar year, with the Big Bang at midnight on January 1, the formation of the earth would have begun about September 14; the first worms appeared about September 16; on December 31, at about 1:30 p.m., Proconsul and Ramapithecus arose, ancestors of apes and humans; and at about 11:59:59, the Renaissance began. Five hundred years equals one sixtieth of a second. Who can calculate a man's days in this scheme of time? Who here can do that? Who?"

Dutch appeared out of the network of leaves wearing what looked at first to be some sort of garish medallion, but when he came forward, gun first, Matthew could see that it was a hand grenade hanging down to his sternum from a brown ribbon fastened around his neck. Hulda asked what that thing was, the words piping out of her, but Andy was shouting that he'd moved the log far enough to give the door a try. Dutch did something with the panel just above the door and the flaps rushed outward on compressed air.

"OK, men," Dutch said, waving the gun in front of him. "Let's go. Out."

Matthew worked his way to his feet and shuffled toward the exit, not taking his eyes off the Luger pointed at his chest, and Dutch asked him did he have paraffin in his kneecap. Matthew shook his head, not knowing what he was talking about, and Dutch turned his attention to the boy in the back of the bus.

"You. Coming? Or you not a man when I say 'men'?"

The boy did not move and Dutch said that answered that and he joined the men outside. He told Matthew and Andy to stand up against the bus to the right of the door and keep their hands at their sides while he stepped back to get a good look at their positioning. Then, with the heel of his boot, he plowed a line in the dirt about ten or twelve feet away, beginning at a point parallel to the front bumper and running down along the side to the rear. He strained in the labor, breathing hard with his mouth open, dropping blood, but it was obvious that the fresh air was reviving him. His one eye focused with greater invigoration, and when he ordered Matthew and Andy to drag loose vegetation and rotting wood—anything and everything in the immediate area that could be moved—to construct some sort of demarcation, his speech, still slurred, shaped sentences with a more viscous timbre.

This "defilade," as he called it, was to follow the line he had just made and curve around the back of the bus so as to abut the dense forest on the other side, marking, he said, the opposite flank. While he spoke Matthew could hear the women inside talking in low voices. Grace must have caught Hulda sneaking a sip of the gin and wanted some for herself, and Erica was whispering for her to keep it down.

It was a fallen branch barring the front side door of the bus and it was this that they used to start their project. Then they fell into a system whereby Andy would shuttle back and forth from the thick woods on the other side of the bus, dragging out anything not rooted down, or breaking the dead low branches off trees, and Matthew would stack them waist-high along the line. Dutch watched them work from the shade of the tree the bus had struck. Sometimes when Matthew grimaced or grunted he would detect what looked to be a grin cutting into Dutch's bloodied jaw, but his face was such a mess it may only have been Matthew's imagination. When the boy stepped off the bus, Dutch shifted his attention to him. The kid stood in the clearing for a moment with his arms folded, chewing hard on a wad of gum, as though this whole thing didn't surprise or impress him in the least. But his eyes moved side to side, and when he swallowed his throat clenched.

Dutch said he wanted a word with him and the boy swaggered into the shade, jaw stuck upward, and spat at the ground near Dutch's polished boots.

"Whatta ya want, George Fucking Patton?"

"Have a fresh stick," Dutch said, holding out a yellow pack of Juicy Fruit.

The kid looked back at Matthew, shrugged, and plucked a stick out of the pack. He let the wrapping fall at his feet and added the stick to the gum he was already chewing so that his cheek bulged. When he saw Andy dragging a rotten log out of the woods toward Matthew, he shook his head and spit again.

"I ain't gunna haul no shit around like some convict."

"Uh-huh."

"You can't make me do what I don't want."

"I can see that."

"Damn straight."

"You took that hit I gave you pretty good."

"Thought I wasn't no man."

"In the army, officers goad tough guys. To make a point to the pussies."

"Who died and made you boss?"

"Heh-heh. You got spunk, kid."

"Well, just don't mess with me, mister."

"Dutch."

"I'll call you whatever I feel like callin' you."

"What do you feel like calling me?"

"How about Asshole."

"You wouldn't be the first. Just remember that even the biggest assholes in creation have their story. Their reasons."

Bad let out a Bronx cheer and rolled his eyes.

"I bet people have some nasty things to say about you," Dutch said.

"Yeah, well, fuck them."

"Right! Who needs 'em?"

"Damn straight. And I don't need to hang around listenin' to some fat-ass GI Joe give me shit, either. I can walk away from this gig whenever the fuck I feel like it. I ain't afraid of that gun or stupid little grenade, so don't think it makes any difference to me."

"You want to take off, then go."

Bad looked at Dutch, then at the woods, chewing hard. "Some real shit gunna hit the fan here," he said.

"Uh-huh."

"And they're gunna fry your ass."

"Naw. I'm the cook. I do the frying. You know all about that."

"What you know about what I know?"

"Control. Taking care of yourself. Making your life work because nobody's going to make it work for you. You do it every day."

"Whatta you talkin' about?"

"I seen you downtown, Bad. From my bus. Waiting at BC Junction. Where the buses park. You're one of those guys hangs out across the street at the Washington Street Mall, near the transit info booth. Skipping school. Skateboarding. First kid out every morning."

"So you seen me. Big woop."

"So my guess is you live alone. No place to stay. Sleep out-side—maybe under one of the bridges over the river. Look at you. You're filthy. Steal from the Woolworth's, right? Penney's? Fowler's if you're feeling lucky? Sell the stuff for a bit of the ready?"

"Hey, man, I don't cop to nothing."

"Do what you have to do. People shit on you, shit back."

"Damn straight."

"Old man probably doesn't give a rat's ass. Glad to have you gone."

"Stepfather."

"Right. You're in the way of the relationship with the old lady, right? Oldest story. Beat you?"

"Worse."

"Bastard!"

"He's a fuckin' asshole."

"Bastard!"

"I almost iced him once, when he was drunk, which is most of the time anyways. I woulda, too, but I figured it wasn't worth it."

"You ever want someone to teach that son of a bitch a real lesson, you call on Dutch Potter."

"Sure. I'll phone the city morgue tomorrow."

"Naw. I'm a survivor. All Potters are survivors."

"I don't know, man. You might not even make it to when the cops get here to blow your brains out. You don't look so hot."

"This? Just a scrape."

"I don't think so, man. Look at you. And you're still bleedin'. Right there at your forehead. You're gunna at least have one mother megascar, right down the middle of your face. Amtrak City."

"I was never much to look at anyways."

"Yeah, well, the luckiest you'll get is a crib in Attica. No way you'll beat the pigs on this one. They got a *real* army, if they want to put it all together. Whatta you got? One puny grenade, if it's even real. Big fuckin' woop."

"I'll tell you what I got that they don't got, Bad. *Will.* It'll be Nam all over again, because they don't learn."

"What the fuck is Nam?"

"*Viet*nam! We had all the power—warships, satellites, missiles, napalm, choppers, Agent Orange, ICBMs, name it. And what did the gooks have? Sticks and stones. 'Blast them back to the Stone Age' is what the generals said, like the yellow bastards weren't there already! And who won?"

"America got its ass kicked, man."

"By a piddling backwater smaller than Jersey. The struggle was beyond our strength because it wasn't really against someone else. Uncle Sam didn't read his Samuel. Forgot David slew Goliath with one stone. Forgot a giant could choke on a gnat. Look at Iran a few years back. What did those towelheads have?"

"Hostages."

"And will. The people with *will* are people with *power*, Bad. They don't have to know shit about fission or fusion or firepower. The people with imagination who are willing to risk everything— and I mean everything—are the ones that got power."

"Sounds like bullshit to me," Bad said, shaking his head.

Andy came out of the woods rolling a rusted metal barrel, smiling as if he'd found treasure. When he saw Matthew looking at him, he stopped, stood erect, slapped his hands together, and said, "This'll help, hey? And there's three more back there."

It was empty, and he stood it upright against the branches he'd been stacking.

"I put up a few fences in my day," Andy said. "Stone. Wood. Wire. The works."

"Yeah."

"My father used to do odd jobs on farms north of Johnson City. He grew up on a sort of farm in the Ukraine."

"You men don't talk!" Dutch shouted.

He was slouching beside the boy at the edge of the clearing, daring another word. Even the low chatter on the bus ceased, and after a brief staredown Matthew set back to work, righting the barrel against the pile of forest junk while Andy returned to the woods for another one. It was bullshit labor; something to do while they waited for whatever was going to happen, a way for Dutch to scope the terrain, get out of the stifling bus.

"So why you call me your buddy?" Bad was asking. He'd

taken out a pocketknife and begun whittling the bark off a stick. "I don't remember us tradin' calling cards."

"You remind me of a good pal. Tough. No-nonsense. Honest. Here . . ." Dutch leaned toward him, tugging at the brown ribbon around his neck. "He gave this to me . . ."

As he chattered on—the war this and the war that, bombs, buddies, bandages—aimlessly, it seemed, Matthew tuned him out. Judging character was part of his job, and this guy, this Ralph Cramden gone full-blown wacko, wasn't all that difficult to read. Willing to risk everything, he said. Even his ego? Even the impulse to impose one's will? Who didn't entertain the idea of letting go, of seizing power? What a luxury! And look at him over there, flapping his arms like a bird! Free, for a moment. Cashing in all moments for just this one. Even now Matthew could hurl this jagged rock at his skull and finish off the job begun by the crash. This slab of oak, used correctly, could smash his bones to powder. But let the law that Matthew served serve Matthew and do the job. That's what it was there for.

Working his way around the back fender of the bus and looking up to face the steep grade of the hillside in the dark woods, Matthew understood that even if his ankle weren't broken or sprained it would be too much of a risk. Through the open window he could hear the voices of the women more clearly. Hulda had admitted to having the pint bottle of Gilbey's, and Grace kept interrupting one or another of them, saying "Give it here! Give it here!" He listened to them talk about men and love, Erica with bitterness, Heather with soft dreaminess, until Grace told them enough already and demanded another one of those questions, and Heather said OK, where did the expression "All roads lead to Rome" come from? "Rome, girl," Grace said. "Where else? C'mon, gimme a *challenge*."

They had all been drinking the gin; even Hulda, whose hands

hadn't stopped shaking since the crash, sounded calm, if not relaxed, when she asked Heather if Rome really was the answer.

"It just says it grew from the fact that the ancient Romans built good roads radiating to all parts of the country, and then the empire. Then it says how they were dug and laid with stones and mortar. Stuff like that."

"The question was who said it, not how they was made. That book talks too much. Hit me with another one—a good one this time."

Above the trees, a pinprick of sunlight—a jet at thirty thousand feet etching a line of vapor onto the blue—and Matthew wondered at its destination. Chicago or Denver. Maybe Texas. The people on board would be eating breakfast, chattering about this and that, some of them glancing down at the green undulation of the Endless Mountains and, to the north, the gentle hills of southern New York State. This God's-eye image of where he lived his life—his office in Binghamton, his home in Endwell, the commute between these existences that afforded him an additional forty-five minutes of work each way—ambushed him with the realization that his wife no longer loved him, though he could not say why or how or where he would have gotten such an idea.

Whitey Davies might have spotted that same jet if he were not legally blind. As it was, the blur of the sun-lacerated woods of northern Pennsylvania had him in mind of a picture in one of his ex-fiancée's textbooks from an elective she took in college— Cézanne's *Rocky Scenery in Provence*—then of the picnic at the Chestnut Hill Reservoir her casual indication of it was designed to inspire, then of her. It was in the happy hour of their relationship, all booze and mushy emotion, when she began feeling comfortable enough to ask about his albinism. "I mean," she'd said, "is seeing for you like, you know, an impressionist painting?"

He thought of her round face, her portly bearing, the sex they had the night before in Binghamton, yet another tumble in the hay for old time's sake, how his huffing then was like his huffing now as he strained to keep up with the oddly dressed woman—who, once they'd put a safe distance between themselves and the crippled bus, had curtly introduced herself as "Ms. Breyer," a name that popped up, as it were, out of incessant grumbling against what she called "the stupendous inconvenience." "I mean, my God! Why now? I've got my major field exam in two days. I've got a metric ton of studying to do. Three years of work coming down to this!"

Whitey wanted to remind her that a man was dead back there and who gave a shit about a test? But he already knew she was as sensitive to the slightest rebuke as his eyes were to light, and he couldn't get out of this mess without her help, such as it was. They'd been hiking for over an hour and had yet to find any sign of civilization. He'd dared to wonder out loud if they might be going in the wrong direction, but she insisted that her navigational skills were "beyond reproach," that she almost made Torch Bearer in the Camp Fire Girls when she was fifteen, and they would find their way soon. "This way," she kept saying. "The thing is, we got to keep moving; we'll get somewhere, and when we do, it'll be over."

But when they entered a small clearing that looked familiar, Whitey, who was unaccustomed to exercise of any sort, and badly hung over besides, sat on the trunk of a fallen tree, removed a bandanna from his knapsack, and wiped his face and neck.

"All right," she said. "But only for a minute."

She sat Indian-style on the ground, set her tote bag on her lap, opened it, and pulled out a clear bottle of something green. She removed the cap and, pinky curled, like a child pretending to be an adult, took a sip, closing her eyes as she swallowed. She offered none of it to Whitey before screwing on the cap and placing the bottle back in her bag.

"We shouldn't have left that dirt path," Whitey said.

"Don't start. You ever experience the wrath of a skunk?"

In fact he had, late one night on Kilsyth Road in Boston where he lived. Anyone else would have seen it and dodged disaster. He took the requisite tomato-juice-and-vinegar baths, and for weeks afterward the regulars at the bar where he worked ragged him about it, renicknaming him Caesar, after the salad. So when he and Rose had encountered the skunk and her two babies on the side of the dirt road, it was Whitey who first ran deep into the woods they were lost in.

Rose sighed again and whined something about her exam.

"For fuck sakes," Whitey said, "enough already."

"Well, I can't help it. My blood is at a boil. And don't swear."

"Don't tell me how to talk," he said. "It's my language, too."

"It's our language. We share it. I don't take kindly to its molestation."

The students from Boston College who frequented the Tam O'Shanter on Beacon Street for the fifty-five-cent drafts made him uneasy in this same way. They were lightweight drinkers, most of them, and they admired the infallibility of his memory for sports trivia. That was all right. But they were college kids after all, a little arrogant with privilege, and he sometimes feared they listened too closely to the way he spoke, diagramming his sentences in their heads to find grammatical gaffes they would chuckle about in their dorm rooms. Maria, of course, had been different. She was studying to be a nurse, something practical and real, and was paying her own way.

This Breyer woman was earning a Ph.D. in medieval literature, she'd told Whitey twice already and was now telling him again. In fact, she had been on her way to her library carrel at the university to study when this whole thing happened. For all her yapping in that high-pitched, girlish voice, she never once asked Whitey where he was going, where he had come from, what occupied his time. He framed her dark form in a squint and wondered what she would think if he told her that, with the aid of genius unspoiled by higher education, and brass balls, he had devised a scheme of collecting disability in three states. Every thirty days he took the Greyhound from Boston to Hazelton, Pennsylvania, where his parents lived, and then up to Binghamton, where Maria had returned after her graduation to work in the emergency room of the hospital she was born in, and then back home, where he had season tickets at Fenway and the Garden, bet on the dogs in Revere and the horses at Foxboro, played poker with the boys on Monday nights—if there were no home games to attend—and, when he'd had too much to drink, which was often, crooned with Elvis at the Tam O'Shanter juke box and pined for Maria. She couldn't make up her mind about him, but she loved him. It wasn't because he was older; it certainly wasn't because he was albino. She wanted to get married to him, she really did, but commitment scared her. Would he be patient? Would he love her no matter what?

"Shush!" Whitey said, and Rose stopped speaking and heard it too: a percussion of air in the distance, a helicopter. In a moment, it was gone, but back at the bus Dutch herded Matthew and Andy into the open door, saying, "Move it, move it."

Andy tried to sit beside Grace, but she told him he smelled "like shit," so he chose the empty seat in front of her and sat studying his hands. Matthew heaved himself into the seat in front of Erica and Andy turned to him and said, "Jesus, look at this." His palms were blistered. "Hurts like hell!" he rasped, wiping them on his shirt and looking at them again. "What *is* it?"

The boy, shirtless now and carrying the spear he'd made, swaggered down the aisle between them on his way to the back of the bus; he stopped at the next-to-last seat, bent over, picked something up off the floor, and said, "Yeah!"

Dutch's presence cast its spell; even the wind-rousted leaves fell silent, or seemed to. He strode up the aisle toward the front of the bus and then turned to face them.

"Yo, Dutch!" Bad shouted. "I found the last battery. It was right back here all the time, plain as day."

"It's like that, Bad," Dutch said.

Bad set his spear against the window, sat in the back seat, and began working the last battery into the compartment of the boom box. "I think I can get this thing humming. You wanna try to catch some news? You know, hear what's goin' on with them stiffs back home?"

"Bring it here, Bad."

"What's this?" Grace said. "Benedict Fuckin' Arnold?"

The boy snapped the compartment shut, tucked the boom box under his arm, grabbed the spear, and made his way down the aisle, settling himself in the seat beside where Dutch had stationed himself. As he fiddled with the dials, Dutch picked up a scrap of paper off the seat next to him—one of Matthew's business cards—and looked at it quizzically, then down the aisle at Matthew.

A noise that sounded like the shattering of dishes filled the bus and Bad shouted, "Yeah!"

He lowered the volume and searched for a station. A violin weeping a concerto and he shouted, "No way, José!" and cranked the dial into a reggae thump, the twang of a country tune, the refrain of Mel Tormé's "I'm Getting Sentimental Over You." Station after station and it was like traveling to different places. When the word "bus" blared out as clearly as if one of them had said it, Dutch shouted "There!" and Bad went back through the white noise to find it.

"—suspended late last year for disciplinary reasons, Petoski said, but that things had been going very well with Potter since that time. However, WBNG news has learned that in April Potter was detained by Binghamton City Police after he had broken into a woman's East Side apartment in the middle of the night. The woman, Po Chamleunsouk of Town and Country Arms on Chenango Street, said she was asleep in her bed when she heard a noise and saw a man she had never seen before standing at the foot of her bed—"

"Lies!" Dutch shouted. "Lies, lies, fucking lying!" and with the gun still in his hand, he tore the boom box away from Bad, raised it over his head, and hurled it down into the well of the seat to his right, where it clattered to the floor.

"Fuck!" Bad yelped over the voice of the news announcer, who had changed the subject to British ships and the Falkland Islands and dead Argentines. Dutch went for the radio again and Bad scampered across the aisle and under the seat to get to it first, and when he did, and succeeded in switching it off, Dutch stood erect and backed away, breathing loudly through his mouth, pulling at the grenade hard enough to come close to snapping the ribbon that held it around his neck.

Erica stood and said, "Please. It's OK."

"OK?" he spat, glaring at her. "OK? Do you know what she is? Do you?"

"Tell me," Erica said.

Dutch did not take his eyes off her, still breathing hard but thinking now. "Makes me sound like some lowlife! Didn't we speak at length three times in that flea-infested dive? Stranger, she says? She knows Jom and she doesn't know me?"

"People spread lies about me, I get mad," Erica said. "But I make sure I set the record straight. I make sure the truth gets told."

"Oh, the truth," he said. "The *truth*!"

"That's all people want. In their hearts. You've been hurt, wronged. I know how that feels."

Erica's hands were gripping the rail at the back of the seat in front of her, and Dutch said, "Screw the pain."

"Pain is eased when it's shared," Erica told him. "Isn't that true? OK, we were taken by surprise at first. But here we are. Like you said, we're all in this together. You might just as well tell us. I mean, for starters, who is this woman? Who does she think she is?"

"American," he said. "She learned . . ." He stopped and then started again, stopped and started, his voice sliding into a tone so soft they had to strain to hear. At first they thought he'd begun to babble pure nonsense again, but after a while they picked up a thread of real story, or something that made a kind of sense. The boy, still on the floor, crawled out from under the seat and rested his back against it, looking straight up into Dutch's bloodied face—first in fear and anger, but then with concentration that might have been a kind of wonder, like a child healing from discipline might listen to his father explain the moral of a tale.

EIGHT

It had something to do with dreams, insomnia, nocturnal pere-
grinations, the deep voice itself cadencing in a brisk stride past
images of warehouses and shops and churches, through vacant
lots and alleys and philosophical thoughts every bit as complicated as the schema of streets he negotiated. His narrative didn't
move forward, it swelled against the cracked and littered by-
ways of Johnson City, the warren of West Side lanes, the amber-
lit blocks downtown where, between two and three o'clock on a
weekend night, bars vomited patrons that drained into parking
garages in swirling flows. Dutch liked to spy them from a distance, breathe perfumed chatter, consider a life from a sentence
or phrase. Often he'd find himself in the seedier sections where
even the street light felt like grime—the Susquehanna Street
projects, the East Side viaduct, alleyways near the Greyhound
Station. Sometimes a hooker appeared out of shadows to ask if
he wanted love. Who didn't? But who believed it came so
cheap?

The voice—crackling in weak transmission through a gust of
spring air and gum—might merely have been a thought, a bad
idea on a bad night, and he did not look up from the mesmeric

sparkle of sidewalk until he saw, or rather sensed, a shifting of the dark near a doorway. But he was in the core of the ward where offers of this kind were made freely, and when they were made, he'd move his hand in front of his face as if to confuse an odor, not bothering to break stride or look back—except, sometimes, to think of them later, if the body appealed to his memory in boredom.

But when he adjusted his course around this one she sidled in to intercept him and he hovered in the exosphere of her perfume, something saccharine and floral, his penny loafers inches from the tips of her black stilettos. Fishnet stockings hung loose on her legs, even at the thighs that disappeared just before pay dirt under a skirt of black leather. Her mouth, small, open for business, worked hard at a cud of gum. A flaxen scar crossed her jaw ear-to-chin, quartering a face that might otherwise have been attractive. Something in the eyes, dabbed like commas in a slathering of rouge, held him where he stood.

"I know you?" she asked, turning her better side to him.

Jagged teeth and too many of them diced syllables into smaller bits of sound. He assessed the silken contours of her body and asked where she was from.

"Where you want I from, John?" She ran the flat of her hand over his collarbone, his neck, his cheek. She held a small purse in her other hand and he stiffened when he felt it brush against his spine. Her mouth hovered near his nose and her breath smelled of strawberry and rice. He reached back and grabbed the elbow of the arm and twisted it. "Don't play games with me, lady."

"Oooooh," she said, wriggling free. "You like rough, John? I play. But it cost more."

When she moved toward him again he shoved her and she tumbled back against the plate-glass window of the Elks Home Antler Lodge. The warbling pane strobed street light as she raked back her hair, sneering like a wolf. He left the way he came and she shouted after him in language that sounded all the more profane, echoing off brick and glass.

Working the 15 Vestal route the next day he wondered why she said he looked familiar. No, she asked if she knew him. Still, a strange come-on for a prostitute—unless he'd surprised her because he did look familiar. He thought again of that scarred face, the eyes hard as diamonds under the streetlight, and was certain he'd never seen her before. Asian faces looked so similar to him, one and another, and there were many more in the area since local churches had begun sponsoring 'boat people.' But who could forget a beautiful and mutilated one like that woman's?

Hookers were as territorial as forest does and rarely strayed from the parcel of city block to which they laid claim. Or so he guessed. But coming down off the East Side viaduct late one night at the same time he ran into her before, the block between Lewis and Eldridge was empty. He made his way down the gentle gradation of the viaduct, hands in his pockets, the long sign over Fred's Big Bargain Corner calling out to him in large lettering. WHY FRET? STOP HERE! BUY! SELL! TRADE! BEST FOR LESS! He'd sold quite a bit of salvaged merchandise there in the sixties, when he and Jom repaired appliances others had left on the curb for junk. He used to be known there as Mr. Fixit, and Fred himself had to haggle with him because Dutch Potter knew a few things about bartering.

He stopped in the doorway of the five-story building that came up to the edge of the sidewalk across from the Wilson & Fritz Lumber Yard. Judging from the style of blinds on the upper windows, it might have been apartments. But a sign in the window at street level called it the Triple Cities NY Temple #1344 I.B.P.O.E. of the World. He followed the business of a cloud of moths against a streetlight on the corner. He had heard once, probably from Pastor Philips, that before electric lights they navigated a great migration by the stars. Now, with the glitter of civilization jamming their senses, they were doomed to lose themselves in lesser lights.

From where he stood he could see the tower of the train station rising above the viaduct. A light shone in the tower, though the station had been closed since 1964, when the *Phoebe Snow* made its last run through Binghamton. Freight cars still used the tracks, and when the circus came to town by train every spring it was there that they would unload their cargo of lions and elephants and tigers and trainers and clowns and march in procession down Chenango to the Arena. But it had once been the hub of Binghamton's hail-and-farewell. As a child he attended the departure and arrival of aunts and uncles and friends of the family with destinations and points of origin as exotic as Niagara Falls and New York City and "points west." On the platform just at the base of the tower, before boarding a train for Fort Dix, Sarah standing at his side waiting to hold him one more time, his father would not let go of his hand when he told him, again, to fight well, make them proud, keep out of harm's way if he could.

A lone car sped down the road, a ragtop, radio screaming rock and roll to a nest of teenagers. In his day, they went only where feet could take them. Or they just milled about on one corner or another in the neighborhood, bunched at the streetlamp like those moths. He scratched the sole of his right shoe over the sidewalk, bothering the silence left in the car's wake. He took a pack of Luckies out of his jacket pocket, shook one free, smoked it, and then another. When nothing happened he felt foolish and left. On his way home he cut through the alley between the Greyhound station and the Press Building. The bus platform, where he'd last seen Jom. "You take care of yourself," he'd said. "Be brave, but don't be foolish." He'd felt like his own father seeing him off to war and did not like that. "Count on me," Jom said, slinging his duffel bag over his shoulder. Then he turned and boarded the bus without looking back. Words after that were delivered on onionskin paper in his looping script, the first of them an excruciating two weeks later.

On the bus in the Pennsylvania woods Dutch rummaged through a black metal box in the aisle behind where he had been standing and in a moment came up with something that looked like a diploma. He stroked free the rubber band, unscrolled the papers, shuffled through them, and passed one over to Bad. "Read."

"Huh?"

"Here."

" 'Well, I'm here,' " Bad read. He looked up at Dutch and then down at the sheet of stationery again.

" 'Our plane stopped at Anchorage, Alaska (cold!) for an hour, then a long ride to Tokyo before getting to Tan Son Nhut (the airport in Saigon). At each stop they announced the correct time and we kept setting back our watches. It felt like we were going back in time. You know, like *The Time Tunnel*? Ha! The first thing you notice coming down the ramp is a sweet kind of sicky odor. I smelled it once before and I couldn't figure out where but it came to me the next day that it was a hot summer afternoon at Floral Avenue Cemetery when I was a little kid, poking my head into the open door of a vandalized mausoleum. (Not my work, Pop, I swear!) Anyway, the customs building was just an old makeshift thing where the heat was even worse, and there you were supposed to hand over any weapons, drugs, whatever. And wait. That's something I've already learned to do a lot of over here. Waiting to change money. Waiting to draw equipment. Waiting to be assigned to a unit (which I'm doing

right now). Waiting for transportation. Waiting, waiting, waiting. Jesus!' "

Dutch went on subsequent nights to the viaduct by the train station, sometimes without having planned to go there. He was
propositioned on a few occasions by different holy women of
the evening, as he called them to himself—one of them a blonde
that could not have been more than sixteen years old; she said
she did it all, everything, and loved it, and rattled off her special-
ties. It so depressed him—or his momentary excitement so disappointed him—that he did not return for a week.

When he did, he stood in a doorway where he could see but
not be seen, as if he had become the whore he was looking for.
He'd stand for a long time, breathing the smell of urine and damp
cement, sometimes chancing a cigarette. The odd car would zoom
by and sometimes a pedestrian—a man walking alone—would
pass into view. Being there reminded him of sentry duty in camp
after they crossed the Rhine, where any movement in the dark
could herald death. He remembered Goddamn Rokos getting
it in Frankfurt, where a woman lured him into an alley with
promises.

He stood in that doorway the night of Jom's thirty-eighth
birthday and the only living thing he saw for an hour was a rat
the size of a gopher hobbling across the lumberyard. But two
nights later, a Saturday, he saw the Asian woman after waiting
only forty-five minutes.

Her hair was short and blond, splayed like Lady Liberty's
crown, but when she looked up at the stars he could see the
slash of cicatrix in the light. Before he stepped out of the doorway a car cruising over the viaduct stopped and he could see the
outline of her bony backside when she leaned into the driver's
window. No sooner had she begun talking than the car, a blue

Honda, peeled out and away toward the city, and when she regained her balance she threw her handbag into its wake, yelling
something complicated and Asian. The handbag had landed
against the curb ten feet away. She was still grumbling when she
bent down to pick it up, and when she rose she found herself
face-to-face with Dutch. He thought later that it was odd she
did not seem the least startled, though he'd taken her by surprise, or thought he had. The wig was not blond but a metallic
green and pink and had fallen out of place, exposing her black
hairline near her temple.

"The man who like it rough," she said. "You going to run
away like baby again?"

"I want to talk," he said.

"Dirty?"

Another car turned onto the street from Lewis and he took
her elbow and guided her into an alley between two buildings.

"You want do it here?"

"Look," he said, backing her against the brick wall. "I just
want a word."

"You cop?"

He shook his head. She looked him over for a moment and
said, "OK. But it cost you anyway. I busy woman."

"I can see that."

The curling lip exposed bad teeth, but when he opened his
wallet and removed a twenty from the wad he'd loaded it with
she smiled and folded the bill in half with three fingers of one
hand. "So talk."

"You Vietnamese?"

"Maybe."

"When did you leave?"

"I been here two and half year. And I'm legal, man."

"When you were over there, did you ever see . . . did you ever
see any Americans?"

"Sure. I see a lot American before I come here. Too many, you ask me."

"I mean after the war. After the Americans left."

He looked hard at her, leaning into her face. She swept the hair away from her mouth and ran her tongue over her lips, pursed them.

"What if I did?"

"I'll ask the questions."

She shrugged, staring at the wallet in his hand, then looking off over his shoulder. "Yeah. I see. A few."

"Where? When?"

She shrugged. "Different place."

"Were they on the street? In camps?"

A squad car cruising down Chenango slowed as it passed the alley, then coasted out of view.

"Look," he said, stuffing the wallet into his back pocket. "Can we go somewhere?"

"I get room," she said. "This way. But it cost, mister. I sorry, but my time, you know."

He took her by the elbow and looked both ways along the street before escorting her out of the alley. They walked quickly down Chenango Street, turning onto Lewis and then Fayette, the woman indicating directions, Dutch setting the pace. She told him her name—so multisyllabic it could have been a motto—and then said he could just call her Po. "Fifty dollar for hour, OK?" she said, working to keep up with him. "This take time from work."

"Uh-huh," Dutch said, walking briskly.

When they turned onto Pine she said, "Up there," pointing at a three-story brownstone calling itself the Confederate Hotel by way of a half-lighted sign over the front door. The faces of sagging houses along the way whispered their hard-luck stories into the breeze. A neighborhood bar bearing no name adver-

tised Genesee Cream Ale in green neon at a window translucent
with grime but through which Dutch could see, illuminated by
the blue semaphore of a television, the form of a single man at a
table bent over a glass.

Inside the Confederate Hotel a bearded man watched them
enter from his seat at a desk behind protective glass. He took
his eyes off Dutch only when Po leaned into the speak hole
and began talking. The "lobby" was no larger than his dining
room at home; garish wallpaper peeled like leprosy, water stains
ruined the ceiling. Po traded a few bills for the key in the tray,
saying something to the man that must have been funny because
they both laughed, and then turned to beckon Dutch up the
darkened stairway.

On the second floor she stopped in the middle of a narrow
hallway and worked the key into one of the doors. Rock music
with a ponderous bass thudded from one of the rooms; a
woman screamed once, then again. An odor of disinfectant
escaped the room as they entered. She shut the door and flicked
on the light. The room was sparsely furnished: a bed, nightstand, dresser, two wooden chairs. He sat in one of them and
took a deep breath, watching Po adjust her wig in the mirror on
the door of the closet.

"Take that thing off."

"You don't like? Some man like." She pulled it off and
smoothed down the hair before tossing it onto the bed beside
her purse. "Make girl look punk."

She removed the bobby pins holding her hair and it cascaded
over her face and shoulders. She shook it out, combing it back
with her fingernails, and sat in the other chair facing him. The
harsh light of the lamp on the end table was not kind to her; the
broad cheekbones, the crowded teeth—and that scar, starting,
he could see as she reached for her handbag on the bed, from
somewhere behind her ear.

He leaned forward in his seat and said solemnly: "Now tell me about these Americans you saw."

She slipped a pack of Kools from her handbag and shook one out. Dutch went into his jacket pocket for his Zippo and when she leaned into the flame he could see into her blouse. She watched him watching her and blew smoke into his eyes.

"Yeah. I see some. Sure."

"How many is 'some'?"

She wrinkled her mouth. "Ten, fifteen? Maybe more."

"This was after the war, right? After 1975?"

She nodded.

He took out his Luckies and his hands shook when he lighted one of them. Their smoke mingled and he asked, calmly, where she saw them and what they were doing when she saw them.

"I see them different place different time. Not all at once, you know. Sometime in group, but small group. Work, you know. Hard labor. Rice paddy. Coal mine."

"Camps? You ever see any camps where they're held?"

"Oh yeah. In country. Sure."

"They're held there by force, right? POWs from the war?"

"No one want to be in Vietnam, mister. It awful place. War-war-war. French, American, Khmer. China. It never stop. Where do it stop? I pay all I have to get out. What do you say . . . bribe? Yeah, I bribe. I risk life to leave, you know. Many die. I'm boat people."

"This was when, around '78, '79?"

She nodded.

"And when was the last time you saw an American?"

She shrugged. "Soon before I leave. In Quang Nam. Near river there is camp. Was, anyway."

Dutch drew smoke from his cigarette, held it in his lungs, then exhaled through his nose, watching the smoke fly into the room in two white streams. A cockroach scuttled across the floor, stopped, turned, and disappeared under the bed.

"You work for government or something?"

"Ha!" he said.

"Why that funny?"

"If I worked for Uncle Sam I wouldn't give two shits about Americans rotting in some jungle. I would've forgotten about them years ago. *C'est la guerre* and all that crap."

"So why you want to know about American in Vietnam?"

"I want you to look at something." He removed his wallet from the back pocket of his trousers, opened it, and worked out a photograph from its clear plastic covering. "Now," he said, "I want you to think hard. It's not the greatest picture in the world, doesn't really capture him, but, well, here."

She took the picture and leaned back in her chair. Her eyes widened a little; her lips parted, then pursed. He could hear her swallow in the quiet room. He waited another moment and said, "What? Familiar?"

"He look like GI I know during war. But," she said, putting out her cigarette in the ashtray on the night table, "can't be. Too coincidence. Maybe he just look like him."

"You knew him how?"

"Somebody I meet. Talk to. You know."

"Saigon?"

"Yeah. That it."

"Do you remember his name?"

"I forget so much. Long time ago, you know?"

"But you saw him?"

She stared at him through small parabolic eyes. He leaned over and took her elbow.

"Yeah. Yeah. OK. I think maybe."

"Tell me about it."

"You hurting me."

"Tell me."

"He handsome," she said.

"Yeah?"

"He GI. You know."

Dutch leaned back and gazed at the frayed hem of the bedspread. He took a deep breath, then another. The woman coughed once from behind a curtain of smoke and asked if the boy was his son.

"He look like you," she said.

"Yeah. Yeah. He's . . . Yeah. Jom. Look, tell me what you know about him. Tell me how you met."

"Hmmm, well," she said, pushing her hair back over her shoulders with her free hand. "It was long time ago. Or it seem long time ago. I am prostitute during war. You know, I need money for my family, for me. I meet Jom. Know him for while. OK?"

"This was what?" Dutch said. "About '69?"

"Late sixty, I think. Yeah."

"Go on."

"He come into bar. Saigon. With buddy—other GI, you know. I notice him right away. I think, wow. You know? He handsome man. Those eye, so very blue. You know? Seeing thing around him? Like, I don't know. Child? That first time, I go up and ask if he like me. You know what he say? He say, 'I not sure. I don't know you.'"

"That's Jom!"

"Yeah. He say, 'I don't know you.' Then he say let talk. He just want to talk with me. First. Like you. I say OK. But you know what? He don't want to talk about hisself, he want to talk about me. Yeah. He ask me question about me."

"Ha! That's him all right. Curious as Lot's wife."

"Yeah. Most GI, they just want fuck. They fuck, they go. Jom, he listen. He very quiet sometime. Like mystery."

"Yes!" Dutch said.

"We talk long time. Then we go to room. When we fuck, it nice. He gentle. We meet other time after that. We have special relation."

Dutch massaged his temples, clenched his teeth, inhaled.

"You sad your boy see prostitute? You disappoint?"

Dutch laughed in a great release of air. "No, no, no . . ." he said. "Oh, God no. Well, I mean, heh, heh . . . Ha! Well . . . But," he batted his hand in the air, "hell."

"Many GI do, you know," she said. "During war. It common thing."

"Of course. And Jom was probably first in line. You know, I once caught him in bed—my bed, mind you—with a woman."

"Oh," she said, smiling and then covering her mouth with her hand.

"Yeah. I was coming home from work one afternoon—this would have been, what, '67? In the spring."

"What happen?"

"It was a silly little thing, when I think of it now."

"No," she insisted. "Tell."

He began speaking, reluctantly at first, and was soon carried away in a deluge of words. What began as a simple narration of the afternoon he sneaked up the stairs with a badminton racket, thinking a pigeon had gotten into the house, became a saga digressing into elements of his son's character and certain events in his life that might have portended this incident. He told her about Jom's propensity for running away, his résumé of rakish shenanigans, one more outrageous than the other. He told of his wife, how she spoiled him—but first had to go back to how he was away at war when he found out she was pregnant, what he felt upon hearing the news. But mentioning that he had to tell about George Conklin and their relationship, that moment on the beach in southern England. How he found out three weeks before the invasion that he was a father of a son bearing his name. How he lived for mail from Sarah telling of his boy's progress—that it was what kept him going, kept him alive. How he met him, finally, in October of 1945, when he was almost a year and a half old, walking around the apartment like he had run of the house!

And then this, twenty years later: seeing him tied up to the posters of his bed, a woman riding him like a bronco buster. "Both of them naked as God's sixth day," he said.

"Jom like fuck. He good, too."

It wasn't so much the sex, Dutch told her, as his own sense of failure regarding the boy's upbringing. He felt he had been too easy on him, too detached, and he saw in one simple act how easily his life could be ruined. His first impulse was to expel the boy from the house, force him to earn a degree in the school of hard knocks. But he dismissed this as too risky, because it would exile him from Dutch's watchful eye. The boy needed direction, and Dutch meant to give it to him. It was as if Jom were on a raft awash in a turbulent sea, and Dutch was hopping aboard to navigate. He would have to understand his son's life to change it, and this he set out to do.

He spent as much time with Jom as he possibly could, drinking beer with him at Swat Sullivan's on Saturday nights, meeting him for lunches downtown whenever he could get a split shift, getting Jom to tinker with him on one contraption or another, like the old Philco TV someone out in Vestal left on the curb for the trash collectors—their first successful collaboration. Dutch would stop into the Leroy Package Store to check with Cohen on Jom's performance as a stock control clerk, and sometimes even go down into the basement and help Jom with his work.

They learned from each other. Jom's interests became Dutch's passions, Jom's friends—particularly that Meehan boy—became his friends.

He remembered one night in particular when the three of them sat out on the upstairs porch off Jom's room drinking Rolling Rocks into the small hours. Dutch had broached the topic of the war and, egged on by the boys' questions, brought them with him, in story, across a Europe in ruins. When Meehan finally left, Jom continued to stare at his father in what Dutch believed to be awe. He had not known that all these monumental historical events had been part of his father's own personal history. The stars were out, questioning the sky with twinkling persistence; a soft breeze enveloped them as they sat shoulder to shoulder, watching the universe, father and son, and Dutch was sure at that moment that he had never been happier, that all the suffering in his life—the early poverty, the trial of adolescence, terror of war, marital strife, tedium of work—was a small price to pay for what life could bring, that no matter the suffering paid out in one's sweat and tears and boredom and blood and loss, love, when it came, was a bargain.

In the room at the Confederate Hotel where he had been leaning forward in his chair—elbows on knees, hands clasped at his forehead—he looked up from the floor as if waking from a coma. "It had to be handled right," he said. "You know." The lamp on the night table cast shadows. A puff of breeze filled the curtains and disturbed the formation of smoke above them. The woman quashed her cigarette amid a pile of butts in the ashtray, the filters blood-red with lipstick. She picked up her pack. Empty. Dutch held up his Luckies and she took one. He took one himself, and when he planted it in his mouth Po leaned forward with her Bic lighter. He bent into the flame, then sat back. When he spoke the words came out in a white rush that hung in the air like the thought bubbles in comics.

"Tell me," Dutch said, leaning toward her. "Did he ever talk about, you know, me?"

"Oh yes," she said, shaking her head. "I say father his favorite subject."

"Really?"

She nodded again. "He say you strict. Very very. But that OK, he say. He know in heart you want good for him. He care about you."

"He said that?"

"Yeah," she said. "He tell me many thing, when I make him talk. We have relationship, really. Yeah, we really did. When he come to Saigon, he look for Po. You look after him, he say. He even tell me about girl he fuck in your bed. But . . ."

"What? What?"

"Well, he say he love this woman."

"Yeah," Dutch said, leaning back and shaking his head. "Yeah."

"Then after he see me second time he say I remind of her."

Jom had always been attracted to people who were different from him. One of his first girlfriends, an Orthodox Jew from the West Side, coerced him into accompanying her to temple on Friday evenings. The colored students at high school loved him, and he seemed to be more comfortable with them than with white boys. He picked up their phrases and mannerisms. That immigrant Polish couple he shepherded to the store, doling out what little money he'd earned, teaching them street English. All just so, Dutch knew, he could learn what it was like to be Jewish, black, Polish. Then his letters from overseas, long passages of which he had committed to memory, spelling out his fascination with the Vietnamese.

"I didn't think he was seeing her anymore," Dutch said to Po. "I thought he was telling me everything. I thought we had an understanding."

Ashes fell from Po's cigarette to the floor. She stared at the bed, then at Dutch, with the same look of bemusement that flashed across Zulik's face when he told him.

"I never had a black woman," Zulik had said dreamily though smoke. "But what healthy white sonofabitch . . . ? Well, I'll be."

"Snap out of it, Zulik. This is serious. The kid's twenty-four going on fifteen. I tell him the stakes get higher the older you get, but he can't get it through his thick skull. He's happy to make a life out of drinking beer, being used, bossed around. You know where that goes. The kid's bright. He's got so much going for him if he'd just use it. I mean, he really could make a difference in this goddamn world if he saw it as something more than a carnival."

"So what's wrong with this woman besides she's black?"

"Mulatto."

"Mulatto."

"I'm not prejudice, Zulik. I'm not like that."

"As long as it's not one of your own getting involved?"

"She's a loser—black, yellow, red, or white. Don't look at me like that." It was in Zulik's office at his insurance business in Endwell. He rose from the chair and paced in front of the desk. "I did some research. The facts bear me out. Listen: her name is Bekka, or that's what people call her. She lives over on the North Side with her mother, has two kids. This girl's twenty-five years old, never been married, has a six-year-old boy and a little girl in diapers."

"What color are they?"

"Seems she's been a barfly since she got off the tit," Dutch went on. "Has a reputation around town like the Magdalen, with none of the hope for salvation. Mouth like a yeoman, morals that makes *you* come off like Pope Pius."

"Jesus H. I'm in love."

"C'mon, Zulik. This is life, not some locker-room yarn."

"You're getting excited over nothing, Dutch. It'll pass. Let him have his fling. It'll be a good story to reminisce about at the country club."

"You don't know her, Zulik. She's treacherous, a real black widow. She knows she'll never do better than my boy, and she's after the whole package."

"What makes you so sure?"

Dutch sat down in the armchair again, rubbing his temples with his index and middle fingers. Zulik held out his dwindling pack of Marlboros before tapping one out, lighting it, leaning back. The air-conditioning blew arctic air into the office.

"I conducted a kind of interview," Dutch said.

"You went to see her?"

"You would too, Zulik."

"What happened?"

Dutch told the story for the second time that week, the first an abridged version softened for Pastor Philips, who, even so, provided little sympathy. Here with Zulik he pulled out the stops, describing the small apartment she shared with her mother and children on the North Side of the city near the old railway station, a cramped coldwater flat on the third floor of a Square Deal tumbledown that reminded Dutch of one of the bombed-out hovels he raided throughout Germany. The carpet bred fleas. Wallpaper hung loosely on the surrounding walls in colors loud enough to hear. The Salvation Army sofa carried a stench in the heat, an odor the electric fan only compounded. Dutch had interrupted her soap opera. Perturbed but curious, she offered him a beer and he accepted because he felt he needed it. He sat on the edge of the sofa. She swaggered to the kitchen and the backside he had seen naked swayed to the rhythm of her indolence and upon her return he noted the halter and faded denim cutoffs left little to the imagination. The children, riled at the presence of company, scurried like rats across the living-room floor, tripping over broken toys and each other. Every so often a groan oozed out of the bedroom, a noise the girl said was her mother, whose supplications for water she batted away like flies.

"Well," she said. "What brings you to the other side of the tracks?"

He thought of the abandoned railway station down the street and the literalness of her phrase; he remembered the day he left for the war.

"I think you know," he said.

She shrugged and said something under her breath. The television blared like the PA system at a bus station.

"Well?" he said over the noise.

She shrugged again.

"He's different since he met you," Dutch said. "I don't like it."

"Does that matter? This is between me and Jom."

Dutch took a long draw from the can of beer, a tallboy, and it cooled his stomach. He held the can up to the side of his face and swabbed his cheek, then rested it on his knee, the aluminum crinkling under his grip.

"It can't work," Dutch said. "Don't you see? I have nothing against you. It's Jom. He's just a boy. A boy in a man's body."

Bekka rolled her eyes but said nothing. Her son crawled up to Dutch with a red and yellow toy truck and ran it over his shoes, making wet engine sounds with his mouth.

"What if you get . . . you know?"

"I won't," she said.

"That's confidence!"

She looked away, staring at the television, where a woman in bed called for her husband to turn on the light. But the light on the bed stand was on, and her husband, interrupted from his reading, looked down at her. The organ struck a major chord; the camera zoomed in on his terrified face as she persisted in her request, groping before her. The little boy had the truck climbing Dutch's leg up onto his lap, where it shifted gears and rammed into his crotch.

"Jesus!"

"Omar, go play somewheres else."

"A ballsy little vixen," Zulik said from behind his desk. "What did you do then?"

"What could I do? I got down to basics. I asked her if it was a matter of money and she said she was no whore. I said there was evidence to the contrary, that she was the heroine of every bathroom wall from here to Kirkwood. That got her attention. Names were pitched like rocks, both of us shouting like fools over that damn TV with the kids wading at our feet. It was ugly. Even the mother joined in from the bedroom, shrieking like a keener. I tell you, Zulik, the woman's trash."

Zulik's office went cold and Dutch stared down at his scuffed shoes—one of them untied. He had not shaved that morning and his fingers rasped at his chin.

"And I admit for the moment I was trash too. It brings you down to its own level. It scares the hell out of me when I think of Jom carrying on with her."

"Why?" Po asked Dutch, stretching her legs across the bed, propping her head with the flat of her hand.

"Why what?"

"Why it scare you?"

"Because she was trash, like I said."

"Why she trash?"

"Forget it," he said.

"Why? Because I trash too?"

"He's not dead, you know," Dutch said. "Listed MIA by

the do-nothings in D.C. Twelve years. But I know he's alive. I know it."

She appeared to think about this. Silence in the room pressed down on them. The wig on the bed looked like roadkill. Dutch reached over and picked it up, studied it for a moment, put it on his knee, ran his hand over the sheeny hair.

"He was stationed as a forward observer in I Corps. His second tour. He went out on a walk one evening outside of Dong Ha. His first there. A friend of his in H&S Company said he just went 'sightseeing.' Well, you know Jom. Jesus! Sightseeing! But he didn't come back. The men searched for days. Never found a trace. Like he just disappeared into thin air."

"VC?"

"That's the way I figure it. His buddies do too. POW. What else? I mean, if they killed him, they would have left him there for the other soldiers to see. An example. You know, 'This is what'll happen to you, Yankee Dog.' "

"That long time ago."

"Tell me about it. But to your people it means nothing. In 1973 a CIA intelligence report documented over a hundred American POWs in confirmed Commie prison camps in Laos alone. A hundred! None of them were returned after the war. That same year Vietnam gave our government what they called a short list of POWs to be returned in Paris, but nothing came of it. And listen to this . . ." Dutch removed his wallet from his back pocket and took out a piece of old newspaper. "This is from a CIA intelligence cable dated March 9, 1976. Just six years ago. 'As of December 1975 some Americans were being held as prisoners of war in North Vietnam. These Americans are being used for bargaining purposes by the Democratic Republic of Vietnam (DRV) in any future negotiations with the U.S.' Now," he said, folding the piece of paper and putting it back into his wallet, "what does John Q. Public make of all that? I'll tell you. It means of the two thousand plus MIAs, a good number of them are still alive, probably incarcerated in labor camps in Nam, Laos, even Russia, I hear. Guys like Jom, excellent soldiers who gave their hearts and souls, waiting to be freed themselves. And our government just doesn't give a shit."

A puff of air from the window touched the room with the scent of lilac. Po sat staring into his eyes and Dutch broke her concentration by asking about the camps she said she saw.

She nodded and looked away. Her cigarette had burned down to the filter and she snubbed it out in the ashtray. "I have many thing to tell you. But no more tonight. I must to go. Meet me again."

"Just tell me a little about it. A few details."

"We talk later."

"Tomorrow."

"Not good. Monday."

"When? Where?"

"This place. Midnight. The man downstair, he tell what room. Say you want Po."

"Just one question—"

"Monday. I wait."

Dutch took a deep breath, tossed the wig onto the bed, and stood. Po extended her hand and said, "One hundred fifty. You got?"

"Yeah."

"I hate do this to father of Jom. But I see we need talk, and this take time. I sorry."

NINE

Al Meehan received news of the bus's location while sitting in the rectory of Saint Patrick's Church on Leroy Street speaking with Father Toibin, a former schoolmate, about what had happened at the Potter house the day before. Toibin resided at the rectory and assisted with confessions and Sunday Masses, but his primary diocesan assignment was to serve as chaplain at Wilson Hospital in Johnson City, where he offered counsel to the sick and extreme unction to victims of trauma—thus the police-band radio in operation on the shelf behind the desk where he sat facing Meehan. Whenever the rush of static broke into the room, Toibin would stop talking and listen to the orders from dispatch or dialogue between officers in the field before continuing with his story.

Dutch had been standing on his front stoop and didn't see the priest coming until he was only a few steps away. Even then, Toibin said, he had to say hello to him twice. Dutch had been surveying the neighborhood, holding an open bottle of Burgundy by the neck, and when he realized he was being addressed he tossed it over the porch railing into the shrubbery.

" 'Looks like you're dressed for battle,' I said," Toibin told Meehan. " 'Old uniform, is it?' And I tried to make a joke about his paunch. He didn't say anything, so I held up the pyx and said I was there to give Ruth communion, like I do every Sunday, and he says, 'She just sits here at home waiting for the body of Christ to show up, and bingo, there it is. How wonderful!' "

Meehan shook his head and Toibin nodded and said, "Yeah." Even the dead-serious countenance could not bring the priest to look closer to his age. His albuminous skin was splattered with freckles the same sorrel shade as his hair, and his grin, nearly perpetual, was so wide and white and boyish that the joke in the parish went that he could be his own father—to which he would reply that, since his ordination some twenty years ago, he was.

" 'Funny thing, Tim,' Dutch says to me. 'She's not here. I say funny because she receives the sacrament at home and she does this because she's not able to go out and get it herself and, lo and behold, she's out. Gone. But isn't that just like life? The lesson we all have to learn?' he says."

"Christ," Meehan said.

Toibin shifted in his seat and tossed the curl of hair off his forehead before continuing. "Then he gets into the idea of taking communion, asking if I knew beyond any doubt that it was Jesus himself I carried around in the pyx."

"What did you say?"

"We got into kind of a debate on faith and empirical knowledge, on believing in God and knowing God. At one point I admitted to moments of doubt but said that was part of the grace of faith—it's what it was about. But he kept pressing me. 'How does one *know* he exists?' he kept saying, over and over."

It was then that word crackled through the radio that the bus might have been located down in Pennsylvania. Toibin held his hand up and Meehan leaned forward. Dispatch was ordering patrol cars to stay in state; Pennsylvania State Police were being

notified of the possible approximate location and would con-
firm ASAP.

The radio went silent and they waited. A few cars called in to
have the message confirmed and when there was a pause in the
transmissions Toibin picked up the phone and dialed the police
station, where John Cosell, a member of the parish council and
friend of Toibin's, worked the front desk. Meehan watched
Toibin waiting on the line, the phone pressed to his ear, his other
hand busy looping the cord on the desk, and when Cosell's baritone shot through the wire—no words, just the sharp electric
tone—Toibin pronounced his name into the receiver and asked
him if he could say anything about the sighting of the bus. While
he listened to what Cosell had to say, Meehan got up from the
chair and walked to the window that looked out across a strip
of grass onto the east side of the church. Three stained-glass
windows were visible from that angle, a triptych of martyrs in
the attitudes of their demise, one of them on his knees as if having fallen or been pushed, arms up in supplication to the heavens. Two robins hunted for worms on the lawn. The dispatcher
came on the radio trying to get hold of detectives Curley and
Lynch, but there was no reply, and in the silence Toibin said
"Good Lord," but Meehan had to wait another few minutes
before Toibin hung up.

"Four people walked into the station ten minutes ago," he
told Meehan. "Two of them claimed to have been on the bus
this morning when Dutch drove off route. Said they went down
Penn Ave. into PA about two, three miles. They're pretty upset
and it looks legit. The long and short of it is that the bus hit a
tree and Dutch was killed."

"*Shit.*"

"There were seven other passengers—all of them OK, I guess.
Just scraped up and scared. These two left to get help, got lost,
and after a while came across a hermit, some Amish guy living

in the woods who guided them to the nearest road where they were able to flag down a ride."

"But Dutch is dead."

"Head injury."

Meehan slumped back into the chair and rubbed the front of his hand over his mouth, his chin, his neck. "Must have fallen pretty far to have risked taking others with him."

"I should have done something yesterday after I saw him like that."

"Such as?"

"Something. I don't know."

"You said you called the house later and Mrs. Potter said everything was OK, not to worry."

"Sarah puts on the good face."

They sat in silence for a few moments. Meehan picked up a copy of the Sunday bulletin from the desk, turned it over, put it back on the desk.

"I of all people should have gone over there more," he said. "Just to check up on them, say hello. I realized that this morning standing on the Potters' porch and knocking on that door. I was family to them, Tim. Me and Jommy were like brothers. Hell, I spent more time in that house when I was growing up than I did in my own."

"OK." Toibin pushed back from the desk and got to his feet. "I won't beat myself up about what I should have done if you don't. Deal?"

"I don't know why I stopped going over there," Meehan said. "I can't even remember when I stopped."

Toibin planted his knuckles on the desktop and leaned toward Meehan. "Al. You and Jommy weren't like brothers, you *were* brothers. Like Siamese twins, for God's sake. I was jealous of you guys at Catholic Central. I didn't have a friend anywhere near as close as you guys were. You more than any single person would remind the Potters of Jom. You showing up in their living room *shouted* Jom. My guess is you stopped going over there because you intuited that, and I'm thinking maybe you were wise to stay away."

"You're a priest, Tim. Aren't you supposed to be nurturing my guilt?"

"I'll work on that another time—like, maybe if you started coming to Mass."

"There you go."

With the cardigan pulled on over his blacks and his Roman collar fastened he made his way to the door, and Meehan followed him out of the office into the front hall.

"I'm going over to the Potters' now," Toibin said. "I want to be there for Sarah when she hears. You want to come with me?"

"Thanks, but I think I'll head over to the police station and see what's up with those people who came in."

Meehan's Dodge Dart was parked on Leroy Street directly in front of the rectory and Toibin's car was in the back lot, so they parted in the foyer, a bear hug and then a handshake, and Meehan asked him what answer he finally gave Dutch.

"About what?"

"How one can know for certain God exists."

Toibin shrugged, and before he let go of Meehan's hand he told him he would have to ask Dutch.

"That's far enough!" Dutch shouted, and the words rang inside the bus like an alarm. He yanked the grenade free from the scapular ribbon, jammed the gun into his belt, and pulled the ring, holding tight to the handle which, if released, would be the end of them all.

Hulda watched Grace and Heather and Andy and Matthew looking out the window, one or another of them turning to look at Dutch, then out the window again where a voice, deep and official but ruffled with a treble of desperation, or fatigue, said something about assistance.

"I'm telling you to hold it right there!" Dutch said. "At the wood line. I'm armed."

He said this as though shouting to a neighbor that he would be by in a minute, and the nonchalance of his tone frightened Hulda all the more. She shut her eyes hard and darkness came like a blow to the skull. Cicadas rose in aria. The caw of a bird, birds, in excited dirge. Distant voices rumbled in low conversation and Dutch said to Bad, "The volkstern are murmuring against me."

"Sir? I'm William Taggart of the Pennsylvania State Police. I'm only here to help. It appears you've had an accident. Will you let me help?"

"Listen to that," Dutch said, nudging Bad. "He's in denial. And schooled to boot." He mimicked the trooper's question in falsetto and Bad chuckled roughly, nodding, and then fidgeted in his seat, the spear he had whittled moving in small clockwise circles as though he were churning butter. The trooper repeated his question and Bad snorted.

"No, but thanks for asking," Dutch shouted.

"Good one," Bad said. When Dutch was telling the passengers about Po he had painted his face and chest with lipstick so that he looked like a little savage.

"Is everyone on board all right?" Taggart asked. "Is anyone injured?"

"We're all fine," Dutch said.

"How many people are on the bus, sir?"

"They're not people, they're hostages. And I'm your host, Dutch Potter. And I'm armed."

"So you said, Mr. Potter. Let's stay calm. I only want to help."

"So you said."

"What can I do, then, Mr. Potter?"

"What a guy!" Dutch said to Bad.

"Yeah, right," said Bad. "A pig's a pig, man."

"That's good to remember, Bad."

"Mr. Potter?"

"Snort snort, right, Bad?"

"Fuckin' snort, man," said Bad.

"Mr. Potter, can I ask what is it that you want? Why you're doing this?"

"You come one step closer, Taggart, and I'll blow this bus to smithereens!"

Hulda shut her eyes again and waited, listening to the silence, then opened her eyes; everything was still there, and she closed them again.

"Let's stay calm, Mr. Potter. I'm moving back. It's just a few steps. See? There's no point in anyone getting hurt. You won't get whatever it is that you want if you hurt yourself. Right?"

Dutch looked away from the window, his eyebrows crowding on his forehead.

"Is it a bomb you have on board, Mr. Potter? Can I ask you that?"

"Tell them," Dutch said to Matthew.

Matthew cleared his throat and projected his voice out the window to his right. "He's got a grenade. He's removed the pin and is holding in the handle."

"Who is that speaking?"

"My attorney," Dutch shouted.

Bad swung his head around to face Dutch and said, "There's something going on over there. See? On that side of the woods. There."

Dutch nodded calmly. "It's all in the book, Bad."

"Shouldn't you get down?"

"Nah. I don't think they'll be stupid enough. Not these guys, anyway."

"How many people did you say are on the bus, Mr. Potter? Seven?"

Dutch nodded to Matthew, who looked over the group of them quickly and then shouted, "That's right. Eight including Potter."

"*Mister* Potter," Dutch hissed.

"Mr. Potter."

"To them."

"Mr. Potter!" Matthew shouted out the window.

"Yes?" Officer Taggart said. "Are you trying to say something?"

It took a moment to clear up the confusion, and then Taggart said, "And nobody's hurt, right? Everyone is OK?"

Matthew opened his mouth to speak but Dutch cut him off. "You," he said to Heather. "Talk." She slid further into her seat, biting her lower lip, and Dutch said, "Too slow. You."

Without taking her eyes off Dutch, Grace shouted, "We're all either alive or sorry-ass dead and gone to hell. Nobody's hurt. Bad, at least."

At the mention of what he thought might be a reference to himself, Bad was momentarily pulled from his stupor. He looked at Grace, then up at Dutch, then, slowly, back inward to whatever thoughts were running around inside his head.

"Mr. Potter, would you put the ring back into the grenade? I promise you we won't make any move. We just don't want anyone hurt. That's our priority."

"No."

"Would you at least consider letting some of the people go? Maybe just a few?"

"No."

"I'm just thinking, Mr. Potter, that in cases like this, three or four hostages, say, are as good to whatever purpose you might have as seven. You know?"

"I know. Two thousand two hundred and forty lives, a thousand, a hundred. All the same."

"Sir?"

"Look, Taggart. I don't have a bone to pick with you. Pennsylvania's a good state. Keystone, Penn's Woods, all that. I know people who have died here needlessly, but I don't blame you. That was . . . well, *c'est la guerre!* No. *C'est la mulatta!* Anyway, Gettysburg was something, and how about Valley Forge?"

"Mr. Potter?"

"These are times that try men's souls, fellas." He paused for a minute and then said to the passengers, "Hah! *They* think *I'm* nuts. Look at 'em standing out there. A nice group of 'em now, hey, Bad? Like in front of a pay toilet with no dime. With their funny little uniforms. Look at those hats!"

Bad nodded. In the distance, more sirens.

"But what's this Altoona, Taggart?" Dutch shouted. "How do you people come up with names like that? Sounds like a luncheon special. And King of Prussia? Down there by Philly. Is that a name for a place?" He tapped Bad's shoulder with the back of his free hand. "Listen to this, Bad. There's a town in Pennsylvania called Intercourse. Did you know that?"

"Of course," he said.

"I have to agree with you on that, Mr. Potter," Taggart shouted. "Lots of funny place names in PA. I'm from a town called Jersey Shore, and it's in the middle of the state."

"That's what I mean," Dutch said.

After a pause, Taggart said, "Can I get anything for you, Mr. Potter? Are you and the others hungry? Can I bring you in some food? Do you need any medical supplies?"

"Hungry, Bad?"

"Maybe," Bad said. "Yeah. I could go for a burger. Some fries, too."

"Hey, Taggart!"

His voice sounded metallic now, as if his throat were made of brass, and its volume had Hulda reaching for her collarbone.

"Yes, Mr. Potter?"

"Burgers. Fries. And tell your beans to bring in some battery acid." To the other passengers he said, "You want a hot pie? Taggart! Couple pizzas. What you want on the pies? You, Andy."

"Um. I don't know. Maybe pepperoni?"

"How 'bout you?"

"Me?" Heather said. "Oh, I don't care."

"Anyone else? No? Pepperoni on the pies, Taggart."

"We'll have the food for you as soon as we can get it. Is there anything else we can get for you? How about something to help us communicate a little more easily? So we don't have to do all this shouting? I don't know about you, but my larynx is getting sore."

"Don't get cute, Taggart."

"Sorry, Mr. Potter. It's a fault of mine. The guys I work with say I complain about my physical ailments too much. After you turn fifty . . . well. Anyway, what do you say? Can I bring in a radio?"

"Bullhorn!" Dutch shouted, and it sounded at first like cursing. "I think that would be more appropriate."

The sirens grew louder until they were nearly upon them, on the dirt road atop the hill—three, maybe four more cars—and Dutch told Bad that the cavalry had arrived.

"Mr. Potter, are you sure you wouldn't prefer a hand radio? It might be more convenient. Easier to use."

"Bullhorn!" Dutch shouted again.

"OK, Mr. Potter. We'll have one for you momentarily. It'll just take a short while. The food too. In the meantime, can we keep talking? Can I ask you a few questions?"

"Go ahead, Taggart."

"Call me Bill. What the hell."

"OK, Bill. And you know, you been such a good cop I'm gunna let you call me Dutch. You guys like to make it personal, right?"

"That's the way it's done, I guess. But what the hell, it makes communication a little easier, doesn't it? As long as we're going to be in this situation? Takes some of the starch out?"

"I guess. But you gotta admit it's kind of phony."

"What do you mean?"

"Well, I got at least one rifle pointed at my head. Hard to enjoy my new friendship under the gun, if you know what I mean."

"No one's out to hurt you, Dutch. If you know how things are done, you know we just want everyone out of this alive. Including you."

"Sure," Dutch said. "Human life. That's the most important thing in situations like this. I seen it in the movies."

"I do want everybody to come out of this, Dutch. I really do. So we have some problems. We'll work them out. We'll deal with them. Let's at least try. Do you mind if I ask what this is all about?"

"I'm waiting."

"For what, Dutch?"

"For the feds. Just like you."

"Excuse me?" Taggart said.

"The feds. G-men. The big guys. You know, Bill. The ass-wipes who run this place. Or think they do." Dutch turned to the passengers and said in his quieter voice: "*Think* they do. 'We the people'? Ha!"

Another long silence fell on them. Dutch dropped into a daze, staring at the floor of the bus as though something there interested him. Hulda thought that he might be losing consciousness, but he began humming a tune. It came out in dry rhythmic exhalations at first, then took voice, out of key and then working its way into key. Then he began singing, shyly, it seemed, until he increased the volume:

> . . . *below me, that golden valley,*
> *This land was made for you and me!*

"C'mon, everybody!" he shouted, and launched into the refrain, waving the grenade in the air over his head—either absentmindedly or to punch a threat into his command, and everyone sang, softly at first—except Grace, who scowled at the window, and Bad, who seemed exempt.

> *This land is your land, this land is my land,*
> *From California, to the New York Island,*
> *From the redwood forest, to the Gulf Stream wa-a-ters*
> *This land was made for you and me.*

He knew all the words to the song—the diamond deserts, the wheat fields waving, the dust clouds rolling, everything—and when they got to the end he started them going again, and then again, and yet again after that. Heather sang beautifully. She was loudest, after Dutch, sitting there with her white fingers woven neatly on the apron of her dirndl, her watery eyes fixed on the ceiling of the bus and catching the light from the window as the words poured out of her. From where she sat Hulda could not see Erica, and with the grenade looping through the air not ten feet away she dared not turn around, as if a breach in her vigilance might cause its detonation.

She was in the midst of a darkness she had feared for so long from the safety of her apartment: that the world could get this bad this suddenly, that it could be so terrifying when it did. It's why she stayed indoors for a year and a half, and almost a year before *that* single disastrous trip. She yearned for company, sure, but the only people who came over were delivery boys from the Triumph or Lane's. She'd try to get them to stay and chat, presenting them with plates of her fresh-baked chocolate chip cookies or apple or cherry pie, but they'd beg off, say they had to get back to work, like Hansels from the fairy tale grown wiser.

After the bus had sped off its course, the fear felt so fundamentally familiar that she wondered if it had happened before and was happening again, like this verse they were singing yet another time. "Déjà vu" was the term—a psychic explained it one morning on *Donahue*—and she couldn't help thinking the obvious, that a person kept living the same life over and over and over in a world that didn't end. A little private world repeating itself ad infinitum, the human being trapped and ignorant inside it, except for little spasms of knowing that came infrequently enough for the phenomenon to be doubted, or explained to oblivion by science.

If Hulda was going to return and live this same life again, then perhaps death wouldn't be so bad, because it wouldn't really be the end. It would simply be like night before another day, or like the reset button on the alarm clock. It would mean that the world for her would go on and on. But repetition was tedium, and tedium was hell—so was there then no heaven? Maybe it wasn't hell but purgatory, a temporary hell. Maybe people kept getting chances at the same life until they got it right, achieved a kind of perfection, like the Hindus claim, and once it was achieved, they could enter heaven. There would be a party of congratulatory multitudes. She'd know then how many lifetimes it took her to get it right. People, angels now, would compare themselves, and she wondered if there would be shame in those angels who had to have the most tries at the world. She wondered how many times she'd already been through her life, and what she needed to do to break the cycle. Maybe this was the end of her life right here, the grenade being the period of the last sentence of the final chapter, and that was why this awareness came to her with such clarity now. Then what could she do in these final moments that she hadn't done before? What single act would direct her into heaven rather than back to the life where all this would happen again? Was it too late?

Her father, top-heavy with imagination and stories to exercise it, would have appreciated this theory, and she would have bathed in his appreciation; and yet she ended up marrying an intellectually nomadic skeptic who'd have questioned such an idea to tatters, and she loved him too. It was a different love, of course, but why at all? Why him of all? She could already hear Peter asking how the mathematics of this spooling reincarnation meshed with the different timing of people's heavenly attainment. When she said "achieve perfection," did she mean that literally or figuratively? If the former, it was blasphemous; if the latter, then to what degree? It was all too confusing, and anyway, how could a person figure out life in general when it was hard enough to make sense of the little bit left of one's own?

TEN

Going to the police station would have been a waste of time for Meehan, and when he got downtown he took the spur by the Veterans Memorial Arena over the Collier Street Bridge, slipped onto Route 434, caromed around the Pennsylvania Avenue exit ramp, stopped for the light at Vestal Avenue, and wept. Mr. Potter had been, after all, more father to him than his own father. Deeply flawed, yes, but a good man who'd always meant to do the right thing and often did, even if in spite of himself. Meehan couldn't see this when he was growing up; he thought Dutch too serious, too taciturn, too hard on his children, the perfect diplomat (the "poster child," as he once put it to Jom) for the "Establishment" against which his generation rebelled.

But Meehan was fifteen years older than the Jom he had last seen; he'd gone on without him, aged without him, suffered and reveled without him, and he wondered when it was in that process he had begun to understand Jom less and Dutch more. Jom, whose dream life *was* his life in the world, who was pulled by desire more than pushed by fear, who held forth rather than back, who was all heart and adrenaline and laughter and trust. Anything was possible to Jom, for Jom, about Jom, with Jom, because he had no prejudices, no preconceptions, no forebodings, no unflinching opinions, no steady resolve.

Nor, Meehan thought, when the light changed and he headed up Pennsylvania Avenue, an ability to think clearly enough, or at least find sense enough, to avoid the catastrophes that resulted in his going AWOL from life.

It was Dutch who knew the Byzantine difficulties of marriage, the tribulations of rearing children, the anxieties of work, of making ends meet, of fear for others' lives and suspicion, if not antipathy, for one's own, day after day. His days, too, had been tutored by Jom's relentless absence, and he knew as Meehan knew the excruciation of living in a state where hope and dread are held dear for one more day, one more week, one more year, year after year. Meehan already believed he was the only one who would understand why Dutch stole the bus into these woods: to make the world wonder what the world had made him wonder. To force it to find the missing. To do something. It was terrible and brilliant, thoughtless and necessary as his death.

The last time Meehan had spoken with Dutch was on Main Street one night during the winter when he and a woman he was dating, an accountant named Ellen, also divorced, also with children, were walking out of the Turf Exchange riled with beer and early possibility, and there he was walking by so deep in thought Meehan had to call him three times. They hadn't seen one another in two years and Meehan was surprised at how gaunt he looked, how frail. But his spirits were high, even exuberant. He was just out to stretch his legs and had stopped in to see a movie at the Crest, which he said he liked very much and gave a strong recommendation. Meehan went to see it the following night and saw Mr. Potter down in the front row, but did not sit with him or talk with him afterward. On a hunch, he went to see the movie again two nights later and again spied

Mr. Potter down in front. It had become his church service, his ritual of presumption, the cultivation of the second soul of the unhappy, and Meehan understood that, too.

It was as if Dutch and not Jom were Meehan's de facto brother, a shift that may have been inevitable with the years but began when Jom was still with them, the night Dutch had burst into one of the backrooms at Swat Sullivan's where Meehan was drinking alone and slapped a half-sheet of paper torn from a spiral notebook onto the table. "I found this in Jom's room. She says she's ready to make the move and meet him here at eight o'clock. What move?"

"Look, Mr. Potter, I gave my word . . ."

"No, you look. That girl's got catastrophe graffitied all over her life and I'll be goddamned if I let her make a mess of Jom's. If you care about him, you'll help me out here."

"She's not a bad person, Mr. Potter. If you just gave her a chance."

Dutch sat in the chair next to him and leaned forward over the table. "You got a lot of common sense, Al. Or at least I thought you did. Your fiancée is a good girl. College degree. Responsible. Now what's Jom getting himself into here but trouble? And what does it say about you if you let your friend destroy his life while you sit in a bar drinking beer?"

"Mr. Potter, the idea was Bekka's and she insisted on it so that Jom *not* destroy his life."

"What are you saying?" But before Meehan could answer him Dutch slumped back in the chair, staring blankly at the two empty glasses on the far side of the table. "Jesus! I thought she—"

"Jom tried to stop her," Meehan blurted. "Nothing he said would change her mind and he asked me to meet him here so I could help him try one more time. But she wouldn't budge. She kept saying another one would be too much. She wouldn't do it.

But when Jommy went to the men's room she told me it'd ruin him, he'd wreck his life by insisting they marry. Believe me, Mr. Potter, she thinks less of herself than you do."

"Where did they go to? Hey!" Dutch took Meehan by the shoulders and one of the empty glasses smashed onto the floor. "Where?"

"Bekka has a friend who once went to this guy in Scranton," Meehan said, twisting himself free. "In the inner city. Someplace on Franklin Street."

Dutch shot up from the table, taking the wet note; it dripped beer onto the floor when he strode through the two rooms leading back to the bar.

"Mr. Potter, it's too late," Meehan said, close behind. "They left here almost an hour ago. Mr. Potter!"

Outside, he ran across the gravel parking lot behind Dutch, who got into his pickup truck, slammed the door, and started it up. Meehan slipped in beside him and shut the door just as the spinning tires catapulted gravel against a wood fence. Dutch recklessly negotiated the South Side streets toward the highway and as they whirred at gathering speed on Route 81 south Dutch pounded the steering wheel with the heel of his hand. "Shit! Didn't I warn him? Didn't I warn *her*? Shit! Shit!" And then, five minutes later when they passed the sign indicating that Scranton was fifty miles off: "Shit!"

They braided through light traffic on the interstate as fast as the truck could go, wind whirling through the open windows, and in twenty minutes they were closer to Scranton than Binghamton.

"How far along is she?" Dutch hollered.

"She wasn't sure."

"Shit!"

"I tried to stop them, Mr. Potter. I did."

Dutch said nothing, glaring at the road as if it were to blame, his knuckles white over the steering wheel. But for a moment Meehan's words seemed to shift Dutch's resolve, because his face softened. But then he shouted, "Why is she only now concerned about Jommy's well-being? Why not months ago, before all this? Don't shrug at me like that—why?"

"She loves him, Mr. Potter. Very much. She didn't want to let him go. She couldn't."

This silenced Dutch, but ten miles later he said, "A single life is like history. You do one thing, another happens. Effect shadows cause. You can't pretend something didn't happen when it did!"

This, Meehan thought, as they passed a Volkswagen sputtering at the speed limit, is what Dutch would drive home to Jom. Down in the valley to the east the lights of Scranton blazed like a galactic cluster of stars, and Meehan felt weightless speeding through it, suspended between Jom's recklessness and Dutch's practicality. When Dutch jerked the truck's decelerating careen into an exit lane, the centrifugal force threw Meehan's shoulder against his until they approached the stop sign at the foot of the ramp, which Dutch ignored except to slow for the turn left toward the brightest coagulation of city light. After a few blocks they stopped at an Esso station and Dutch demanded directions to Franklin Street from an attendant pumping gas into an Impala.

"Uh-huh," the man said, one hand on the pump, the other rubbing his cheek with grease-dappled fingers. "You keep going down this street here six, seven blocks. Take a right on Olive Street and she's back there somewhere. A whole tangle of streets named after presidents and such."

Olive opened into a ghetto of darkened tenement buildings and vandalized warehouses and empty storefronts, and as they proceeded down the avenue it felt to Meehan as though they were descending through the cornices of an abandoned hell.

"Turn here," he said, guessing, and four blocks and two turns later they found, by pure chance, Franklin. No sign of life anywhere, just the dark, broken neighborhoods. They cruised slowly, like a trawler in enemy waters, and after a few more blocks Dutch slammed on the brakes.

"Isn't that Jommy's?"

On the left side of the street a half a block ahead, a yellow Falcon, and when they moved in they could see the red windbreaker hanging over the seat, the *Playboy* air freshener, the plastic Saint Christopher carrying Jesus across the dash. Dutch pulled in behind, parking the wrong way on the street, and got out of the truck. Broken glass crackled under them as they walked along the sidewalk.

"Try this one," Dutch said, pointing at the nearest brownstone.

Meehan jogged up the steps and yanked at the door handle. Nothing happened, and he visored his eyes with his hand and peered through one of the windows. "It's all torn up in there," he said. "Abandoned."

Dutch stood at the curb with his arms at his sides, sniffing like a hound. "He's got to be around here somewhere." He went back to the Falcon and opened the passenger-side door. Only Jom, Meehan thought, would fail to lock his car in a neighborhood like this. Dutch ran his hands over the vinyl, then spotted, on the floor under the glove compartment, a scrap of paper— the other half of the notebook page upon which Bekka had written her message. He read it under the car's map light: a crude map, and under it, "205 Franklin, back entrance." He tossed it back onto the floor, backed out of the car, slammed the door, and strode up onto the sidewalk, studying the building in front of him and the one across the street. "This way," he said to Meehan, and headed down an alleyway between two buildings.

It was darker back there, and some movement stirred the shadows—a rat or a tom, darting through the narrow draft. A puddle of light seeping from under a door spilled over the ledge of the stoop at the end of the alley. Dutch took the five steps in two bounds, Meehan right behind him as he twisted the metal knob, pulled, and entered. A moth battering the ceiling lamp struck Dutch's forehead as he appraised the hallway before them. A noise like a song echoed from deep inside the building: a radio, perhaps, or a baby cooing. Dutch moved his head slowly, cupping his good ear. The moth struck his head again.

"Down here," Meehan said.

They descended a stairway into pure opacity, the wood treads groaning underfoot as Meehan felt his way along the wall until he found and turned a doorknob. A fog of blue light splayed over them from a room furnished with a committee of folding chairs around a rectangular table. The light came from the mouth of a hallway off this room, and Dutch pushed Meehan aside and went ahead.

When Meehan entered the room he had to cover his eyes until they adjusted to the brilliant light and then he saw that the source of the noise was Jom singing, or mumbling something in a soothing cadence. There were two green tanks set against the wall with black hoses looped to the table he seemed to be sitting on.

"Jom?"

He didn't turn, or even stop the eerie crooning, but when they came closer they could see Bekka slumped against his chest, her face buried in his T-shirt, her arms, flecked with blood, dangling at her sides. There was a smell of vomit, footprints of it mixed with blood trailing from the table to another door on the other side of the room near a chair where Bekka's clothes had been folded so neatly it was as if they were on a display in a boutique. When Dutch called his son again, inching closer, arm outstretched, he fell back as if the force pulling him had let go. He bumped into Meehan, whose shoe sent something spinning across the room—a steel curette flashing like an explosion in the light of the single floodlamp.

When Jom turned around, Meehan could see in his palm a human form no larger than the hand that held it, sitting upright, sculpted from a clot of blood, it seemed, its arm extended, finger up, as if making a declaration.

"Lord!" Meehan said.

Dutch said to call an ambulance and Meehan ran from the room.

The baby, a boy, would have been fifteen this summer, Jom thirty-eight, Bekka forty, and perhaps all of them friends and, with luck, enjoying some moments of life as they could. But instead Jom fell into a depression that, months later, only the idea of enlisting seem to ease. He was going to be responsible, he promised with something like the old exuberance, the familiar grin. He was going to show his father, show him, Meehan, show his mother and sisters, everyone and anyone who cared, that he wasn't a total waste, a complete fuckup. He'd come back whole, he said, and live a real life instead of having life live him. That was the plan. That was his promise.

A chorus of sirens grew close quickly and Meehan had to pull the Dodge Dart to the shoulder of the road and let two state troopers and an ambulance pass. Before he could speed back into the lane another ambulance flew by and behind it, a Binghamton police patrol car and a gray Ford Escort carrying a crowd of men in shirtsleeves. Meehan accelerated to gain on them and hung behind the Escort at seventy miles per hour. There were more sirens in the distance behind him, and it was as if the hills themselves were wailing. Out the window to his left the blur of trees rushed past his vision, and on the opposite shoulder a splash of roadkill as fast as a single aberrant frame in a film, a wound slashed into the day, closed as fast as opened, and he glared over the concatenation of hills at the frothy sky, to wash the image from his thoughts.

ELEVEN

Hulda thought maybe she was going crazy, because she wanted to scream, but she only sang louder—it was "God Bless America" now—until she heard a voice pitched lower than Taggart's, more sonorous, less friendly, more detached, like a question in *The Book of Knowledge* shouted from the woods. The passengers fell silent and Dutch craned his neck to better see out the window past Bad.

"I'm Special Agent Beikirch of the FBI. Tom Beikirch. Officer Taggart tells me you've been waiting to talk with a federal agent."

Dutch turned to the passengers and whispered, "You see, if you wait long enough . . . Well—no. Not true. I don't think. Is it?"

"Mr. Potter?"

Dutch's body began to shake so badly Hulda thought he might be having a fit, except his eyes weren't white in his head but gleamed in convivial warmth, and she realized that he was straining to contain laughter. Movement outside rustled the brush at the edge of the clearing. It sounded organized and Dutch's mirth ebbed.

"Mr. Potter, can we talk?"

"Bad," Dutch whispered. "Tell him you don't know where Mr. Potter is. He's gone. Vanished."

Bad looked up as if to see if this might be true before clearing his throat and shouting the message verbatim. Dutch patted the boy's shoulder and kept his hand there.

"Who is that speaking?" Beikirch asked. He waited a moment and when Bad did not answer, he said, "But I can see you, Mr. Potter. I know you have a grenade and I know you want to speak with me. I'm here to talk. Maybe we can work something out. But I can't help you if you won't let me. Right?"

Dutch stood thinking, or maybe, from the look on his face, daydreaming, if that was possible in a situation like this, and then he turned to Heather and said, "You."

"Me?" Heather said.

Without taking his eyes off her he ordered Bad to fetch him a pen and a piece of paper. The boy worked his way out of the seat and with spear in hand strutted down the aisle, scanning the floor and seats. When he spotted the briefcase on Matthew's lap he snapped his fingers and motioned for him to turn it over.

"Dutch? It's Bill Taggart again. What's up? Why the silence?"

Bad slid back into the seat in front of Dutch, propped the spear against the window, and opened the briefcase on his lap.

"Bad, tell our friend Officer Taggart to tell Efrem Zimbalist Jr. out there that Jonathan Potter is busy right now and he'll get back to him when he has the time."

Bad nodded and as he rummaged through the briefcase he shouted the message with a bright spin of vernacular. In the silence that followed he held up a yellow legal pad and a silver pen, and Dutch said, "Write this down, kid."

It took the boy a moment to figure out how the pen worked; it did not have a cap to remove or a clicker at the top, and by the time he discovered that he needed to twist the bottom half in order for the point to emerge, he had to interrupt Dutch and ask him to start again.

"Potter's demands," Dutch said, his gaze back on Heather, who inched from the middle of her seat toward the window. "One. Bring back Lieutenant Jonathan Potter Jr. from Asia. Two. Bring back Lieutenant Jonathan Potter Jr. from Asia. Three. Bring back Lieutenant Jonathan Potter Jr. from Asia."

It was like listening to nails being driven into wood, and with each command Bad would cock his head to one side and look up before writing it down.

"Anyone want to add something?"

The passengers each looked away, except Grace, who grunted hard, tossing her head back as she did.

Dutch took the sheet of paper from Bad and looked over what he had written.

"It's not OK?" Bad asked.

"'Lieutenant' is all wrong. But it'll do. You," he said to Heather. "Take this to our Zimbalist out there."

"Excuse me?" she said, but when she could see he was serious she rose slowly from the seat and took four steps down the aisle where three would have been enough, and even then had to reach her hand a full arm's length to take hold of the sheet of paper. Then Dutch slipped into the well of the seat across the aisle from Bad and indicated with a sweep of his arm that he wanted her to use the front door of the bus. After she made her way past him, and then through the splaying leaves of the branch, she turned and asked Dutch if he wanted her to return. When he said no she stood facing the other passengers and it seemed to Hulda that she looked hurt, as if she had been rejected rather than freed. It must have been an expression common to her; when the men had been off the bus and the women were talking about men in general, Heather spoke of her boyfriends and their betrayals with that same expression on her face.

It was clear she had chosen men poorly, or let bad men win her too easily, yet she so staunchly defended romance against the onslaught of Erica's and Grace's cynicism that Hulda wondered if she was of the type who so believed in love that she dared not practice it in earnest lest reality molest the beautiful image of it that sustained her.

"Go!"

"The door is closed," she said. "How do . . . what do . . . ?"

Veins pronounced themselves in Dutch's neck, but his voice was calm when he asked Bad to escort the lady out of the bus. Using the spear as a fulcrum, Bad pulled himself up out of the seat and made his way down the aisle in long loping steps, then pushed himself so roughly past Heather that she fell back against the edge of the partition dividing the driver's seat from the row of seats behind it. As she regained her balance, Bad, straddling the stairs, jammed the spear into the rubber strips between the door flaps and wedged them open with something like a rowing motion. When they were separated wide enough for a person to pass through, he looked over at Heather and jerked his head once toward the opening.

"Mr. Potter?" Beikirch called out. "What's going on?"

Heather looked back and said, "Goodbye, everybody," and then, before stepping down, waved the sheet of paper in the air and shouted, "I'm coming out! I'm Heather Reed and I'm coming out of the bus!"

Between the dirt road and the lip of the hill over which the bus had tumbled the FBI established a command post in a beige Winnebago. Inside, men and women moved past the windows and its perimeter buzzed with law-enforcement officers whose vehicles lined the opposite shoulder of the road—New York State Police, Susquehanna County sheriff, Pennsylvania State

Police, Broome County sheriff, fire medics, a BC Transit vehicle—all parked at equal intervals, as if readied for inspection.
Squad-car radios scratched the pastoral air, and twice a helicopter warbled at low altitude. An open ambulance idled in the
middle of the road, and from where he stood Pastor Philips
could see into the back, where a woman sitting on a stretcher
wept into the neck of an EMT. Sarah saw her, too, and the pastor, with the help of Father Toibin, tried to usher Sarah out
of view but she would not move. He thought she might say
something to the girl, or at least to the deputy stationed just outside the ambulance, when the Binghamton policeman who had
brought them there turned and said, "Let's go. Minister Philips.
Mrs. Potter? Father? This way."

They were led down the road to the command post—Sammy
Corcoran and Dutch's daughter Georgia and her husband right
behind them—and introduced to Special Agent Gouldin of the
FBI, a portly man with black hair who had just come out of the
Winnebago. The food had arrived and Gouldin, alerted to this,
ordered two New York troopers to bring it down to a man
named Blaszczak, a Bureau psychiatrist stationed at the bottom
of the hill. "Easy does it," Gouldin warned. "Quickly, quietly."
Just as the troopers began their descent, one cradling three pizza
boxes and the other with a large white bag and a beverage tray
with three large coffees, another officer, this one a Pennsylvania
trooper, climbing up the steep grade, hailed Gouldin.

"He won't buy it. Blaszczak says we better go with the bullhorns."

"Get two from inside," Gouldin said, jerking his head
toward the Winnebago.

"Another thing," the trooper said. "Blaszczak said to nix the
chopper. It's bothering Potter."

"When you go in, tell Kavanaugh to get on the radio and get
it out of the sky. We don't need it anymore anyway. The area's

sealed off and we got men interviewing locals for a survey of the area. Mrs. Potter? Reverends . . ."

"Philips. This is Toibin."

"And you," he said to Sammy and Georgia and Bummy. "Move over this way and stay out of the road, please. I'll be with you in a few minutes. Officer? Yeah, you. Stay with these people."

All of them moved across the road from the Winnebago near the line of trees. Sarah, her arm still locked tightly onto the pastor's, leaned closer to him and said, "Dieter, what's Jack doing? What's he doing?"

The pastor shook his head, not looking at her but at the area of woods into which the trooper had entered with a bullhorn in each hand. Beside them an albino was embracing a short, portly woman, who kept declaring her love in an hysterical whisper as he hummed "Love Me Tender."

"A grenade, that man said," Sarah said. "Where could Jack have gotten such a thing?"

The pastor freed his arm from hers and wrapped it around her shoulders, drawing her closer, and was relieved when she took a deep breath. But she tensed when her husband's amplified voice echoed in the air around them. They could not make out the words at first, but it was unmistakably Dutch, and it drew the pastor back across the road, leaving Toibin to take care of Sarah. It was a dialogue; the negotiator from the Bureau was saying something about the bullhorns they were using, and Dutch said he liked it loud because he had nothing to hide. The negotiator said he had nothing to hide either, though if they both turned them down there would be less feedback.

Dutch refused—"Feedback be damned," he said. The pastor could see nothing through the cluster of trees but judged the distance of the bus to be fifty or sixty yards from where he stood.

"The food OK, Mr. Potter? Can we get you anything else?"

"Yes. My son."

"Can I call you Dutch? Is that all right?"

"Call me 'Mr. Potter.' I'd like that better from you guys. A little respect, for once."

"Who do you mean when you say 'you guys,' Mr. Potter?"

"You. And the guys you work for. You. Guys. See?"

"I think you and I have more in common than not. I'm a war vet—Korea, '52, '53. I'm a father; I got two sons. Sure, I got my job and I try to live day in and day out, just like you. My job here is to try and make sure we all get out of this alive—hopefully in a way that will satisfy you, if we can. But I got to tell you, Mr. Potter, nobody's going to get anything if we get hurt. Understand?"

"Where are your boys? Your sons, I mean."

"Tom Junior's down in North Carolina. High-school teacher. Mike, he's in college up in Buffalo. Canisius."

"And you can call them whenever you want. Say 'Hey, what's up?' and all that?"

"Yes, Mr. Potter. I can do that."

"Nice."

"Mr. Potter, I can't even imagine the agony you have gone through all these years. I can't. And I hope to God I never have to go through anything like it. But please do me a favor and just look at those people on the bus there in front of you. They have family, too—brothers and sisters, mothers and fathers, maybe some of them have sons and daughters of their own. If any of those six passengers were, God forbid, harmed in any way, think of the pain that would cause their loved ones. I think you know that we can't ease our own suffering by inflicting it on others, Mr. Potter."

"Bring my son back to me and everyone will be OK."

"Please, sir, let's be reasonable."

"I already tried that."

"Mr. Potter . . ."

"No. My boy or nothing. Period."

Everyone on the bus listened to the silence that followed as if some meaning might be hidden in its swells. The smell of hot food had filled their confinement. Hulda wasn't hungry—no one but the boy even touched the food. He had an open box of pizza on his lap and was going at it like a wolf at a carcass.

"Mr. Potter, would you at least let a few more of the hostages go? You don't need all of them. You know that or you wouldn't have let the girl go. Right?"

"How many would you like?"

"How about letting the women go?"

"No. They make the place homey."

"Just a couple of them, Mr. Potter? Two?"

"No."

"How about the older woman, at least. Just that one person."

Erica cleared her throat behind Hulda and said, "Yes, please, Mr. Potter. Just let Mrs. Lambert go. You'll still have your hostages."

Spittle flew from him when he asked who was running the show here.

"You are," Erica said. "I'm just saying—"

"I know what you're saying. You know what she's saying, Bad?"

Bad nodded.

"Is everything OK in there?" Beikirch asked.

"Dandy," Dutch said into the bullhorn. "Family discussion."

Hulda looked at him and then at the row of windows across the aisle, shining like the white light at the end of the tunnel. She wanted to turn and offer a smile in thanks to Erica—a social worker, she'd said she was, a single mother with more to lose than Hulda—but she sat still, eyes fixed on the window two rows down from where the boy sat.

"Well, Mr. Potter, what do you—"

"No hostages, Zimbalist. We're not playing poker here."

"I just thought . . . well, you let Miss Reed go, so I thought maybe you'd be good enough to let another go. That's all."

" 'Good enough,' Zimbalist? Ha! 'Good enough,' you say?"

"I'm appealing to your better side, Mr. Potter. I know you're a good man."

"How do you know that?"

"I been around the block a few times. I'm betting you don't want to hurt these people. I'll bet you've never hurt anyone in your life. You just don't know what else to do to get your son back. Just let me suggest there's a better way."

"Oh, but I *have* hurt people, Zimbalist. I've killed people."

"Are you talking about the war? About Normandy? The Ardennes?"

"*This* is war, Zimbalist!"

"Hold on now, sir. I'm on your side."

"No. You're flying by the seat of your pants."

"Maybe we both are. I really, really don't want anyone hurt, and I don't think you do, either. I just want this to be over. Can't we make this thing be over? Would you work with me to make that happen?"

"There's only one way."

"But how can we do that? Do you really think the government wouldn't have brought back your son long ago if they had the chance?"

"Don't you read the papers? It's money! Pride! Nixon! Hanoi! All that shit. Get me someone who knows what's going on, man."

"OK, OK. Let's say I agree. The government's not been forthcoming. OK. We'll go with that for a minute. Let's say they even know where he is. It would take time to get him here, time we don't have."

"I got all the time in the world."

"You can't keep a grip on that grenade forever. You must be exhausted as it is, and you're hurt. Can we make an agreement? Put the ring back into the grenade, we'll take a breather, and we'll work together on this?"

"I was born at night, Zimbalist, but it wasn't last night."

"I'm just trying to make sure we all get out of this OK. Is that so bad?"

"Safety at any cost?"

"For the innocent, yes."

"There are no innocent, Zimbalist."

"Some are less guilty than others, Dutch. I'm sorry—Mr. Potter. Are you sure I can't just call you Dutch? I'm afraid I'm not a formal kind of guy."

"Go ahead. Have a blast with your informality."

"It's sort of like loosening your tie, you know? Look, how about letting me take the place of a hostage or two?"

"No."

"Why not?"

"You know why, or you should. The government doesn't care if you die. This is chess, and you're a pawn. How do you feel about that?"

"Assuming that's true, and really it's not, but for the sake of argument, let's say I am expendable. It's what I signed up for. It's sort of what Jom signed up for, too. Twice. We know the risks. Jom knew."

"Jom had every right to believe the Corps valued his life. It's been twelve goddamn years. Twelve! And the replies? Shameful!"

"But you know better than anyone how war can be, Dutch."

"Oh, yeah. I know all right."

"Let's say the government has acted shamefully—"

"They have."

"OK, then. What can we do about it now? I mean this minute?"

"Get me my boy."

In the silence, Hulda could not even look up in front, where her death would come from, but stared instead at the floor between her feet wondering if she would suffer much before she breathed her last. That was the thing to worry about. The actual death—well, who knew, and she was done making guesses except to hope it was more like sleep than anything else, because she was tired and would take that as her reward. What made suffering so terrible was the being aware and knowing. She closed her eyes and did not open them until Agent Beikirch spoke once again to say someone with him wanted to talk. Dutch leaned in to get a better look out the window, the grenade in his left hand, the bullhorn in his right.

"Jonathan? Jon?"

"Oh, no," Dutch said to Bad. "The clergy." And then, into the bullhorn, "Well, Pastor Philips, and what has you out of the parsonage today?"

He turned to the passengers and winked, as if they were all in on the joke.

"Jon, you're hurt. You need medical attention."

"Surely you didn't come all this way to discuss my health? Let's talk about something important. Goethe? Schiller? One of the nice Germans. C'mon, impart an interesting fact. Feed me some fruit from the Tree of Knowledge. I'm famished."

"Jon, please let those people go."

"Pastor Philips is smart," Dutch told the passengers. Then, into the bullhorn: "The pastor knows a lot. But it's no good. I ask a question, he knows the answer. Most times. Right, Dieter?

I'm not talking two-times-two. Watch." He clicked off the bull-horn and said, "Name something in the Bible. Anything." He was addressing Hulda and she said the first thing that came to her mind. Dutch nodded, keeping his eyes on her for a moment, and then said into the bullhorn: "Tell us, Pastor Philips, where in the Bible is Lucifer mentioned?"

"Jon, please. What you're doing isn't right. Look at yourself. Look around you, for godsakes! Look what you're *doing*."

"Where in the Bible is the story of Lucifer?"

After a pause, the pastor said, "Isaiah. Fourteen."

Dutch handed the bullhorn over to Bad, plucked his metal-plated Bible out of the front pocket of his army jacket, and flipped it toward the back of the bus, where it landed in the aisle beside Andy.

"Read Isaiah 14," he said.

Andy picked up the Bible and turned it over in his hand for a moment before flipping through the little pages.

"Jonathan . . ."

"Isaiah, Andy, c'mon."

"The print is so small," he said. "Oh. Here. I found Isaiah."

"Now see if you can find Lucifer in that haystack of print."

Andy screwed his eyes tightly, bringing the book—which was smaller than his blistered hand—within a few inches of his face. Dutch took the opportunity to switch the grenade to his right hand, a process Hulda shut her eyes from witnessing. When she opened them Dutch had the bullhorn in his left hand.

"At least let the women go, Jon. At least them."

"You talk too much, Dieter. Now it's time to listen. This is *my* church. My congregation. Nobody yawning in these pews, man."

The pastor's ashen silence blew through the bus. Dutch licked his lips and put the bullhorn down at his side. "Whatcha got there, Andy?"

"Right here," Andy said, "it says 'Lucifer.' Isaiah 14, um . . ."

"See?" Dutch said to the passengers. "Is this Pastor Philips an amazing piece of ministerhood or what? What's it say?"

"Um, it says—geez, this print is so small—"

"Jon, you've put these people into a terrible situation. Please let's end this before someone gets hurt."

"Get up here with that, Andy. Yeah. Come on, you're OK. Don't lose your place in the book. Now, take hold of this. You turn it on by clicking this here. Jesus, man, what happened to your hands?" Andy started to say something but Dutch cut him off. "Speak clearly into the horn and read about Lucifer to our friends outside. Go ahead."

"Um, it says . . . Let's see. It says, 'How art thou fallen from heaven, O Lucifer, son of the morning!' "

"Go on, Andy. That's good. 'Son of the morning.' "

"Um, 'How art thou cut down to the ground, which didst weaken the nations!' Should I keep going?"

"What the hell."

" 'For thou hast said in thine heart, I will ascend into heaven, I will exalt my throne above the stars of God: I will sit also upon the . . .' Um, it's smudged here and I can't read the next line."

"That's OK, Andy. Sit down right here. Now, we know how smart the pastor is, but we don't know how smart he *isn't*. Give me the bullhorn, Andy. Do you know, Pastor, what Lucifer went through? There's a lady here who thinks I'm him, and I think maybe she's right. History is written by the winners. But is Lucifer really a bad guy? He was good enough to be God's best angel, the apple of his eye . . . Hah! Then Christ comes along and . . . I don't know. *Used,* you know? I understand that. Do you? Knowledge isn't just what you know up here, it's what you feel, right here, in your heart. That's where I'm smarter than you. Oh, I know what you'll say to my little Lucifer story. Christ was God's son, so the Almighty would do anything for him, right? To sit at his right hand? Any way you look at it, Pastor, I'm right."

Grace, shifting in her seat, said, "What's all this bullshittin' talk supposed to mean?"

Dutch lowered the bullhorn and raised the grenade as though he were toasting her. "In hell's service."

Grace sneered at him again and looked back out the window.

"Anyway," Dutch said to the passengers, "the pastor knows the Bible pretty good, huh? All those prophets and their numbers. He's one of the best ecclesiastical accountants around. Got it all figured out."

"Jonathan, you need help. You're not well. Let us help."

"You ever turn that sharp eye in on yourself, Pastor?" Dutch lowered the bullhorn and turned to the passengers. "Safety is a culture for Pastor Philips, like a country, a civilization, a way of life. Me, I'm in top form with a little danger in the air. Give me a grenade and my wits get prickly."

Hulda unfolded her hands on her lap, folded them again.

"Go back to where it's safe and sound, Pastor. Skedaddle. Your education doesn't count for much here. Like trying to buy hamburgers with Roman coins."

"Jon . . ."

"Zimbalist! Give him the hook!"

"Jon, wait a minute. You're right. I've been too much minister and not enough friend. I went professional on you. I blew you off, especially these past few years. I didn't give you the time or the comfort a real friend would give."

"So tell me something I don't know."

"I've felt for you, Jon, what I knew you must have been going through, but . . . I'm no good at . . . I just didn't know how to, what to . . . I'm sorry. Forgive me, Jon, please. I'm sorry."

Dutch didn't say anything for a while, he stared out the window, then down at the floor, then out the window again, and then he called out to the pastor without the use of the bullhorn and asked his friend to pray for him.

"That's one thing I never stopped doing, Jon. I've prayed for you every single day. At least I've done that."

Dutch began to weep, then laugh, then seemed to be doing both at once. When he calmed a little, Andy asked if he wanted his Bible back and Dutch shook his head. He put the bullhorn down in the seat across from Bad and sat beside it.

" 'Something about this war,' " he said, " 'this place, I feel I got to figure out and the way to do that I guess is to stay titi longer and keep being a part of it. I'm confused so bad my head hurts most of the time. What else is new? Except here in the Land of Make Believe there isn't a whole lot to keep you sane. Reality dodges you. It shifts. It changes its rules.' "

"What the fuck you talking about, Dutch?"

He pulled an airmail envelope from the front pocket of his shirt and handed it to Bad. The boy examined it and removed two thin sheets of stationery covered on both sides with looping script. He looked again at Dutch, who resumed speaking his nonsense in a wistful voice that didn't sound anything like his own.

" 'What do you do with all this?' " he said. " 'What's it for? Everybody's got opinions and it all sounds like thunder to me. I've been in Nam for twelve months and twenty-two days. I'll finish this extension in September. That's not so bookoo, right? Six more months? Maybe it's true that I've taken so many chances I think I'm invincible. That happens here. I got a friend, a Captain who happens to be a shrink, and he explains it. He explains everything. Nice guy, but everything is a syndrome. He also has a theory that he calls "short-time syndrome," people who get nervous just before going home. He says it's a sign of their reluctance to face relationships and responsibilities back home. Maybe that's true with me. Maybe it's not here but there

I got to figure out. I don't know. But I do know I want to finally
grow up. I guess part of me is afraid of losing what it is I need to
lose to really do that. Something I can't name, but I know it's
there. Does that make sense? I want to be old enough to be the
father of the kid I am now, to know what it is I'd tell myself.' "

He stopped speaking and just stood in the aisle squinting at
the light pouring in through the window. Bad waited to see if he
would continue; there was more to the letter he had been recit-
ing verbatim. But Dutch said nothing and Bad silently read the
last paragraph wherein Dutch's son described the thick humid-
ity of the jungle and reminisced of springtime in Binghamton
and promised—gave his word—he would return and all would
be made right and there would be peace in the world and in his
heart, and then he concluded by asking forgiveness for what he
called this loose bunch of words which, with a declaration of
love, he signed "Jom in Nam."

TWELVE

Men moved through the cramped command post—two, four, five of them, and one woman—feverishly, one or another leaving the vehicle and coming back, or not, and another person Meehan had not seen before climbing aboard. It looked staged, like a rehearsal for a farce, and it became clear as he watched them that they had no cohesive plan. He heard one man say to another that they had a "real sphincter-tightener here," and another kept asking, "What next?" Surely they were desperate if they thought Meehan could help. When Mrs. Potter had introduced him to Gouldin as Jom Potter's best friend, and Sammy Corcoran chimed in by calling the boys "frick and frack," inseparable, as they'd been, since grade school, the agent ordered Meehan to come aboard the Winnebago.

Three telephones had been set up at another table against the wall opposite where he sat, and two men were on separate lines talking in low voices. One of them was gathering data from Quantico on the success rate of defusing a Mark II fragmentation grenade with a rifle shot from twenty yards; the other held his hand over the speaker of his phone and announced that the contents of the grenade included filler TNT, ammonium nitrate, and sodium nitrate producing up to a thousand fragments that could travel up to fifty yards. "The time delay," he said to Gouldin, "is 4.8 seconds, tops." At another table a man wearing earphones was communicating with someone stationed down near the bus by speaking into a microphone. Agent Gouldin, leaning over him, his hand on the man's shoulder, was telling him what to say.

Through a speaker placed somewhere near the front of the command post Meehan could hear what was going on down by the bus with more clarity than he had outside, where he had to strain to pick up the dialogue through the bullhorns. Dutch was ranting on about springtime in Binghamton, an interminable digression on lilacs and crocuses and a garden he once culti-vated, what he planted in that garden and how much of that was harvested, and then a litany of all the springtimes that had come and gone since Jom had reupped. He counted off the years start-ing with 1971, telling a little something about each, as though introducing guests on a dais. He got waylaid for a time at 1975, in April of that year when Saigon fell. At 1978, when Pintos were exploding and boat people were drifting across the South China Sea in droves and Jom had been gone eight years, Gouldin slid the microphone back in front of the radio operator and before leaving the Winnebago lifted a finger into the air to indi-cate to Meehan that he would be back shortly.

Meehan watched him through the window walking toward another agent, the man who called the situation a sphincter-tightener, and joined his conversation with a man with an IBM identification tag clipped to the pocket of his white shirt. Two Pennsylvania state troopers made it a huddle. Gouldin did most of the talking. Across the road from them Bummy and Georgia were standing between Sarah and Pastor Philips, each of them— Corcoran and Toibin included—staring at the ground, listening to Dutch's harangue. Corcoran had said Bummy unloaded on

Dutch the day before at the Potters' house, and Meehan could imagine most of what he said, as could anyone who knew Bummy. He was three years younger than Meehan and Jom but he cut a figure for himself in the mid-sixties. His brazen iconoclasm was flawless and he used the patois of the time so righteously it was as if he'd coined the phrases himself. He continued to spice his conversations with the old colloquialisms, but his ponytail was graying, his hairline receding, his body thickening into middle age, and to those who didn't know how effective his attitude had once been he appeared not a little pretentious. He squinted up at the Winnebago in such a way that Meehan thought he might be able to see him through the tinted glass, and so he averted his eyes.

Dutch was speaking about Article 12 and how Jom would never have broken a promise such as the one he'd made in his letter—a vow, by the way, reiterated in the few letters he'd sent after this one. Beikirch chanced an interruption to say that of course Dutch must realize that circumstances could easily have intervened to make honoring such a promise impossible.

"*Every* soldier expects to come home," the agent said. " 'Make the other SOB die for his own country,' you know?" During the silence that followed, Meehan could hear Dutch's breathing through the radio speakers. "You remember good buddies that didn't make it back from Europe, right, Dutch?"

"What kind of question is that?"

"I'm just saying that probably all of those men told fathers and mothers and wives and girlfriends they'd be back. That they'd make it. Don't you think?"

"What do you know?" Dutch barked.

"I'm just trying to be reasonable, Dutch."

But being reasonable with Dutch Potter was, Meehan thought, not itself a reasonable act. His actions, though proceeding through a kind of logic, or at least seriality, had little to do with the common sense the world supposed itself to operate on. Dutch might have told the agent, if he even realized it himself, that Jom's did not, either—especially toward the end.

A shudder of feedback reverberated through the woods, ushering a deep voice over the bullhorn, a man introducing himself as Dawson, from Owego.

"Yeah? So?"

"These guys here, the FBI, they asked me if I'd talk to you man-to-man from a common experience."

"Like what?"

"U.S. Army. Sixteenth Regiment, First Division, Omaha Beach, D-1."

"Owego, you say?"

"That's right."

"The Sixteenth?"

"Yes, sir. Easy Red. E Company. We went left and you boys in the 116th went right."

"And we met in hell."

"You know it, brother."

"And here we are again, Jackson."

"Thirty-eight years and one day later, yeah."

"But who's counting?"

"I am, Potter. And I know you are too. That day defined my life."

" 'Our great and noble undertaking.' "

"It felt like the end of the world. Most of my company was slaughtered in the first twenty minutes. I saw a lot of them die with my own eyes. Not one day has passed that I haven't thought of those guys."

"I hear you, Dawson. Rodriguez. Conklin. Rokos. Klein."

"Marenowski. Jones. Schuler. Kaheny. I could go on. And I know you could too, Potter. Good lives, good men. Wasted."

" 'Theirs not to reason why.' "

"Right. 'Theirs but to do and die.' "

" 'Someone had blundered.' "

"But we made it, you and me."

"We got off the beach."

"That was everything, right there."

"How'd you do it, Dawson? How'd you get up that bluff?"

"Me and a handful of guys from Companies E and F were trapped behind the shingle, shaking bad. Machine-gun fire hitting all around and nothing to do but keep our butts down and pray to God. Some took cover behind the wall. There was no one in charge, no officer, and it seemed like there was nothing to do on that beach but die. Then this guy you'd never expect—name of Lester Jones—just said, 'There ain't no use stickin' around here, we're all gunna get killed!' Then he runs up to a gun emplacement and tosses a grenade in the embrasure. He comes back with four prisoners and the rest of us thought, Shit, if Jones can do that, so can we. That's how we got off the beach."

"So what happened to Jones?"

"Didn't make it past the hedgerows."

"Those fuckin' things."

"How'd you get off the beach, Potter?"

"Heh! There's a story. Me and some guys from different platoons—you know, we were all mixed up by the time we got on shore—we were huddled, like you, only behind a burning tank. It was from there I saw my best buddy killed. Blown to bits by an 88. A good man. It shocked me into making a move. I told the guys around me to let's get out, to get over the wall, to, you know, just *go*. It was the only thing to do."

"And you did it."

"They followed."

"And you led, Potter. You were one of the guys that made it happen that day. You're one of the guys I wished I had the guts to be."

Silence swept through the grass like a wind; then Dawson said, "It's time to get off this beach, Potter. Forget how you got on it. It's time to get the fuck off."

"I don't see it that way, Dawson."

"How do you see it, then?"

"Look around you, soldier. I ain't doing this for three-seventy. What do you see?"

"I see a man holding people hostage with a pineapple and a hip flask, and I got to tell you, Dutch, your cause may be a good one but you're going about it all wrong."

"Might is right, Dawson."

"It's an impossible situation."

"Omaha Beach was an impossible situation, too."

"Look, Potter, haven't the both of us seen enough death for one lifetime? Enough's enough."

"Enough is never enough if it's not enough. And I say it's not. I'm running the show here."

"Maybe."

"No maybe about it."

"All you got is your life to give, Potter. So you die. Maybe you take some or even all of those people in the bus with you. It makes the papers for a few weeks. It's analyzed to death by a bunch of shithead journalists. Then the world forgets and life goes on and that's that. Take a hard look around you. Those people in there with you didn't do anything to hurt anyone. Shit, Potter, those are the people we fought for."

"If you could see some of them you'd take a different tack, Dawson."

"I don't know if your boy can be brought here or not. I know you got the attention of the feds. They'll stay on it no matter what. All I'm asking—"

"You want me to sit here and second-guess myself. That's where weakness starts. That's what cracks a man's resolve, and the next thing you know he's questioning everything until he can't wipe his own backside. And you know what, Dawson?—if that's what your name really is—you know what? That's what weakness is. Is that what happened to you?"

"I got my faults, Potter. Being weak isn't one of them."

"So maybe you were heroic thirty-eight years ago just for diving out of the LST and making it up the cliff. But you got to earn that every day. Every day is a beachhead. When you were huddled behind that shingle on Omaha, what if you thought, Why am I here? Is war right? Are the Nazis really all that bad? Mmm. I wonder if it was wise for me to sign up for this—blah, blah, blah. The next thing you know you're a real philosopher sitting there with your fist under your chin wondering if you actually exist. That's the best way to make sure you won't exist for much longer, let me tell you! Because thinking like that is wrong, Dawson. You see what needs to be done and you do it. End of story."

"OK, so you're doing. What's it going to prove?"

"I'm not trying to prove anything. I'm willing to fight for what I believe in—remember that?—and what I believe in is my son. If the government that I fought for, that I pay hard-earned money to every goddamn day, that is supposed to serve, won't do their job, by God I'll make them do it. I'll lead, as you call it."

"Even if you got to hurt innocent people to get your way?"

"Did you ever use a body for cover that day, Dawson? If you didn't, do you know somebody who did?"

"These are living people, Potter."

"Now look, Dawson. You tell those FBI boys and staties and SWAT teams and whoever the hell else is out there that they can crouch behind their own shelters or they can move. Tell them to get off their own beach. The best move they can make is to get my boy here ASAP."

"Potter, look—"

"That's enough, Dawson. You're relieved of duty. Go back to Owego and do whatever it is you do."

"Fine, Potter. Just let me say you disappoint me and every respectable soldier who goes on day after day in this world. You besmirch the glory of the memory you contributed to."

"Oh, you're memory's spokesman, are you, Dawson? Who appointed you scribe? Huh?"

"Mr. Dawson is gone, Dutch. I'm back again. Let's stay calm, shall we?"

"Listen, Zimbalist, quit playing *This Is Your Life* and get to work."

"We're trying our best, believe me. How you holding up in there?"

Dutch handed the bullhorn to Bad and looked out the opposite set of windows, absently switching hands on the grenade, mumbling "Disappointed!" and "Besmirched!" and mimicking Dawson by wagging his head from side to side.

"Thinks the sun falls out of his asshole," Bad offered, but Dutch did not hear him.

"History is going to give my way of thinking its due," he said to the passengers and then spat on the seat beside him. "Yeah. Not that zipperhead's out there. Thinks you fight once and it's over. Thinks wrong and right is black and white. You don't know who's your enemy and who's your friend. Goddamn disguises."

"Yeah," Grace rasped, almost loud enough for Dutch to hear. "Like, I thought you was a bus driver and this was a bus to downtown. But what does this dumbass nigger know?"

She'd drunk too much gin and needed to watch herself. The empty pint of Gilbey's lay facedown on the seat beside her; she hadn't had a hit in a long while and was sleepy. This situation was getting old and she had to go to the bathroom. Over there was the nut job with the grenade, here were the hostages, and the whole thing was surrounded by an army, and talk, talk, talk. To her, that was white folks—all weirdnesses and talk.

She wondered if the old lady might have another bottle stashed away but figured probably not. Most of the stuff in that Jacqueline Farrar handbag, a big old thing right out of the JC Penney catalog, had spilled out during the crash, and Grace didn't see her or anyone else pick up another bottle when they were cleaning up the bus. She tried to remember her name— Helga? Hilda?—something weird, and looking at her sitting up there closest to the driver, shaking like she had the palsy, Grace felt bad for the poor hag, all dressed up like the biddies do when they go out for anything. Like it made some difference. That smell of piss, ten to one it was her. Old and scared out of her bladder, like most of the hospice patients Grace cared for.

At least she had a good excuse for missing work; they couldn't fire her now. Not that she liked feeding people too sick to have an appetite in the first place, emptying their bedpans, listening to their cries of pain and complaint. But it was money, and the people she home-cared didn't give her too much trouble—or at least any trouble she couldn't handle with a voice and some sass. They were at death's door looking in, and she was the person cleaning up their last earthly messes, like the sweeper at the end of the parade. Niggerwork in a white world, is what she called it when she discussed it with her friends. With little money, two kids at home, no man (most of the time), she had to scrape by with her smarts and her guts in a world so bleach-white it could blind a girl—especially in a town like this. So the few brothers and sisters around were close, or at least knew each other, or at the very least knew *of* each other. They were a little society spreading out inside the bigger one, like a stain on a white shirt—that was the way she believed whites around here saw the black community. You can do this but you can't do that, was what that was all about. You can wipe the wrinkled bums of octogenarians when their kids are too busy making money, out having their wine and cheese, but if you leave your own kids alone—sound asleep—for an hour, for a little relaxation at Sugar's, and you get caught because the guy in the other upstairs apartment can't get to sleep because of the radio you left on loud so if the kids wake they'd think you were home, say, then you are "possibly unfit" and "warned" because even if you did have baby-sitting money, what blue-eyed parents would allow their pigtailed Suzy to come to an apartment like yours anyway?

Abraham Lincoln, Martin Luther King, hell: still two sets of laws. If this crazy bus driver were black, and somehow survived this stand-down, Grace wouldn't give two cents for what they'd do to him. But this white guy would get some smartass big shot lawyer to say he was temporarily insane, stressed out—though the point was moot because there was no way he was going to make it to a courtroom. The FBI man was saying they were "working on it," and Grace knew they must be up to something. To her, white people spent a lot of time thinking of tricks—like that grenade, for example. That was smart, she had to admit that—but smart, finally, how? It was major law out there he was dealing with; he was messing way above his head. He was using his smarts for something so dumb she had to wonder how he got the smart idea in the first place. Maybe TV. Even Andy could appreciate smart ideas on TV.

Her tongue felt large and she could swallow only air. She took the empty bottle from the seat beside her, sniffed the neck, licked it. Sugary, like Sugar's, where she'd go tonight if she got out of this. If she got out of this, she'd be famous. At Sugar's, at least. A kind of celebrity for a while, till something else came up, or time just wore down the story to nothing. Robert, Marcia, Rodney, Safiya, Shalim, all them. They'd want to know just what happened and she'd tell them. *I was just ridin', you know, like goin' to work. This driver—get this—he's wearin' a army uniform, I swear, you'll read it in the papers. Shoulda known somethin' was up with him when I got on. Then we're going down Main Street and the man goes wacko! Drives haul-ass into the woods I don' know where. Someplace down in PA. Way the hell down. Crashes into this big-ass tree, got his face all bloody 'n' all. He call for help? Nah! Pulls out a grenade. A grenade! You'd be scared too, man. You're lookin' at death and it ain't pretty. And you're thinkin', Shit, I don' wanna die. Specially on accounta some fucked-up white guy losin' it.*

She looked up at the driver, who stood listening to the FBI man, and she wondered how he could keep on holding the grenade like that all day. It had been hours now, and he wasn't steady on his feet, weaving as he was. He'd lost a lot of blood, too. There was a trail of it from the steering wheel to where he stood. Smatterings on the aqua seats up front, blots of it on his army jacket and shirt. Half his face was covered with it, caked now, like a mask.

It looked like, you know—who's that guy in the funny pages? Yeah, the Phantom. 'Cept the driver's was side to side, not up and down, like, and nothing funny about it. I'm sittin' in the back like a good nigger. You know. Let's see—one seat up from the one goes 'long the side like this way? You know what I'm sayin'? On the right side lookin' up. The driver, he's one, two, three . . . seven seats up, standin' in the aisle, talkin' and such to the feds, and they bring in some people to, you know, calm him down. Some priest guy, and a guy he was in the army with. But the driver won't budge. He says he wants his son or he'll blow us all up. Problem is this: the son is MIA from Nam for like I don' know how long, but you and me know he's dead as dead gets, you hear what I'm sayin'? So we're up the creek, sittin' and sittin' like we got all day, sometimes there's talkin'—him and the feds—sometimes there's no talkin', and all the time we don' know if we're gunna die or what. Uh-huh. It's afternoon a long time, we been on this bus since, shit, six o'clock in the morning. I'm thinking, I need something to drink—you hear what I'm sayin'? I'm thinkin' of being right here at Sugar's tellin' you all.

Then what?

You know, he's just standin' up there, ignoring the fed that's tryin' to talk him down—'cept sometimes he says, barkin' like a dog, "Bring my boy," like that. And you know the FBI wants to take him down. I mean, you know he's already dead, right? Question is whether we go with him.

Go on, girl.

But Grace doesn't know. She's stuck, like the bus. She looks around, memorizing details: the driver's blister-white knuckles, the precision of the lawyer's haircut, the nervous movement of the boy's spear, the two pages from the old lady's book on the floor in front of the seat across from her. Questions and answers out of the reach of her focus—blurred words, like lines of ants marching across yellow leaves. The trick was not to die, so she could tell it all—and not from a hospital bed, either.

Finally I just had enough and called the crazy man's bluff. Just got up and walked out.

No, he was too riled for her to be fool enough. And nothing she could think of—him just giving up, the grenade being dropped but not exploding, the feds storming the bus and some people getting hurt but not her—nothing she could think of felt possible right then. She looked out the window. The FBI man with the bullhorn was standing at the edge of the clearing, just where the driver had told him to, an audience of trees crowded in behind him. She spotted three men up in three different trees, blending with the foliage like birds or squirrels in a *Highlights* magazine sketch, one of them a brother, rifles she couldn't see but knew were aimed at the bus, and she thought that being safe seemed so close. She shifted focus to the pane of the window

three inches from her face: smudged, scratched, lightly tinted—a
shatterproof membrane between her and the world.

So what happened next?

*We all died. Commended our spirits. Happened so fast, I
don' even know how. That's the awful truth. I'm just the ghost
of Grace at Sugar's come to say goodbye to you.*

No, really. What happened next?

*You all going to miss me? Or you going to just forget me?
Which?*

C'mon, girl, tell us!

*OK, OK. I'll speed it up for you because at the time things
sure went slow. Just sittin' there for long stretches. If I was
really going to die, it woulda been of boredom. Uh-huh. I'm sittin' there thinking what I'd be doing on a regular day at that
time, probably, you know, sittin' at home with my feet up waiting for Shauntay and Michael to come home from school.
Thinkin' that way. You know. Then—you remember that boy?
With the spear? Uh-huh. The one helpin' the driver? He's all
gussied up like a savage—makeup and no shirt. Did I tell you?
Well, he's sittin' up there beside the driver, and the driver—after
just lookin' at him real strange for a while, he says something to
the boy, and the boy thinks for a minute and says something to
the driver, who says something back to him. They're up there
whisperin' away for a while and the driver, he takes up the bullhorn and says—*

"I got a favor to ask, Zimbalist."

"Now, Dutch, you got us scrambling here as it is."

"This one's simple. I want you to find a guy for us, but he's in
town. In Binghamton. I even got an address. Name of Williams.
Lives on Chenango."

"Who is he?"

"A sex pervert, the stepfather of the kid on the bus. Abused
him, and I think he ought to be strung by his balls and given a

taste of his own medicine with a two-by-four. What do you think, Zimbalist?"

"It's not for me to say, Dutch. If he's guilty, he ought to be punished, yeah. There are procedures to follow for these things."

"Procedures! Listen to him, Bad. If it's not one book they throw at you, it's another. If it isn't the Bible, it's the law. If it isn't the law, it's a contract. Excuses not to act."

Bad stared at the floor, his hands gripping and regripping the shaft of the spear.

"Those are the kind of people you ought to be after, Zimbalist! Fatherhood is an important thing, a position of responsibility. That's what this little adventure of ours is all about. You know."

"It sure is an adventure, Dutch. You got that right."

"Let's just make sure it has a happy ending."

"We're doing our best."

"There's only one way this is going to have a happy ending. You know that, right?"

"I'm aware of the situation, Dutch, and I'm doing the best I can."

"What is it exactly that you're doing?"

"I know what you're asking and I'm trying to answer you. You holding out OK?"

"Never felt better, Zimbalist."

But I tell you he didn't look so hot. And the FBI guy, he knew there wasn't a whole lot of time to play round with. I mean, how could he hold that thing all day? Probably built up his strength playing with his little weeny all his life. Still and all, we was just waiting and waiting and I got to wonder if they really did care if we was going to live or not.

"Jack?"

Dutch raised his head as if sniffing the air.

"It's me. Can you . . . Oh, Jack!"

Dutch shook his head, as if to confound orbiting gnats, cleared his throat, began to speak but stopped. He raised the bullhorn, then lowered it.

"J-Jack, just come out of there. Please? Please?"

His countenance collapsed and his voice cried out as if he had been struck across the back. "Sarah, no, please. Not you, not here. Please leave. Please."

"Listen to Mr. Beikirch, Jack. They'll do what they can. They promised. Please let those people go. Please just come out."

"I'll come out and everything will be OK? Everything will be back to what it was before?"

"I'll be better, Jack. I will . . ."

With his lips trembling Dutch mumbled something to Bad, or to himself, something about Sarah, and his eyes glazed and he said, or rather whispered, "It's not you."

"Those people in there, Jack. Their loved ones are scared for them. I'm scared for you."

"I can't, Sarah. It's our boy. Our Jommy, Sarah! He . . . I can't come back without him. I can't keep coming back without him! We can't even say his name, Sarah! And I miss him. I just miss him. Oh shit, Sarah, Sarah . . ."

"You always promised to come back to me, Jon Potter!" she shouted. "Now come back to me! Come back!"

"I'm not worth it without him! I'm not!"

"You're Jack Potter and you're my husband and I love you and I want you to come out now, Jack! Please! Please!"

He tried to speak into the bullhorn, but his voice choked into fits of air, and when Beikirch called to him Dutch wiped his eyes but it was a few moments before he could talk. When he did, it was only to say that he was putting an end to words and would speak to no one else except his son.

THIRTEEN

After such a long time with nothing happening it seemed to Hulda that the authorities had given up. Gone home. Decided that they weren't paid enough to face this kind of nonsense and, what the hell, the situation could take care of itself. The way volcanoes and earthquakes do. Let violence take care of violence. Let atrocity settle its own score. Even Dutch's busy agitation had abated. He stood as still as the death he was heading toward, the grenade gripped at his side like a wound, his eyes fixed upon the middle spaces, head bent into the light at just such an angle that the wisps of hair rising from his skull looked like solar flares off the sun's corona. He didn't have a bomb, he *was* a bomb, one with a wife and children and a hair-trigger past that could give it all up with him just standing there, Hulda just sitting there, and the others, still as death, too—and the boy graffitied in her lipstick like a savage, even he was staring at the floor or at one of the advertisements or out the window as if time had stopped and the earth with it. Peter once told her that if the earth's rotation ever did cease, landmasses would crash into each other like cars at an intersection. "A continental pileup," he called it.

But no memory of her husband, however vivid his unflap-
pable voice in her head, could snap the spell of this tension. No
birds sang, no insects—or perhaps it was all absorbed into
the white breeze that brought a lucidity to Hulda she knew
wouldn't last. Shapes and colors dazzled her comprehension.
The rugged handsomeness of the driver shrouded in dry blood
the exact hue of a handbag she once owned. The youth of the
boy, hard as fruit, and the throbbing vein at his neck. And
the others, behind her: the lawyer and the social worker and
the unemployed man and the nurse. The waitress who was al-
lowed to leave. All the loved ones of all these people. All the law
officers out there and how everyone had been thrown together
by coincidence—in the right place, as the saying goes, at the
wrong time. Or was it the other way around? If she had left the
house twenty minutes later, or not at all. If Erica's car had not
broken down the day before, or if she had thought to call for
a cab, as she later lamented not doing. For all that, what if the
driver's son had just come home when he was supposed to come
home, or been killed like so many of his companions? How
often had she read in the paper or seen on TV the news of catastrophes occurring to people by timing so perfect it was as if they
were selected by a malicious force? Car crashes. Muggings.
"Freak accidents" that often involved something falling on a
person—a chunk of granite from the ledge of a building, the
wheel of a plane, a meteor. Out-of-the-blue events that mocked
credibility.

    She thought again of the business of *Skylab* just a few years
before, how this aging space station tottering in a disintegrating
orbit was to fall back to earth at a location and time the scientists could not predict. Not all of its seventy-seven tons could
burn up in the atmosphere, and what was left of it could as easily have fallen on Hulda's house as on a hut in the Congo or an

igloo on the tundra. It was frightening, but fascinating too, and trying to figure out the why of things sometimes distracted her from the terror that had always seemed to motor her metabolism. The peril had brought about a sense of community; people around the world had begun to think like her, to feel the world in the way that she experienced it. And it helped her to feel closer to Peter, too, who, in the last years of his life, had followed the career of *Skylab* as though it were a son he had sent off to college. She knew from him that this space station was originally a spent stage of a *Saturn 5* rocket, that it completed an orbit every ninety-three minutes, that it took thousands of pictures of the sun, that it was visited by three sets of astronauts, that it was only three hundred miles above the earth in a career deteriorating faster than expected because of high sunspot activity—being done in by the very thing it studied. Knowing so much about it invested it with a kind of personality. It was like a man who had lived a productive life, worked hard, did what he was supposed to do, but got sick, began to weaken and fall out of the life he had set for himself, like one succumbing to drink or depression or a malignancy on the brain the size of a dime and the shape of a crab. She'd unearthed Peter's globe and set it on the dining-room table so she could place the situation in perspective. It was mostly blue, after all. She'd spin it and watch, sometimes holding an object near it as it whirled round—a tube of lipstick, say, that she'd wobble between her index finger and thumb as she moved it in dreamy motion closer and closer until it struck the surface of a planet moving at 18.46 miles per second. It could happen anywhere, this lethal version of pin-the-tail-on-the-donkey. But because she saw *Skylab* as a friend of her husband, an object of his affection, such as it was, she could not help feeling that it might, in the larger scheme of things (one mostly mysterious and unknown even to real scientists) conceive a kind of attraction to this particular area of the globe. Intense interest did have the power to attract in the physical world. Any courtship provided proof. She'd put her fingernail on the globe and tap at the Southern Tier of New York State, USA, North America. South of Lake Ontario, east of Lake Erie, west of the Atlantic Ocean, north of the Chesapeake Bay. All that blue, yes, but who could say? The human body was mostly water, too, but life was still largely a skin-and-bones affair. It was, after all, what bled and broke. What things happened to, water or not.

She was lucky, that time, as was everyone else in the world, but luck gives out. What were the odds, she'd like to know, that the first time out of her house in a year and a half she would board this of all the buses that had, in that span of time, stopped in front of the Triumph Supermarket on Main Street in Johnson City, New York, USA? Hijackings didn't happen every day. And a transit bus? What were the odds? And the time she'd left the house before that—the business of accidentally stealing the cheap ring that was still stuck on her finger next to her wedding band. Just trying it on at the Comfort Jewelers, putting on airs on a snowy Valentine's Day, and, scared because it wouldn't come off, slipping out of the store with it. If she could believe in luck she could believe in curses. It was enough to justify her reluctance to venture out.

She backed herself further against the window and glanced sideways at Erica, who sat in the seat behind her with her shoulders squared and hands clasped tightly on the nylon mantle of her lap. The sun burned off another minute of hydrogen. Then a voice came from outside the bus, not the FBI man's. Deeper, more official still, and Dutch roused like a bear out of hibernation, shaking his head and actually growling as he wiped his mouth with the back of his hand, stretching his jaw side to side.

"Mr. Potter?" the voice said again, and Dutch bent a little, squinting, to see what was going on out there. "I'm Lieutenant Colonel Frederick Bennett of the United States Marine Corps."

Dutch did not seem to know if the voice came from outside or inside his head and he shook it again as if to dislodge an obstruction. When he tried to steady himself, he screwed his eyes into a tighter squint and scanned the clearing outside the window.

"I've got news of your son, Mr. Potter. Will you please talk to me?"

Dutch looked at the others on the bus looking at him, then out the window again. He picked up the bullhorn, clicked it on, and said that he was listening.

"I served in the South Pacific during the Second World War, Mr. Potter. Korea from '50 to '53. Vietnam from '67 to the end. Since my retirement from the Corps in '76, I have made it my personal mission to investigate the possible existence of living American MIAs in Southeast Asia. I have worked shoulder-to-shoulder with a number of organizations around the country to this end. Your cause is extremely important to me, Mr. Potter."

"So? What is it, you want to be pals or something?"

"No, sir. That isn't necessary."

"Get on with it, then. You said you had news."

"Over the years we've received reports on camps in Southeast Asia. I've taken it upon myself to look into the more credible of these that have come to my attention—particularly those corroborated by operatives in Bangkok. Nothing much ever came of these investigations. Until this past year."

Dutch licked his lips but said nothing.

"There were reports," Bennett went on, "of a particular work camp in northern Laos. One that might have held some Americans. Satellite photos indicated some irregularity in the jungle terrain. We—one of my organizations, privately funded—sent our own flier over the site to take photos. When these were reviewed it was enough for me to get on over to Thailand to snoop around. I came home convinced there was some validity for hope."

"American POWs?"

Then the colonel rushed through details, describing how he was able to gather more intelligence on this camp, chart its movement from the site it was originally located to another twenty miles to the southeast, the methods by which they determined there were at least two, possibly four, Americans among the dozen-odd prisoners of the work camp. By November, enough evidence had been gathered to warrant, the colonel believed, a rescue operation. The long and short of it was that the government's hands were tied in assisting in such an operation, at least overtly, and it was up to him, Colonel Bennett, to pull something together on his own—if anything was to be done at all.

"Strangest thing is," the colonel said, "what ended up happening in real life closely paralleled a movie that came out a few months before we went in. We, a group of vets I had gathered, were training in Arizona—six weeks of intensive preparation— and this movie comes out that seems to be about us. Although I got to say we're a much less dramatic bunch. Hollywood, you know. Still, it was a frightening coincidence, and it got us pretty anxious. I grew concerned that the enemy—the real enemy— might somehow be alerted, the world being what it is today. Too small for all the incongruity, I mean. I made a decision not to say anything about it. We forged ahead, focused on the mission, and stayed pretty much on schedule."

"You actually did it? You went in?"

"Yes, sir."

"Go on."

"Here's where the information becomes a bit sensitive, Mr. Potter. May I come aboard and speak with you? It's not wise to broadcast—"

"I'm sick of sensitive, Bennett. I'm sick of secrets and back-rooms and shame. Out with it."

The colonel said something to someone standing back in the woods, then put the bullhorn back up to his mouth.

"Very well. They had moved the camp yet again during our training, but my people were able to track them and pinpoint their location for us. This meant that we had to train for a longer period of time—you know, learn details of a different terrain, different configuration of the camp itself, et cetera. Yes, sir, we went in. April 13, a Tuesday. We rescued two American POWs. One of them was your son."

"My—Jommy?"

"Yes, sir. Lieutenant Jonathan L. Potter Jr., USMC."

"Alive?"

"Yes, sir. But very, very ill. And you should know that he is still very ill."

"Where? How?"

"Here's the situation. We flew out of Bangkok to a hospital near Agana on Guam to get him medical care. Malnutrition, malaria, dysentery—and that only scratches the surface. There were injuries from maltreatment in the camp that had not healed properly, ongoing infections from untreated abrasions, a bad case of dysentery from poor sanitation, amebiasis. The list goes on. We had him there for a period of eighteen days, at which time medical officers thought it safe to move him to the mainland, where he could receive more extensive care. On Sunday, May 2, he was flown to Andrews Air Force Base and immediately brought into Bethesda Naval Hospital for continued treatment. He has been there since."

"Bethesda? Maryland?"

"Yes, sir."

Dutch slumped down onto the nearest seat, staring dazed at the floor. "Bethesda?" he said again, this time without amplification.

"The prognosis is good, Mr. Potter. With time and proper care he could reach pretty close to full recovery."

"If what you're saying has a shred of truth to it, Colonel, you're a son of a bitch."

"Sir?"

"You're either a bald-faced liar or a son of bitch, take your pick. If my boy's been three hundred miles from me for five full weeks, as you want me to believe, and you haven't had the *decency* to tell me . . ."

"Let me explain, Mr. Potter. There's very good reason for not letting you, or anyone else, know right away."

"When were you sonsabitches going let me know? Ever?"

"Of course we—"

"Oh, I know how the politicians operate. And their lackeys in the military. I know all about it, Colonel Bennett. How they all either lie or hush the truth. Which is it this time?"

"The operation I undertook grossly violated international law, sir. It was not sanctioned by our government, but the government would have to take the heat anyway. Big time. But beyond that we had to consider your son's well-being. The physical damage he incurred over the past twelve years does not cover all the injury done to him. A great deal of psychological harm was inflicted on this boy, sir. He's at a very shaky phase in his recovery. The smallest thing could push him over the edge. We've had to proceed with the utmost caution. A media circus would be devastating. Even a visit from a loved one could so shock his psyche as to cause us to lose him. A decision was made to proceed slowly. Your son doesn't even feel at home in the

English language, Mr. Potter. He wasn't aware that May 15 was his birthday. At that point he wasn't even certain what a birthday was. Trained professionals, the best we have, are working round-the-clock to bring him back, Mr. Potter. We are making progress. He's physically here, back home, but in a more fundamental sense he is not. You must understand."

"What I understand, Colonel, is that he hasn't returned home until he returns *to his home*. That's what he needs—not a herd of whitecoats stampeding at him night and day."

"Not informing you and your family was a decision made only after a great deal of earnest deliberation, Mr. Potter. I certainly wasn't convinced they were doing the right thing and I said so. I took the position you are taking now, and I argued till I was blue in the face. They assured me that they were prepared to notify you at such time that they believed there would be no risk to Jom's physical or psychological well-being. They finally convinced me beyond any doubt that your son's health, his life, was the primary concern. I'll be honest with you, Mr. Potter— what finally convinced me that they were doing the right thing was the issue of your personal troubles."

"What's that mean?"

"You being jailed recently after harassing a young woman— actually breaking into her apartment in the middle of the night. Your suspension from work last fall for a series of incidents on the job. The drinking bout and breakdown in Rhode Island last summer. These events suggested to us a pattern of behavior that exhibited a fragile psyche that might cause a threat to your son's recovery."

"How dare you! Who do you think you are?"

"We're on the same side, Mr. Potter. Remember that our objective remains exactly the same as yours. We want what's best for Lieutenant Potter. Period."

"Did you ever get off your high horse long enough to think that those 'events,' as you call them, happened—if they happened in the way you heard them—out of frustration of being deprived the decency you say you withheld? They were symptoms of the pain you caused by keeping me in the dark, and then you blame me for the pain?"

"No, I don't. I admire you for the patience and fortitude you have shown, Mr. Potter. I mean that. Over the years I have spoken with hundreds of loved ones of MIAs—mothers, fathers, wives, brothers, sisters, sons, daughters, sweethearts. Their sorrow and frustration and anger has become my own. It's why I do what I do. I tell you with all due respect that you're badly mistaken if you think I don't understand. It's a rotten situation and you've been treated awfully. I'm deeply sorry if I contributed to that indecency. But I did what I did for what I believed to be the best for everyone involved. I didn't make the world, I only try to fix it where I can, Mr. Potter. Before you pass judgment on me I ask you to remember that I have spent the past six years of my life on behalf of people like you and your son. I ask you to remember that me and seven good men threw our lives into peril to save a few of our brothers from that hellhole over there. I lost two of those men in the operation. Good and decent men who died so that people like your boy could have a chance. Remember that before you fly off the handle, sir."

A long silence followed, during which it appeared that Dutch had fallen to sleep. But at last, without lifting his head or opening his eyes, he put the bullhorn to his mouth and asked the names of the men who'd been killed.

"Robert Brown and James Davall. Brown took a bullet in the head, Davall shrapnel from a grenade."

"And the other POW you mentioned. Has his father seen him?"

"He wasn't as lucky as your son, Mr. Potter. He was wounded in the escape and, being in the health he was in, died en route to Thailand. His father had died four years ago. We have briefed his mother, yes, but asked her to keep silent. She understood and has been cooperative."

"I want to see him, Bennett. My boy. If you really have him."

"Of course. Under these circumstances, what's happened here . . . Of course. I am prepared to fly you down to Bethesda any time you are ready. But I warn you, Mr. Potter. We need to tread lightly. He's still in a fragile state."

"You want me to walk off this bus, hop on a plane with you, and fly down to Maryland just on your word?"

"We can get a chopper to Griffiss and board an Air Force transport from there. We can get to your son in less than two hours. Sooner, if we leave right away. I can brief you further en route, better prepare you for what you'll find, his debilitations, injuries incurred, what topics might best be avoided for now. Those sorts of things."

"You bring him here, Bennett. If you really do have him, I want him here."

"But, Mr. Potter, his health would be severely compromised by the activity, the noise. We'd be putting him in a tense situation. All these people—"

"But you have no choice, Bennett. You bring Jommy here and you make sure his health isn't compromised. That's your new mission. Understand?"

"Mr. Potter, can I just say—"

"No, you cannot. You'll take all the necessary precautions to ensure my son's safety. If you can get him from Laos to Maryland, you can get him from Maryland to this bus. I have full confidence in you."

After a few moments Colonel Bennett got back on the bullhorn and told Dutch he would see what he could arrange. "In the meantime, though," he went on, "would you give your decision a little more thought?"

"I don't have second thoughts, Bennett."

He passed the bullhorn across the aisle to Bad, but the boy didn't take it, and so he tossed it onto the seat next to him and the passengers winced at the racket it made when it fell to the floor. He chewed on the inside of his cheek and his eyes flashed occasionally, like warnings from a lighthouse.

"April, they say they did this," he said. "One, two, three—five, six, seven weeks ago? Eight?" He stood as though lifted by a gust of wind and began pacing up and down the stretch of aisle between Bad's seat and Grace's, muttering at the floor, jerking his head side to side as if shaking off palsy. "Bad, light me a cigarette," he said clearly, though the boy didn't hear him. "Reconsider! Like I'm as fickle as them! April I was doing what? Getting strung along by that woman. And they say they had Jom three fucking hundred miles from his home? Jesus! Bad, how about that cigarette?"

But the boy didn't move except to swallow hard.

"I told you these people will yank your chain like you were some dog. This dog's biting back, Bad. The squeaky wheel gets the grease, the barking dog gets the bone. Where's that cigarette?"

"I ain't your slave, man," Bad said. "And I don't like you telling people my business."

"What are you talking about?"

"It ain't their business, man. The thing about me you told all them."

"About your old man?"

"Stepfather."

"So I ratted on him. So I took him down."

Bad kept his back to Dutch and said, "I don't need you tellin' the world my problems, man. What was said was me and you. It was private."

Dutch looked out the window and then down at Bad who stood up and made his way down the aisle and threw himself into the seat at the very back of the bus. He folded his arms across his chest—nostrils flaring, lips pressed hard together—and Dutch stared at him for a long while, ignoring two attempts by the colonel to get his attention. Under the heat of Dutch's gaze the boy seemed to melt, to actually become smaller, softer, and, finally, Dutch picked up the bullhorn and answered.

"You know there's only one thing you can say that I'll accept, don't you, Colonel Bennett?"

"Yes, Mr. Potter."

"So what is it?"

"We're going to do our best to get Jonathan Potter here as quickly as we can."

"Your best better be good enough, Big Boot."

"Here's the plan, Mr. Potter: we'll fly him by chopper from the hospital heliport to Andrews, where he'll board an SR-17, which is currently fueling. Preparations for this this leg of the trip have already been set into motion and your son should arrive at Andrews in twenty, maybe thirty minutes. The SR-17 is our fastest recon jet—hell, it's our fastest aircraft, period. With a little luck we can land it at the strip at Hallstead after a twenty-, twenty-five-minute flight. We'll have a chopper waiting there for transport here. It's now 1345 hours. Lieutenant Potter should be at this location by 1500 hours, give or take a few minutes. Can you hold out that long, Mr. Potter?"

"Colonel, I've held out for twelve years and three months and four days. I can hold out for another hour and fifteen minutes. But I tell you, this better be on the up and up. I've had it to here being jerked around. It better be good."

"This is a legitimate operation, Mr. Potter. You have my

word as a soldier on that. I'll keep you posted as we move along. In the meantime, can I get you anything? Some coffee, maybe?"

Dutch looked at his watch as though he were reading banner headlines at a newsstand. He bit his lower lip, squinted out the window, looked back at his watch. He mumbled something to himself, a declarative sentence by tone, then addressed the bus.

"Amebiasis," he said. "What's that?"

"I think it's diarrhea," Erica said.

Andy said he'd had that plenty of times and Grace told him he had amebiasis of the mouth.

"Malaria and dysentery," Dutch went on. "Who knows about these?"

No one said anything at first and Dutch goaded the silence with a few interrogatory grunts before Grace spoke up again.

"I had a friend went to Africa. He saw *Roots* and thought he was Kunta Kinte, but all he came back with was malaria. You know, you get bit by a badass mosquito, makes you all lazy 'n' shit. But with Robert you couldn't tell the difference. I used to take him to the doctor. He got fever and chills and all this sweating. Something about the liver and then the red blood cells rupture, is what happens. That means there's more and more white cells, and less and less colored cells. That's bad. The body gets all fucked up. But there's ways to take of that."

"I know something about dysentery," Erica cut in. "My mother had it in Treblinka."

Dutch turned to face her but his eyes were unfocused and he did not so much see her as, it seemed, something behind her, or around her, or something happening in the air between them—dust particles floating, sylphs dancing, molecules joining.

"It's a disease of the intestines," she said. "There are sharp pains. Bloody stools. From bacteria."

He seemed hardly to hear Erica at all. Whether he believed the colonel's story or not might not matter after all, because he had noticeably weakened, to the point where it was doubtful he'd last the hour it would take to find out.

"Completely curable, right?" he said in a low voice.

"My mother recovered. From that." Erica paused for a moment and then went on. "She was sent there in 1943. My mother, I mean. She also contracted a number of diseases. Dysentery was only one of them. It's amazing what the body can put up with. At least when it's young. You know, don't you, Mr. Potter? You must have endured quite a bit. Physically, I mean. During the war."

His middle and index fingers tapped the grenade as if it were a flute. "We liberated Bergen-Belsen," he said. "Never seen anything like it. Bodies stacked like Lincoln Logs. I could take mayhem better than I could take order like that. I got sick against the side of the crematorium. The fucking thing was still warm. The survivors were skeletons, the living dead, like that horror movie, coming at you and at you and at you, grabbing your wrist, your jacket, trying to pull you down."

He opened his eyes and ran the fingers of his free hand through his hair. He exhaled through his nose and looked as sad as Hulda had ever seen a person look.

Erica said, "That experience must have, in a strange way, helped to give you hope for your son's chances for survival."

Dutch looked at her through narrow eyes and said, "With Jews the Holocaust is the lesson for everything." He looked out the windows opposite the clearing, into the thick, dark trees, contemplating them.

"It tells us a lot about what people are capable of, Mr. Potter, both bad and good." Dutch shrugged and she went on. "I saw a picture of my mother taken in 1939, when she was seventeen years old, then one taken in 1946. It wasn't the same person. I mean, what's seven years when you're a young adult, but the suffering and horror had twisted her beyond recognition. And of course the way she acted, who she was, her personality, had been shattered and needed to be rebuilt."

"What happened?"

"Not all the pieces were there. For example, she could sing beautifully, I heard. But never once did I hear her sing. Not a note. Her voice as I knew it was as thin as wind through wheat. Parts of her youth, which I think was fairly pleasant and happy until the Nazis came, were just blotted out. Or drastically revised and different, depending on when you asked her to tell a story about herself. She'd tell me about her life in Warsaw at eight years old, or nine, or thirteen. But later she'd tell me completely different versions of what were supposed to be the exact same stories, as though her past was a work in progress."

"She still alive?"

"She was taking my sister from our home on Second Avenue to her violin lesson on the Upper West Side. In New York, where I'm from. To the apartment of a Mrs. Hartman, who had once played in Prague. They had to switch subway lines at Times Square. It was 3:20, a Thursday in May. The eighteenth. She was talking to Deborah, very pleasantly, about the bloom of the plants up on the streets. She loved flowers. She loved the springtime. She knew all the flowers and was naming what she had seen and where, when Deborah, who had already heard the litany, interrupted her to say the train was coming. 'Yes,' Momma said, leaning to have a better look down the tunnel, where she must have been able to see the light of the train, and just before it rushed into the station she stepped into midair and was gone."

"That's pathetic," Dutch said.

"No, Mr. Potter, it's not."

"The coward's way out. Life's tough—who's going to argue? But you got to deal with it."

"You can't even imagine what her life was like."

"More horrible than most, sure. But killing herself? That's being the Nazi to what she had left. And Jesus," he said, spitting into the aisle, "right in front of the kid!" Erica looked down at the yellow sputum on the rubber matting, then up at the mouth he was wiping with the back of his free hand. "Just *shit*," he said, but it sounded more like a cry of pain.

FOURTEEN

In interviews afterward the only hostage who admitted to believing that Bennett would actually deliver Dutch's son was Andy. The colonel was sincere, he said, and stranger stories have turned out to be true. The precision of details and the manner in which they complemented one another made it difficult to believe otherwise, or at least did not discourage an aversion to believing otherwise, a presumption nurtured by Bennett's frequent updates: Lieutenant Potter boarded the SR-17 at 1410 hours and the aircraft was positioned for takeoff from Andrews ahead of schedule; the SR-17 was cruising at an altitude of fifteen thousand feet and was currently positioned 170 miles, 123 miles, 79 miles, from Hallstead Airport; a Boeing CH-470 helicopter, a Chinook, was brought in to take the colonel to the airstrip so that he could escort Lieutenant Potter to the bus. Before he left he had spoken further about what Dutch's son had suffered; how he weighed less than a hundred pounds when he was rescued and had gained some weight since but not much; how his left arm had been broken three times, his right arm twice, and scars crisscrossed his body, some of them evident on his neck and face. His vision had been compromised from the beatings he endured, he said, and required corrective lenses, and he was partly deaf in his left ear.

It was difficult to say if Dutch himself believed the colonel; his only response was to ask more questions in a neutral tone that acquired only a little importunity when the colonel related his conversations with Jom at Bethesda Naval Hospital. The colonel reminded Dutch that his son's speech was disjointed and his concentration erratic and that he often spoke in a mixture of Vietnamese, Laotian, and English that was impossible to decipher, but yes, he did mention his family on a few occasions, asking about his sisters and mother and father.

But to the others Dutch's fate was sealed, stamped, and posted to him, from him. After the colonel departed he continued to stare out the window as if engaged in an official moment of silence. He took the pack of Luckies from the front pocket of his jacket, shook one loose, and pulled it free with his lips. His eyelids were fluttering again, and behind the smoke he looked more like a boy than a man.

Beikirch checked in to ask if he was doing all right, and Dutch said he was. "I'm just thinking, Dutch, now that we're close to clearing all this up—would you think of putting the ring back in that grenade? Your hand—"

"No deal."

"Fine. If you can handle it, that's fine. How about hostages? Would you consider letting a few of them go?"

"Yeah."

"I mean, now that we're able to get your son here, you—"

"I said yeah." He lowered the bullhorn and tried to focus on the back of the bus. "You, kid. Scram. Out." He indicated the side exit door by swinging the bullhorn.

Bad stared at Dutch for a moment, jaw raised, lip curled, before getting up and walking down the aisle. He stopped in front of the door and said, "I ain't leavin' without my box."

"So get it."

But it was in one of the seats behind Dutch, near the front of the bus. Bad hesitated and Dutch asked him what was the matter.

"Ain't nothin' the matter. With me."

He advanced down the aisle and stopped just a few feet in front of Dutch. He said in a soft voice—a child's voice, Hulda thought—"Excuse me," but so quietly she wondered if he'd really said it until Dutch complimented him on his manners. "We're going to have to start calling you 'Good,' " he said.

"I just want my box, man."

"You're not afraid of me, are you, Bad?"

"No."

"So go get it."

Dutch didn't move, so the boy had to sidle into one of the seats and climbed over the backrest, then the next one and the one after that, scampering like a monkey, not once taking his eyes off Dutch. When he was safely past him he hopped into the aisle and retrieved his radio from the sidelong seat up front. Dutch had turned sideways and was watching him tuck the contraption under his arm as he came back down the aisle. Before he turned to go down the steps, he looked at Dutch looking at him, and Dutch dug into the pocket of his trousers and pulled out a quarter. "Do me a favor, kid. Give this to my wife. She'll know what it means."

"Why don't you keep it and call somebody who cares."

Then he was gone. Erica leaned sideways in her seat, but Hulda knew she could see very little of what was going on outside the bus. She had been crying, and eyeliner webbed at her cheeks down to her jaw. She'd said her Jonah was about that boy's age, and maybe she was thinking of him.

"Thank you, Dutch," Beikirch said. "We appreciate the gesture. As we get closer to your son's arrival, I'm thinking of the logistics of how we might handle the whole thing. I'm thinking the ordeal might be less cumbersome with even fewer hostages."

"I think you should stop thinking, Zimbalist."

"I'll volunteer," Grace said.

"Can't," Dutch said. "You're our affirmative action hostage."

Grace scowled and dug her shoulders further into the seat.

"I don't know, Dutch, it just—"

"No, you don't know, Zimbalist. Now it's my turn to ask for something. Clothesline rope."

"Dutch?"

"You heard. I'm thinking logistics, too. Two thirty-foot packs. Nylon. And five pair of handcuffs."

"Dutch, we—"

"Do it."

He tossed the bullhorn into the seat again. Metal rattled on plastic, then silence. He plucked the pack of Luckies out of his shirt pocket, lipped a cigarette out of the opening, stuffed the pack back, dug into his trousers pocket for the Zippo, and lit it.

"OK, Dutch. I've ordered the clothesline rope. Can I ask what you want it for?"

Dutch bent over and scooped up the bullhorn. "You'll know soon enough. Some mystery in a relationship, huh, Zimbalist? Don't forget the cuffs. Five."

"Dutch, I want you to trust me. Can't we proceed on trust now? We've got your son on the way. We're doing exactly what you've asked."

"And you'll keep doing it. Over 'n' out."

He threw the bullhorn down into the same seat to free that hand for another drag on the cigarette. Hulda hadn't smoked since the men were out of the bus, but she did not want to call attention to herself by begging permission. He was reading one of the loose pages from the *Book of Knowledge* that he'd picked up from the seat in front of him, and she could see the question and answer on the backside of it. It was the one about sound she had read while waiting for the bus in front of the Triumph Supermarket that morning. The answer had surprised her and she read it again, and in the context of what had happened it seemed to mean something different from what she had first understood.

Dutch let the page flutter to the seat and he flicked the burning butt out the open window. He removed the lid from one of the Styrofoam cups and took a sip of coffee. It must have been cold by now, but he took another before setting it back into the cardboard holder on the seat with the others. He went for another cigarette but the pack was empty and he crushed it in his fist and tossed it to the floor. Hulda heard herself offer one of hers.

"I got Kents. Right here in my purse."

"Yeah."

She fished through the mess in her handbag and in a moment came up with it. "You mind if I have one too?"

Dutch shrugged and after she removed the cellophane and opened the foil liner she tapped one out for herself and handed the pack over to him. He lit his and offered her a light from a silver Zippo. She leaned into the flame without taking her eyes off the grenade in his other hand, only inches away, sucked in smoke, and sat back in her seat. She told Dutch he could keep that pack, it was his, her gift, enjoy them, she said, she was trying to cut down anyway—for her health, and then giggled and even that too loudly. Her husband called them cancer sticks, she said.

"What's he do? Your husband?"

"Well, the funny thing is, he's the dead one. I mean, it's not funny, but, well, there you have it."

"How?"

"He'd have called it a brain tumor, but the truth is he thought too much and he died of it."

"Huh?"

"That page you were reading there. It was one of his books. He was trying to figure things out through science."

"How long you been a widow?"

"Four, almost."

"What's it like? Your kids take good care of you?"

"I don't have any."

Dutch took a long drag and seemed to think about this.

"We couldn't," Hulda said. "Not that we didn't try."

She was making a fool of herself, but the talking made her feel safer. She wanted to tell him how she'd pretended to have children, how she'd even given them names and how baptizing their nonexistence helped to prepare her for the loneliness of widowhood. Instead, she told Dutch, she had cats. "Three of them," she said.

"I hate cats."

She sat back in her seat and smoked the Kent all the way to the filter before quashing it on the seat next to her and letting the butt fall to the floor. She watched Dutch finish his in quiet languor, then start up another without offering her one. He blew smoke at the window and she half expected it to pass through the glass.

She watched him smoke one after another of her Kents this way, his foot planted up on the seat, his forearm positioned over the knee, and she could see in that comportment and in those fading blue eyes the mystified determination of Peter, and thought that maybe there is a common element in the character of all men, something in the Y chromosome. Donahue had a show on that—the "macho thing," everyone kept calling it—

and one of the guests suggested it had to do with the fact that since childhood men could urinate wherever they wanted and this somehow kept them thinking like children and many of them became stuck in a state of adolescence; women, on the other hand, menstruated and that taught them something about the passage of time. It ritualized aging by means of a kind of biological mythos. The result was that women created and men made; men needed to know and women needed to apprehend.

It all sounded like psychobabble to Hulda, but it was certainly true that she and Peter had lived in contrary apposition. Where she looked up and appraised the soft azure of sky, he saw an endless vacuum refracting light. Where she perceived clouds in the shapes of dragons and ducks and profiles of famous people, he saw cirrus and cumulus and stratus formations of fine water droplets. Her fresh air was his wafting percentages of hydrogen and oxygen and nitrogen and whatever else was in what they breathed. Parallel existences, Y and X. It was as if they had met at the same point from different routes and had discrepant tales to tell of what they found when they got there.

The conversation on *Donahue* had moved to sex and how men tended to be more socially reckless about it. Women had something precious that men wanted, one audience participant said, but men would not come out and admit it and they blamed women for their own desperation. Masculinity is jealousy, another woman said, and femininity is fear. Men expelled, women received—except sometimes women expelled boys who turned into men who were always trying to fight their way back into female bodies, like they forgot something there.

Male or female, a baby in the world had the world against it. Bacteria and viruses and electric sockets and sharp objects and heights from which to fall. And then cars and strangers and machinery, planes and just plain crossing the street. Meteors and bullets and knives and all deadly objects in the world and the world as object whirling through the aimless order of cold space. How on earth, she wondered, did young Hulda Wilde of Johnson City ever clear the obstacles of sixty-eight years to arrive at this moment? Was her sitting there in a soiled dress, trembling, thirsty, aching, a miracle? Could she call herself fortunate to die in a violence that seemed to have been stalking her across the century like a fire-breathing dragon? Should she thank God for this moment of her life as she would any other? She sighed so loudly that Dutch, absorbed as he was in his own thoughts, looked over at her, his eye bloodshot, and then offered her one of her own cigarettes. She plucked one out of the pack and he lighted it for her.

"If I had a Lucifer I'd light it with that," he said, putting the Zippo back into his pocket.

"I didn't mean it," she said.

"Maybe you were right."

"Maybe you're trying to be a good father and don't know how."

"Story of my life."

"You got other kids?"

He told her about the girls, all beautiful, all disgusted with him—one so much so that she moved as far away as you could and still be in the forty-eight contiguous states. Her name was Margaret and she didn't even have a phone out there in the Northwest so he couldn't call her. Her mission in life was to be away from him, from our home and what it had become, he said, and frankly he didn't blame her. He talked about all three of his daughters, but mostly her, until he was interrupted by Beikirch telling him he had the material Dutch had requested and asked permission to bring it aboard.

"No. Come out to the middle of the clearing, just like with

the food. That's it. Keep coming. Slow down. OK, far enough. Toss the box to the door. Don't look at me! Do it! Now scram. Shoo."

Dutch put the bullhorn down, pulled the gun out of his belt, and pointed it at Andy, who was watching Beikirch's retreat.

"Yo, Andy," Grace said. "I think you're being paged."

"Whoa!" Andy said. "What?"

"Get it when I say. Don't screw up." Smoke from the cigarette lodged between the middle and ring fingers of Dutch's hand made it look as if he'd already fired a round.

Andy rose slowly from his seat and shuffled over to the stairwell. Dutch brought the grenade up to his face to wipe his forehead with the sleeve of his jacket. When Andy finally took the steps, Dutch scuttled into the well of the nearest seat, pointing the gun out the window. In a moment Andy was back inside, cradling a brown box about the size of a case of liquor.

"Bring it up here and put it in this seat. OK, take one of those packs of rope and sit in the seat. There. Open the pack, take the end of the rope, and tie it around your neck. Just a simple knot."

"OK, Dutch. I'm back at the edge of the clearing. Are we all set?"

"C'mon, Andy. The guy who relaxes is helping the Axis."

"Huh?"

"Just move."

"Dutch? Can you hear me in there?"

When Andy finished he looked up at Dutch like a dog on a leash. Dutch ordered him to stand and then jerked at the slack. Andy rose to his feet, holding a coil of rope at his chest as though it were a snake, and he kept it there for a moment before passing it over to Erica, who was also ordered to her feet. Dutch positioned the two of them so that Andy stood to his side and Erica just behind him in the aisle. After doling out another six or seven feet of slack, Andy was to loop the rope three times around her neck. Once this was complete he called up Matthew, and when he was finished looping the rope around his neck, it was Grace's turn.

"And let me just say this to all of you," Dutch announced. "You better be tied up good, because if the noose is loose . . ." He paused for a moment, as if the rhyme had confused him. "Then we will rest together in the dust."

When Grace finished looping the rope around her neck Hulda closed her eyes, waiting for her name to be called. But Dutch addressed Andy instead, demanding that he open up the second pack of rope, which he handed to him, and cut a seven-foot length of it, and then he told Grace to unravel what was left of the rope and pass the end of it down the aisle to him.

Hulda felt apart from the group and did not know if this was a good thing or not. She wondered if Dutch had forgotten her, though with the exception of Andy she was sitting closest to him.

"Um, excuse me," said Andy. "What do you want me to cut this with?"

He was standing so close to Hulda she could have reached over and touched the loop of rope hanging over his hand. Dutch reached back and pulled out the M-1942 bayonet in the plastic scabbard on his belt, looked at the shining blade for a moment, then pointed it at Andy while looking into his eyes.

"Lift up the rope and pull it taut."

He did, and Dutch sliced it with a quick upward snap of his wrist that concluded with the knifepoint just under Andy's chin.

"Give it here," Dutch said, and Andy, his blistered hands shaking, passed the length of rope to him. "You," he said, and it took a moment for Hulda to realize that he was referring to her. "Tie one end of this around your neck."

Before she could answer the rope was in her hands and he

was ordering Andy to take the handcuffs out of the box and begin passing them down the aisle. "Group effort," he said. "Team play. The second person puts them on the third, the third on the fourth, and so on. Behind the back. I want to hear the snap-snap. The correct click. I'll inspect. Any come off, I get mad. C'mon. Move it."

Andy was helping Erica into hers when Hulda finished tying her knot as tightly as she could; Erica had written something on the inside of her arm in lipstick—she could make out the words "love" and "Jonah"—then she watched Andy snap one of the cuffs around his own wrist and turn his back to Dutch with his hands at rest against the seat of his trousers. Dutch fastened the cuffs together, reached into the box for another pair, and handed them to Hulda.

"Put these on. Hands back. C'mon."

She obeyed, doing just as Andy had done, snapping a cuff on her wrist like a bracelet, and turning around in the well of the seat with her hands together at her back. She felt everyone looking at the wet spot on the back of her dress, could feel it where she'd placed her hands. Dutch said nothing as he fastened the other cuff, but he placed something in her palm, a coin, and when she closed her fist around it he ordered everyone to sit. He collected the three ends of the rope that connected them all, and when everyone had settled he stood at his place in the aisle.

They sat in the same seats, their arms out of sight, their shoulder bones jutting, necks craned, chins up. Hulda followed the concatenate migration of the rope from Andy across the aisle to Erica, back across to Matthew, behind him to Grace, and then returning up the aisle to Dutch, and she thought of molecules from the illustrations in one of Peter's books.

The FBI man called Dutch again, but this time he had information: the chopper was on its way from Hallstead and would arrive in approximately seven minutes. "It will land where it did earlier, just north of the ridge," he said. "Will you come up with me to meet it?"

Without picking up the bullhorn Dutch shouted "No!" and the word whistled past them like something thrown. Erica tried to wipe her cheeks with her shoulders, and when she saw Hulda looking at her she whispered an apology.

"Bring him down here where I can see him," Dutch shouted out the window. "We don't leave the bus until I see him."

They waited. Dutch remained erect, head cocked, jaw out, his one clear eye moving in his head. When he checked his watch, Hulda thought about how silly clocks were anyway. Time wasn't a thing so much to be gauged as felt, and she longed for boredom. The coin Dutch had slipped into her hand clicked against the ring she had stolen and her wedding band beside it, and she wondered if giving this to her meant she wouldn't die. If she did, would she die as stoically as Peter had? His mind was jumbled, nearly gone, in those last days. He couldn't speak clearly, and then he couldn't speak at all, just mumbling and spittle. But she could tell by his eyes he was thinking, or trying to. Sometimes the fear would cast a shadow over him, but mostly, when his eyes were open, they squinted as if counting the atoms in the air above his bed.

She'd tried to keep him comfortable. Sometimes he'd mumble something she couldn't understand. He never complained and often even smiled in a wry distortion of his face when he caught her looking at him. Then he would tumble back into deep thought—or the pose of deep thought, maybe just catatonia.

A rumbling came out of the sky, and it grew louder, and in a matter of moments the trees around them were bowing like a mob swayed by a speech. The noise destroyed Hulda's image of Peter and she thought instead of what the helicopter might look like landing over that ridge, a gargantuan piece of machinery dropping out of the sky. The nightly news in the sixties was so full of such images the percussion of blades had become an anthem of the war. And here it was played live, as in a concert, as though the war had never ended but instead come back like a virus hidden in the nervous system unleashed by stress.

The engine died and after the few minutes it took for the propeller to come to rest they were oppressed by a silence as loud as the landing had been, so pacific and composed that they could hear the cracking of dry twigs in the distant woods.

"Mr. Potter? We're here."

Andy craned his neck to look out the window. Dutch looked at the bullhorn on the seat beside him but did not pick it up.

"With my son?" he shouted without looking out the window.

"Yes, sir."

"Where is he?"

"Prepared to descend the ridge with two Marine escorts. They're unarmed. They will take it slowly. OK, Mr. Potter?"

Dutch licked his lips under nostrils dilated by short intakes of air. "Bring him down to where I can see."

"Yes, sir."

"And Colonel . . ."

"Sir?"

"Get those snipers out of the trees. I see even one of them when I get out of this bus you might just as well radio the coroner."

"OK, Mr. Potter. Done. Let's just take all this nice and easy. We've come this far together."

Dutch stooped to look out the window and searched the field outside. When he swallowed, all the muscles in his neck moved. He licked his dry lips again and stood.

"Ten-shun!"

The passengers looked at one another and Andy said, "You want we should stand up?"

Dutch waited until they got to their feet and told them the plan. "Andy goes out that door first, then you, you, and you," he said, pointing at Erica and then Matthew and then Grace. "You," he said, tugging on Hulda's line. "Follow me, no closer than two steps."

He stole another look out the window and said that everyone except Hulda needed to back up behind the side door. He waited for them to do this and once they settled into position he nodded to Andy, who slowly descended the steps. Once he was standing outside Dutch took a deep breath, announced that they were making history, and ordered Erica off the bus, then Matthew, who was to stand to the right of her outside, then Grace, who was to take a position to the right of him. When they were outside Dutch sidled past Hulda and without looking back ordered her to follow at the distance he had prescribed.

The breeze splashed over their faces like water. Dutch ordered them to spread out from where they stood and the design of his human fortress took the form of a boron atom with Dutch as the nucleus. B was its designation on the periodic table of the elements, like an average grade, a so-so movie, a stinging insect, the command to exist. It was only later that Hulda discovered what boron was—what it did for a living, so to speak—an amorphous yellowish brown substance that could be formed into a conducting metal of great fortitude and value. If the boy had stayed they'd have come together as carbon, and she knew something about that right then, about monoxide and dioxide, for example, both of them lethal.

Out of the dark cluster of trees four men entered the clearing, all in uniform. The breeze had stilled and the solemn air darkened under a cloud. The men halted a few steps past the wood line and stood at military attention. The man with the cane was in full dress but the uniform was too large for him and his body, lost in the stiff creases of cloth, gave the impression of a boy playing man in his father's best clothes. His face was shrouded under the brim of his hat, and only the outline of his jaw could be seen. They stood in all that quiet and Dutch watched them standing there and for a moment the silence felt natural and without expectation. A kind of relief, Hulda thought. Matthew could not feel the pain in his ankle for the first time, as if it were somehow connected to what was happening rather than what had happened to it. He had Dutch's wallet in his back pocket, he could feel it against the back of his hand. Andy swallowed dry air and wished for his pipe. Grace lifted her head back to look straight up at the sky, taking in a deep draft of air that filled her body. Only Hulda could see the note in lipstick on Erica's wrist—and Dutch, if he were to look down. But he was not looking at the backs of the hostages spread out behind the barricade, but beyond them, across the clearing, at the men.

"Jom?" he said finally. "Jommy?"

The man with the cane looked around as though he had dropped something, then turned to Colonel Bennett, who, lifting the bullhorn, said, "This is Lieutenant Jonathan Potter, Mr. Potter. His voice is weak. May we come forward?"

"Proceed!" Dutch shouted. "But only the two of you. The Marine escort leaves."

Colonel Bennet said something to the escort, and after they turned and disappeared into the woods, he took the soldier by the elbow and guided him forward. As they made their way across the clearing it became evident that what had been said about the boy's health was true. His locomotion was impeded by a severe hobble, a palsied gait defended from collapse by strategic use of the cane. They moved slowly and deliberately through the tall grass, and when they reached the middle of the clearing, about thirty feet from the barricade,

Dutch ordered them to stop. They obeyed and stood in the exemplary posture.

"Take off your hat, soldier," Dutch ordered.

The soldier's white-gloved hand shook a little reaching for the brim. He removed the hat and held it against his chest, revealing a disfigurement so strange that Hulda first thought it might be a trick of the light. A surge of white scar tissue twisted the left side of his face from his neck to his temple as though his skin were mortar. His eyes, blue and unmarred amid the devastation, squinted against the sunlight.

"Jommy?"

Colonel Bennett raised the bullhorn to the soldier's mouth, saying something into his ear. In a moment a hoarse whisper came through.

"It's I. Me."

"How do I know?"

"Geez. Not sure myself. Story of my life. Hey?"

Dutch too stood military straight, staring at the broken man claiming to be his son, watching him move his head stiffly side to side in wonder, or shock. The scar tissue appeared to form a caulifloral bump of flesh within his ear, but a closer look revealed it to be a hearing aid of some sort.

"Your face?" Dutch said.

The soldier lifted his gloved fingers and lightly touched his jaw. He shrugged. "I'm ugly?"

"What happened?"

"We used to hunt near here," he said, looking around again. "Remember? The time you got a buck on the way home? Hit it on the road? You said you used V-6 caliber? Huh?"

"What kind of car was it, soldier?"

"Car? Truck, you mean. Ford pickup. Red. How come you call me 'soldier'? You ask questions like doctors."

Dutch's boots remained planted in his stance, but he moved forward slightly and then slowly back.

"Pop? You OK? It's me, Jommy. I waited so long! Don't be mad. Please. My decision it was to wait, not colonel's. I didn't want you and Mom to see me like, you know. This. I wanted to walk into the house. Proud. Me. See you all there healthy and me be healthy. Look at me, Pop. I dreamed of that twelve years. A bed. My porch. Have Rolling Rock. With you. I got thoughts to tell."

"Where'd we go out the night before you left for your tour?"

"The Belmar, Pop. Don't you remember? The triangle table near the window. Hot pies! That neon sign. In the window."

Even with the bullhorn held to his lips some of his whispery words dissolved in the air and Dutch, leaning forward again, asked him to repeat the last part of what he had just said.

"Pop. What's realest about me is you. Please. Don't misbelieve me!"

Dutch wiped his brow with his sleeve, shuddering the web of rope. "C'mere closer where I can see you better."

The two men started moving forward and Dutch said no, just the boy.

"He can't walk without assistance," Bennett said.

Jom said something no one could hear and Bennett once again held the bullhorn up for him. "I fell three times already, Pop. I'm sorry. I will try if you want. But I don't know. I will try, though. If you want."

"Stay there, soldier. Bennett, you're relieved of duty."

"Mr. Potter, I think that—"

"Go."

The colonel pressed his lips together, blew air out of his nose, and let go of Jom's elbow before patting him lightly on the back and turning to make his way across the clearing. He did not turn until he reached the woodline. Jom swayed like a stalk in a light breeze. He had put his hat back on and kept his jaw lifted slightly so he could see out from under the visor.

"OK," Dutch said, yanking once on the rope. "Everyone moves forward, slow."

No one moved except to look at one another, and then Andy cleared his throat and asked about the barricade in front of them.

"Bugger it," Dutch said.

Each of the four in front worked in his or her own way to get over or through the barricade, kicking at the weave of branches, and Dutch growled that bugger meant bugger and to push through the shit. The piled branches just in front of Matthew and Grace were loosest, and with a little effort the two of them made an opening acceptable to Dutch.

"Slow," he said again as they slipped through one at a time, Grace first, then Matthew, then Erica and Andy. With the four of them re-established on the other side, Dutch gave the order to proceed by flicking the reins and then pulling back hard when his leg got caught in the wedge of one of the piled branches. From behind, Hulda watched him work it free and then all of them moved toward the soldier in the field as though he were tracking them in a gravitational pull. When they were within ten feet Dutch ordered them to halt.

"Pop!" the soldier whispered. "You're *you*."

Dutch's eyes bore into the image before him. A runnel of sweat disappeared into his collar.

"You don't look like Jom," he said.

"You don't want me? Back?"

"If you're my son."

"I always run away, you always get me. This is last time. I promise."

When Dutch did not respond, Jom sputtered something in Vietnamese, a burst of syllables ending abruptly in a heavy shrug, his eyebrows arched, his mouth open so you could see the rotted teeth. Dutch shifted foot to foot and realized a complication of twigs from the barricade still clung to his ankle. He shook it to free himself, and Jom, watching him and then looking over at the makeshift fence, asked him what all this was for.

"You had your projects too, remember?"

Jom paused, looking off into the distance, touching the side of his face lightly, then his ear. "You mean the backyard?"

Dutch nodded. "That was one."

"When I dug that hole?"

"Why did you dig that hole?"

"I . . . I wanted to get to China."

"That's right!"

"Dug all day. So deep I hit water."

"Yes!"

"China," he said sadly.

"It was between two trees in our backyard. What kind of trees?"

"Oh! Old crab apple. First tree I climbed. Four years old. Remember?"

"I remember everything."

"And white birch. I love that tree."

"Take off that dress jacket."

"Pop?"

"Do it."

He could not let go of the cane and so he had to perform the task with one hand. After finally unfastening all the buttons, he struggled out of the sleeves and let it fall to the ground behind him.

"Now the shirt."

This time he did not question the order and in a few moments the shirt fell open to either side, filling with air from a breeze.

"Pull back the right side."

He did, revealing more scar tissue below his ribcage.

"How did you get that?"

"You know. That one happened at home."

"Tell me."

"Dog. German shepherd. Rec Park. I was nine. No, eight. You took me to General, remember? This one here, that didn't happen in the World. A knife."

"Jommy? Is it really you in all that mutilation? Could it be?"

"I'm what you see. My life has been a lie, Pop, but this . . . this is truth."

"Your life was no lie! It was more to me than anything in the world."

"I ran away my whole life. But now, it's home! Like a dream. And you, you're there. And these people, though . . . American, scared . . . and I know how they feel and I know how you feel. Too. Like I'm them and I'm you too."

"You're different."

"Sorry. I'll be better. Give me time. I'm always . . . try since Bekka."

"Her!"

"I'm responsible, Pop. Dead because of me."

"No! Because of *her*. Or me. Us. Not you."

"My fault. I wanted to die. Kill pain."

"Not your fault, Jommy! Me before you!"

"I used to tell me in camps that suffering and all the world of hurt was purgatory burning one big sin. You taught me a man must . . . responsible. Take action."

He wept bitterly and Dutch rocked forward once, then back.

"Pop," Jom said, raising his free arm. "Please? I'll be good. I'm so so sorry . . ."

"J-Jom," Dutch sputtered. "My boy?"

He dropped the rope and moved forward, ducking under the stretch of line between Erica and Matthew. Before he could embrace him the cane fell to the ground and Jom wrapped his arms around Dutch, saying "Pop" again and again. They struck the ground in that embrace, disappearing into the grass that swayed in the same breeze rustling the trees and rushing the clouds across the blue expanse above.

EPILOGUE

When you get over here all you think about is getting back to the World. But when your time gets near it sort of scares you because you know in your heart that you're not like the people back home. It's a funny feeling to be afraid to go home, but everyone over here feels the same. There are a lot of mixed emotions—worrying about hurting the people close to you, or maybe your dreams about being home will shatter when you get there. And then there's the way you regret leaving your buddies. Abandoning loved ones to their deaths. In our hearts we all wish we could go home together.

—JOM POTTER, IN AN UNDATED LETTER FOUND AMONG HIS EFFECTS AFTER HE WAS DECLARED MISSING IN ACTION IN MARCH 1970.

S tarting down West End Avenue from Floral near the Red
Apple, where she stopped to buy a pack of Kents, Hulda
Lambert sidestepped a puddle rippled by a westerly breeze. She
didn't need her umbrella after all; the sun had come out blazing
as if it were newly minted in the universe. The storm during the
night portended otherwise; a clap of thunder had released a
flood from the sky, rising, now, in sweet fragrance from the trees
and grass and gardens. Robins consorted on lawns, cardinals
and blue jays and finches swooped tree to tree, squirrels went
about their business. Later, it would a scorcher, but for now she
was glad to be making this trip, if for no other reason than to be
out on such a morning.

She traversed the sidewalk on the even-numbered side of the
street and after a half a block she stopped in the shade of a
maple to entertain second thoughts. Maybe she should have
called first, but she didn't want the poor woman to fuss on her
account. Hulda had only decided the night before to take her up
on her invitation, anyway, and had changed her mind a dozen
times since then. She was still a little ways away; it wasn't too

late to turn back, but she proceeded down the street, though more slowly.

She'd meant to go to the funeral but later thought it was better that she hadn't. She sent the card instead, saying she, too, was a widow and was so sorry for her loss. She didn't think Mr. Potter was a bad man; he just loved his son, and love sometimes made people do things that they probably oughtn't do. He reminded her in some ways of her own husband, Peter, why she'd loved him so much and realized now why she always would: because no matter his faults, and there were many, he cared, and because he could be trusted with her love, and that, for whatever reason, he loved her. Mrs. Potter responded with a note of her own, thanking Hulda for her kindness and her beautiful words and asking would she visit sometime. Hulda took the envelope out of her pocket and checked the address again.

She'd read in the newspapers that Mr. Potter had many friends, which she thought interesting for a man in such mental disrepair. The Lutheran Church of the Redeemer was full to the rafters and the minister gave a moving eulogy—the *Sun-Bulletin* printed it in its entirety beside an article by the young man who had interviewed Hulda. She'd dreaded having to talk with the press, but he'd made her feel like a real person, and she appreciated that. The minister talked about the cardiomyopia as though it were a spiritual rather than physical illness. The heart stuck on one thing and not able to get unstuck, and bursting from it. How it hadn't worked right since his son's war, like the grenade hadn't worked since his. He asked everybody to forgive his friend because he was a good man with a sick heart. He just couldn't work it out with his son gone, but thank God no one else was hurt and it was good, too, that there was a chance he died believing he was embracing his beloved Jom. The reporter said the minister had to stop a few times, overwhelmed with emotion as he was, and so what he said must have been true.

People are more complicated than we usually give them credit for being, he'd said, and there is much more to life than we can ever understand.

She thought that very thought the night of the day it all happened when she got home from the hospital, made a gin and tonic, sat in her chair, looked at the ring she had accidentally stolen, and pulled it off her finger as though she were picking lint from her sleeve. She put it in an envelope addressed to Comfort Jewelers and the next day Gibbs the mailman carried it away.

She started up the front walk of the Potters' house and her shoe hit something, a green bottle, and sent it spinning over the concrete. Rolling Rock, and it rolled onto the grass. A vacuum cleaner was fighting for breath somewhere inside the house. She looked around the neighborhood, then walked up the steps to the door. Before she could ring the doorbell or walk away, a little boy appeared on the other side of the screen.

"Know what?" he said. "I get a new room today."

"What's that, dear?"

"Brand-new. My aunt who came from far away got a new room, and now I got one."

"I see. Is Mrs. Potter home? Sarah Potter?"

"My G-ma. C'mon in."

He opened the door for her and she stepped inside the foyer. He might have been about five or six and he was still in his pajamas.

"She's upstairs in my new room. I'll show you."

"Could you just tell her Mrs. Lambert is here?"

"C'mon," he said from the stairs.

He took her hand and led her up the stairs, telling her that the room used to be his uncle's. At the top of the landing a miniature poodle barked at her and the boy brought her into a bedroom where two women were cleaning. They looked up when she entered.

"My goodness!" the older one said, turning off the vacuum cleaner.

"I'm Hulda Lambert. I've come at a bad time. I'm sorry. I was just in the neighborhood . . ."

"Mrs. Lambert! I'm Sarah Potter and this is my daughter Catherine. You've caught us doing a little cleaning is all."

"It's my new room," the boy said.

"That's my grandson, Joseph," Sarah said. "Catherine's son."

"Pleased to meet you," Hulda said.

"Oh," Sarah said, removing her apron. "Look at me. I'm a mess. Let me take you downstairs where it's more comfortable. I'll make some coffee and we can sit and chat."

"Please don't fuss on my account. Like I said, I was just taking a stroll and noticed I was on your street."

A woman older than Hulda appeared in the doorway and asked what was going on.

"Ruth, this is Mrs. Lambert. Mrs. Lambert, this is my sister Ruth."

"You were the gal on the bus!"

They stood in silence for a moment and then Joseph, jumping on the bed, asked if anyone wanted to join him. Catherine told him to get down and he said she wasn't the boss of the room.

"I was just about to make some coffee," Sarah said.

Ruth turned to make way and Sarah led Hulda out of the room. Before they turned to the stairs the door at the end of the hall opened and a young woman appeared. The hem of her loose cotton dress issued softly at her ankles when she moved toward them.

"This is another one of my daughters, Margaret. Margaret, this is Mrs. Lambert."

"She was on the bus," Ruth said.

She had beautiful skin and dark hair splashing over her

shoulders and she looked Hulda right in the eye and said hello and then kissed her on the cheek. She smelled like lilac.

"You look a lot like your father, dear," Hulda said, "I mean, your eyes," and then felt herself blush for having said it.

But the girl did not seem bothered in the least; she continued looking right into Hulda's eyes as though she knew everything there was to know about Hulda Lambert, and liked her.

"Come, Mrs. Lambert. You'll be more comfortable downstairs. Margaret? Would you like to join us for coffee?"

"I'm having tea," Ruth announced.

"I'm going back up," Margaret said, pointing to the open door behind her.

Ruth and Sarah began downstairs, but Hulda could not take her eyes off the girl ascending the narrow staircase on the other side of the door, the summer dress cascading around her waist and calves and ankles. When she disappeared into the attic, Hulda stared at the doorway for a long while before turning to join the women and the boy, who were already downstairs. But then she stopped and moved back toward the open door. The stairway was dark, the treads loose, but at the top it was so bright with sunlight coming in through three windows that she had to shield her eyes. It was a single large room with slanted ceilings over a tile floor partly covered by a lavender remnant. Margaret was sitting Indian-style on the brass bed in the corner amid an avalanche of photographs and without raising her head she said, "Look at this one," as if the two of them were in the middle of a conversation.

Hulda approached her and the picture she held out was of her father and brother sitting at a picnic table near the gazebo at Recreation Park. Dutch looked to be in his thirties, Jom just a boy of ten or eleven, and they had their arms over each other's shoulders, smiling into the camera. It was a hot summer day, there was sweat on Dutch's brow, and they both wore white T-shirts. Dutch's hair was as dark as Margaret's, not a touch of gray, and his head rested down against Jom's. Hulda didn't know what to say and handed the picture back to Margaret.

"He thought I hated him," she said. "But I just couldn't be here anymore. With him and without Jommy. I couldn't."

"I think he understood, dear. He said as much to me."

"He talked to you? About me?"

"He told me you were out west and that he missed you terribly but did not blame you for being away. A person has to live their life, he said. 'My baby,' he called you."

Her lips trembled exactly as her father's did when he was speaking with Sarah from the bus. "I used to go out to the coast—in Oregon, where I was living—and just sit and watch the ocean. It was a way of being near Jommy. I could talk to him there, looking out over the blue. He was there when we talked."

She wept quietly and without shame, as though it were natural, and Hulda sat on the edge of the bed and put her hand on the girl's back. The photographs around them were of the family over the decades, in this house and other houses, at beaches and in parks—Margaret and Georgia and Catherine, Jom with them, or with his friend, younger versions of the reporter who had interviewed her for the paper, Sarah and Dutch dancing, sitting on the sofa or in the backyard, Sarah with her sisters, the children with their cousins, with their grandparents. But most of the pictures were of Jom and Dutch, together or alone. Jom as a teenager, an infant, a soldier, a toddler hugging the leg of Dutch the soldier, Dutch the young bus driver, Dutch alone with gray hair again, sitting at the kitchen table looking up from a birthday cake. Together they formed a portrait of a life happening all at once, bursting forth out of time's divisions to occur in a kind of simultaneity.

"*There* you are, Mrs. Lambert," Sarah said from the top of

the stairs, and when she saw her daughter she said, "Oh, Mags, Mags," and crossed the room to join them.

The boy scampered up behind her and dove onto the bed. Some of the photographs fell to the floor around them. "Pictures!" he cried. "Tons of them."

Sarah sat on the edge of the bed near Hulda and put her arm around her daughter, leaned into her, said her name again, and then, "Oh my." She picked a picture out of the group beside Margaret and said, "Look here." It was of Margaret and her sisters at play beside a dollhouse in front of a Christmas tree. "You couldn't be more than four in this picture. How adorable you were!"

Margaret wiped her eyes and smiled. "Look at Georgie. What a ham."

"Who's *this*?" Joseph asked, holding up a black-and-white picture of a soldier and a young woman arm-in-arm in front of a house. The soldier looked like Jom, but it couldn't have been, because the style of the woman's dress was 1940s.

"That's me," Sarah said. "That's G-ma."

"*Her*? *You*? Nah!"

"And that's your uncle Liam," she said to Margaret, touching the photo lightly. "Just before he went off to the Pacific." She looked as though she might begin crying herself, and when she saw Hulda looking at her she apologized.

"For what, dear? Looks like you have a fine family. You should be proud."

"Mrs. Lambert said she spoke with Daddy," Margaret said.

Sarah looked at Hulda. "A little bit," Hulda said. "While we were, you know, waiting. He gave something to me." She fished through her purse and came up with a small box of the type a necklace or pendant might be wrapped in at the jeweler's, and handed it to Sarah. "He wanted you to have this."

Sarah removed the lid, and when she saw the quarter Hulda

had set on the cotton lining she smiled sadly. "Look, Mags," she said, and Margaret shook her head, smiling the same way. Sarah told Hulda that it was something she and her husband passed back and forth to one another. It had to do with how they met. She fought back emotion when she explained that she was walking to the Riviera to see a movie with her sisters and was in a light mood—it was such a beautiful evening in May—and she was tossing her quarter up into the air. She took the quarter from the box to demonstrate and it fell to the floor and rolled just as her coin had rolled along the sidewalk in 1941, and Joseph scampered off the bed to retrieve it.

"Daddy sees it and picks it up," Margaret said, "and there's Mom standing in front of him with her hand out and he says to his friends, 'Fellas, you ever seen a prettier panhandler in all your life?'"

"That's right," Sarah said, wiping her eyes. "And I said, 'Hand it over, buddy, or you'll be sorry,' and he says, 'My hard-found earnings?' He was so handsome and charming I fell in love with him right there."

"And Daddy said, 'OK, take it, but you're taking the only luck I ever had.'"

Sarah nodded and said it was why he married her—to get it back—and Ruth called up from the bottom of the stairs to say the kettle was boiling for her tea. They could hear it whistling from across the house and when Sarah said "Well . . ." and got to her feet, Joseph held up the coin and asked if he could keep it.

ABOUT THE AUTHOR

Robert Mooney was born in Rochester, New York, and educated at Boston College and Binghamton University. He currently teaches literature and writing at Washington College, where he is the Director of the O'Neill Literary House. His short fiction has appeared in many journals and magazines. He and his wife, Maureen, and their two children divide their time between Chestertown, Maryland, and Binghamton, New York.